What others are saying…

"I'm still catching my breath! This fast-paced, twisty story is a test of humanity in an alien-invaded world where nothing is as black and white as the alien war would have people believe. I was surprised with the turn of every page! What makes Captive *particularly unique is how it explores the apocalypse within a person as well as on the external world in which they live. Expertly done. My favorite Bradley Caffee book yet!"*

—Nadine Brandes, bestselling & award-winning author of *The Nightmare Virus, Romanov,* and *A Time to Die*

"With its unpredictable twists and heart-pounding turns, Captive *is one of those rare books able to take a perspective and completely flip it. An electrifying tale of flawed heroes, aliens, and militia warring to save an unforgettable world."*

—Candace Kade, author of *The Hybrid Series*

"With a villain who will leave you looking over your shoulder, unexpected twists that challenge what you thought you knew, and endearing characters who grow and change in profound ways, Captive *is a pulse-pounding adventure that looks at prejudices, hatred, and what it means to be truly human. Caffee delivers an adventure sci-fi fans are sure to love!"*

—C.J. Milacci, award-winning author of the *Talionis Series*

CAPTIVE

CAPTIVE

A Sci-fi Dystopian

By
Bradley Caffee

For those on the journey to freedom from whatever burden has held you captive. May you come to know that you are not alone.

*Greater love hath no man than this, that a man
lay down his life for his friends. John 15:13*

Chapter One

The monster stares at me. The barely perceptible movements of slate gray pupils moving across obsidian eyes are the one reason I know this creature is aware of me. I didn't realize it was possible for any creature to sit so still, yet this one hasn't moved. It's taking me in. Studying me. Looking for a weakness I'm sure—a chance to make its move and escape. I don't plan to give it one.

I glance down at the bonds on its wrists and ankles, a silent reminder to the beast that it isn't going anywhere. I'm confident my knots are good. My dad taught me that. That doesn't stop me from mentally double-checking each one. I can't afford to make a mistake if I'm going to get the answers I need.

Dark purple blood oozes from the being's skin abrasions and runs in tiny streams across the pale green skin. The creature's struggle to free itself ended half an hour ago, but the wounds from my well-tied knots still seep. So does the head wound from the rock I'd hurled earlier. A lucky throw, but all the opportunity I needed to get the advantage over this being that is, admittedly, stronger than me. Apparently, this species' blood doesn't clot the same way as a human's blood. Good. Maybe it will bleed out—slowly. I smile at the thought.

Returning my gaze to the alien face, I watch the rhythmic pulsing of the gill-like cheeks that suck in and out. The respirator device that all the beasts wear on their nose to breathe our atmosphere wheezes its quiet whisper. It's their one physical weakness. Without the device, I've heard they can only last seconds before they lose all function. If it won't answer me, I could use that to my advantage, but I'm hoping it doesn't come to that. The alien's permanently pursed lips haven't moved, and my repeated questions go unanswered. I'd heard that some of the creatures could speak English, but apparently my luck isn't that good. My captive remains mute.

Still, it's my captive. I've dragged it to the basement of this decrepit building to see what it knows. In two years, it's the first time I've been able to get this close, and I have to get it to talk. And when I get the answers I want, I will make certain there will be one less Fishface on our planet.

I try again.

"Are you from the Bubble?" I've asked this question several times already, and the creature never answers. Still, it's the only one that I've gotten any response to. The first time I asked, the thing cocked its head like it was considering answering—which it did not. "The one here in Charlotte. Is that where you came from— inside the bubble over the city?"

Respirator wheeze. Nothing more.

"Hey. I'm talking to you!" I kick the creature's leg.

Hisss.

I stare. The airy noise from the alien mouth is the first audible response I've received. I kick again.

"Yeah, you. You hear me. I know you do."

The midnight eyes glance down at my foot and back up at my face, seemingly daring me to try again. I do. With lightning reflexes, the creature grabs my foot with both bound hands, pulling my leg to the side instead of simply blocking the blow. My body lurches with the redirected momentum, and I lose my footing. An instant later, lights flash across my vision as my head hits the cement floor. Hollow pain rings in my skull and pulses through my extremities.

Hissssssss. A sharper noise than before, it draws my blurred vision. I can hear the scraping of the floor grit as the creature slithers away from me—attempting to get on all fours. My head pounds, but I shake it anyway to clear my senses. Reaching out, I grab the rope attached to the creature's ankles.

I yank.

The effort makes my head explode in pain, but I'm rewarded with a satisfying thump as the beast faceplants on to the cement.

Hand over hand, I drag the surprisingly sturdy body of the Fishface toward me. It squirms, but the bonds hold, and my grip is sure.

Our eyes meet again, and I show it the rope in my hands. *You're not going anywhere.* The creature stills as if a silent agreement has come between us—I am still the captor. I take a couple deep breaths to try to clear the rattling in my head.

Perhaps I'll forget my questions. I'll end the creature right here. It attacked me once. It'll do it again. If it gets the jump on me again, I might not get so lucky. Maybe this was a bad idea. I make up my mind that this is the end for my captive. Head throbbing, I force myself to stand. As I do, I grab the rock which had allowed me to subdue it earlier. With my other hand, I wrap the rope around my wrist several times to make sure it can't get away.

Hate courses through my veins as I lift the rock above my head. This monster is no different than the rest of them. No remorse. No hesitation to attack. No sense of a soul. Creatures from another world, but not like us. Alien in every sense.

They destroyed our planet—leaving it in ruins. Millions died after the explosion, which became known as the Cataclysm, from their supposed gift to planet Earth of a clean energy facility. They'd promised access to the technology that ended war on their planet, and we welcomed them with open arms. How could we have been so gullible?

The explosion was simply the beginning. The rest of the planet would die a far slower death. The world quickly regressed from fallout, becoming a wasteland that could no longer produce meaningful crops. Some decided to fight back. With the world's militaries left impotent with no one to run them, small militia groups have managed to continue the fight, which has drawn to a bloody stalemate. Neither side is gaining ground. Lives are lost. Precious remaining resources are expended. Humanity's days were numbered because of this creature's kind. I have spent each of them alone—my father dead from being at the epicenter of the explosion.

It deserves to die. They all do.

My fingers tighten around the stone and my muscles tense. I

glare at its face, the blank eyes staring back at me. With a breath, I raise the rock high to strike my blow. I've never killed before, but I'm surprised at how easy it feels. I am not a violent person, but something in me screams that this is a small measure of justice.

"Pleasssse."

I try not to let the shock of the creature's first word show on my face. I pause. Trembling violently, the bound hands rise, open in surrender. The wheezing intensifies.

I should end this. I should put it out of its misery. But I don't.

Hisss. "Pleassse. I won't esscape. I won't fight anymore."

My hand lowers almost involuntarily. My heart races—not because of the words—but because of the voice. Every Fishface I've encountered has a low, almost growling voice. This is a softer, hushed sound.

"I promisse."

The rock hits the floor, though I don't remember letting it go. It's that voice—*her* voice—that melts my resolve.

Neural Implant Log: Entry 133
Officer: Tash'jya, daughter of Sun'tssh
Rank: Tactician

I have been unable to escape my captor. So far, he seems unaware of my neural implant or my ability to maintain these logs with simply a thought. It is my hope, should my mission fail, that these logs will assist in understanding what took place, so my family is not dishonored by my failure. I have attempted to overpower him, but he has the advantage over me for now. I've lost my element of surprise.

His questions. So many questions about his father and the Bubble over the city. Part of me wants to answer them, but the unanswered questions are the one motivation he has to keep me alive. I cannot complete my mission while dead. I maintain little hope that any human left in this world will be able to fully understand what we are trying to do for them.

The time delay this is causing is unacceptable. Will continue my efforts to escape at the first available opportunity. Mission remains priority one.

For now, the human seems taken aback given that I've spoken. Perhaps guile and not force will be my tool of liberation.

End of log.

Chapter Two

I back into the wall and slide to the floor. My mind races in every direction but always returns to the same question. *Female? The creature is female?* The survivors said the aliens were a single sex, neither male nor female. Admittedly, that was a small sample as most had never personally come face to face with them. They looked the same. Acted the same. I'd never witnessed any behavior that indicated they were separated into male and female.

Yet, the voice I heard was distinctly female. At least, that is what my gut told me. There was no way to be certain—not any way I was willing to find out—except to ask.

"Are-are you a woman?" The question sounded so stupid. If she hadn't answered any of my other questions, why this one?

The creature wriggles over to the wall and props herself upright. It takes some effort, and I loosen the rope a little to give her the slack she needs. Her respirator wheezes. "Yess. I am what your people would call—female—though our speciesss doess not divide quite the ssame as yoursss." I can't be sure, but her tone almost sounds exasperated.

I cannot decide whether I am more shocked by her revelation or by the very fact that she's speaking to me. Her dark eyes continue their blinkless stare. It's clear that she won't be volunteering any information on her own.

"Why are you now talking to me? I mean, you wouldn't before."

"Among our kind, it is courtesssy to begin by asking who someone iss before asking what they are doing. Anything elsse is impolite." She cocks her head to one side, and her lips curl into something like a smile. Did she enjoy telling me that? I'm reminded of how little I know of her species. Whatever the expression is quickly disappears as she shifts, her bonds rubbing her raw skin.

"What do you want from me?" *Hiss.*

My face heats with anger as my intended task returns to me. I need answers. I've been on my own for two years since the Cataclysm. My father worked with the aliens believing they truly meant to help our planet. He and everyone else near the epicenter of the explosion are gone. All that remains is the Bubble. After the explosion, it appeared over the city of Charlotte, covering the center of the uptown area. People attempted to enter it from time to time, but no one has been witnessed returning. It's a one-way trip. Everyone inside, human and alien alike, must be dead. They have to be. That includes my father.

"Tell me about the Bubble. What is it? Why is it there?"

Her cheeks puff in rapid succession. Is she laughing at me? I tug on the rope for good measure, reminding us both of her situation. The laughter, if that's what it is, stops.

"Tell me."

"You would not undersstand, human." She spits, a gob of dark blue gel-like substance hits my shoe. If that is what they have for saliva, it's gross. "None of you undersstand."

"Understand what?"

"That we came to help you. Nothing more. You wage war against uss. Hate uss. Kill uss." She raises her hands to show me her bonds. "You tie uss up."

Something inside of me pinches. Guilt washes over me. What would my father say? *Trust them, son. They mean well for us.* Those were his words for so long. He'd spent nearly every waking moment in his last days working with the creatures to construct the first energy facility. Now he is dead, lost to the Cataclysm or the Bubble. Either way, he is gone.

I rub the back of my head. "Well, that's because it's clear what you'll do if you get the chance."

She touches the still oozing wound on her head. "Nothing you did not do to me firsst, human." Her logic causes my gut to wrench again, and it is clear I won't be outsmarting her. I want to change the conversation.

I don't have to. Sirens blare outside our concrete hideaway. Blasts follow, distant at first but drawing closer. Gunfire follows. A battle between the humans and aliens has broken out. It won't be long before whatever is happening is right on top of us.

The beast looks at the basement ceiling, her lidless eyes darting back and forth. "You stupid human. You will kill uss in this place."

One nearby blast could bring the remains of this building down upon us. Bits of dirt and dust fall in tendrils. I can feel the vibration of the distant blasts in the floor. Images of the ceiling coming down on us flood my imagination. Not how I want to die.

I stand. "We have to move."

She hisses at me, holding her wrists out to me. "Cut my bondss and let me go. I cannot run like thiss." I hesitate. "Let me go, human! Or we will both die."

"Right." I glance around at the beams holding the ceiling up. "And then you kill me. I don't think so."

She hisses and pulls madly at her restraints. My knots hold despite her struggle.

I should leave. I should be running instead of standing here. Two years on the streets has taught me not to stick around when a battle nears. I haven't survived this long by making reckless choices. I've been careful and steered clear of any hostility. Soon enough, both sides will be right on top of us, slaughtering each other. In the chaos, no one will notice me. I'll be shot, blown up, or crushed under rubble. Or worse, I will be trapped under a building and die of thirst.

I should definitely leave.

Fishface will only slow me down.

Perhaps this is a mercy. What I couldn't bring myself to do with the rock earlier could still be accomplished. All I have to do is leave. I'll need to get my answers elsewhere, but if I managed to catch one of them, then maybe I can do it again. She—I'm still digesting calling her she—would be another casualty in a war that her kind brought upon us. The blood would be on their hands, not mine. Yes, this is a mercy.

"Please, human." My train of thought is broken by the creature. Her voice has softened. Her plea rips at my gut. She's moved onto her knees. Her eyes stare into mine. With both hands, she touches her forehead and then her chest.

I recognize the gesture. My father didn't teach me much about them, but I know this.

When the Fishfaces came to earth, their benevolent claims won over the optimists of our world—people like my father. In time, he'd grown to admire their way of life, often telling me about how they'd overcome the pettiness of politics and geo-political conflicts on their planet. In return, he'd won them over with his engineering prowess. Adapting their technology to the resources available on Earth had been a challenge, but my father had been at the center of almost every breakthrough. At the announcement that the first energy facility would be ready to begin operation, several of the leaders had made the head to chest motion to my father and his team. It was a sign of respect—an admission of dependence upon one another.

Now I am receiving the very same honor, but for a very different reason. Her life is in my hands, not because of my benevolent cooperation, but because I am her captor. I leave her here, and I condemn her to die. No, I can't explain her death away. I might be the only one who ever finds out about it, but her blood would still be on my hands.

She realizes it and is reminding me.

I despise her for it. I'm sure I'm going to regret this.

Pulling out my pocketknife, I open the blade and approach. She shrinks backward, her eyes darting to the blade. I stop. *Idiot. I know better*. I make the head to chest gesture in return, indicating I've accepted her honor and will treat her accordingly. Her body relaxes a bit, but she still seems ready to spring into action should I make another threatening move. I can't *blame* her. Seconds ago, I was wielding a rock, ready to kill her.

With a firm hold on the rope that is attached to the bonds on her wrists, I cut a couple feet off the end. Pulling the threads apart, I'm able to produce a slender length of twine. Tying one end to her wrist bonds, I attach the other end to the tube that protrudes from her respirator. Any sudden movement or attempt to fight back will jerk the respirator from her nose, and she'll lose her ability to breathe our air. I raise an eyebrow to silently ask if she understands. I receive a slight nod in return. Finally, I slice the knot at her ankles and step backward. With a couple of tiny kicks, her feet are freed.

I click the knife back into closed position and pocket it. I hold the rope up in her line of sight. "Don't try anything funny. I can still tie you to something and leave you. Understand?"

Hiss. "I undersstand, human." She rises, slowly, to her feet. Arching her back, something like relief washes over her face. Laying on the concrete has not been comfortable, and I am suddenly aware of how sore I am. In this moment, I finally realize how much taller she is than me. At six foot one, I'm not exactly short, but she is easily five inches taller than I am. Like all of her kind, she is slender, but not thin. Muscles ripple under the form-fitting gray jumpsuit that covers her taught pale-green skin.

Before, I hadn't realized that her kind has females, but now I can see it. While still powerful in build, her features are slightly curvier than the other aliens I've seen up close. It is barely distinguishable, but I see it clearly now that I know to look. Why my father had never mentioned it baffles me. Perhaps it was so obvious to him that he didn't think it needed explanation. Not that he was around much to explain anything to me. We were already distant before the creatures showed up in the sky above us. Working with the aliens became his passion. He had such hope for the future, and I mostly got promises that he'd be around more once the power grid was up and running.

A blast, closer than all the others, shakes the walls around us. A cloud of dust fills the room, and my eyes water. My lungs burn as I breathe in, and I pull my shirt collar over my mouth. Her respirator wheezes loudly, filtering out the particles in the air.

It's all the reminder we need. It's time to leave. We've waited too long already.

Chapter Three

Emerging at the street level, my stomach sinks when I see how close I've allowed myself to get to the battle. The night air feels thick with heat and smoke. Flashes light up the sky with crimson glows, and orange balls of fire streak toward their target. Gunfire pops too close for comfort. I can't see either side of the conflict, but I can tell it's not far. It won't take much—a single stray bullet would do it—and my delay would cost me my life.

Fishface stands in a half-crouch taking in the surroundings. If I'm reading her body language right, her anxiety matches mine. I suspect she'd be sprinting away from this place at a pace I could never hope to match if I didn't have her bound.

Giving a slight tug on the rope, I motion her forward. Hugging the wall of the building, I slink to the corner and peer around. I have to figure out which direction each side is coming from. Last thing I need is to get caught behind the wrong battle line. For a while, I see nothing.

Then, movement catches my eye. Figures in the smoke and dust are barely visible. Tall and slender, I'm certain they are Fishfaces. They move in staccato motion from one place of cover to the next. The flash of an energy rifle goes off, streaking away from the moving figures.

I sigh in relief. They're retreating.

The creature firing sends several more energy blasts off into the distance. His comrades take advantage of the covering fire to move quickly down the street. Closer now, I can see them. Each wears a dark gray jumpsuit not unlike my captive, but theirs are covered in panels that look like body armor. Occasionally, I can see the ripple as a bullet from a human rifle bounces off the invisible shield that each panel produces. It's incredible technology for ground combat. Yet, they still retreat.

The alien soldiers pass from sight, and I hold my breath. Stepping out at this point would place me in the no-man's-land between the battle lines and in the line of fire from both sides. I wave my hand at my captive Fishface to make her crouch and point down to indicate we are staying put.

Gunfire reports erupt in the distance, and I see an occasional spray of brick and stone as bullets hit the buildings. An explosion rips the side of a building clean off, and I cover my ears involuntarily. Whoever this human resistance is, they have bigger guns than most. I pray that one of those explosives doesn't hit the building above our heads.

Minutes later, I hear the shouts and commands of the human line. Men and women emerge. Not formal military, but a ragtag local militia of sorts sporting what army surplus clothing they could get their hands on. The roar of an engine drowns out the soldiers as a pickup truck with a mounted machine gun in the truck bed pulls into view and stops. The gunner lets off several rounds, adjusts, and lets off more.

This is our moment.

I stand and start padding my way in the direction the human soldiers came from, keeping our building between us and the crossfire. Blasts shake the ground, and I narrowly dodge a brick falling from above. I am way too close to the action, and I mutter a curse for allowing this to happen to me. Two years on the streets—I should know better.

Fishface has no choice but to follow, but her head is on a swivel. I realize that from her perspective she is behind enemy lines. She could be shot at any moment if we are sighted. It doesn't matter that she's not one of the alien soldiers fighting back. Any militia member in the heat of battle wouldn't hesitate to drop any Fishface they see, bound or not. Again, I wonder if that would be a mercy. We aren't moving very fast, and she's not helping me get to safety any faster.

Block by block, we slowly progress, the sound of gunfire fading into the distance. Now and again, the blast of an explosion causes us to duck. It's only when I can barely hear the battle that I allow myself a breath of relief. We are going to get out of here, and I promise myself to never be so stupid again as to get this close to the fighting.

I'm nineteen and not in bad shape. If I wanted to join the fight, any local militia would take me. Younger people than me have already joined the conflict. Several of my former classmates attached themselves to a militia when the schools shut down. Some wanted to get payback for what the aliens had done. Others simply wanted a hot meal. Many of them are dead. I want no part of it unless I have reason. I simply want to survive until I get the answers I need about why my father deserved to die. If the answers are as bad as I think they are, I may join the fight after all.

What has given me pause, aside from answers, is that what we are fighting over is a mystery. The planet is a wasteland. Disease, starvation, and violence are everywhere. I don't understand why the creatures haven't gotten on their ship and left us to rot in the cesspool they created. Perhaps by some cruel irony they are stuck here. Perhaps they simply want to finish the job they started at the Cataclysm. We are all surviving and fighting for the scraps that remain, but those scraps won't last forever. Humanity is doomed.

Lost in thought, I'm brought back to awareness as I turn a corner faster than Fishface can react. The rope goes taught, yanking her arms forward as she whips around the corner. Her respirator rips from her nose, and an expression of panic washes over her face. The effect is almost immediate. A gurgling sound emits from her mouth, and her skin flushes. She fumbles in the air with bound hands trying to replace the device as she falls to her knees. With every second, she seems more panicked and less coordinated. I retreat back to her and grab the device now hanging loosely from her shoulder. She tries to swat my hands away, but she is getting weaker by the moment. I place the device under her nose, and she inhales. Seeing what I'm doing, she cups her hands over mine and breathes deeply. Several breaths later, she gently removes the device from my fingers and, still trembling, reattaches the device to her nose. A slight click can be heard as it locks into place.

Stepping back, I give her space to compose herself. *Why did I do that? Why did I save her?* Her eyes search mine as if asking the same question. I've been looking for an out, and that would have been it.

Realizing my heart is racing, I sit down beside her to catch my own breath. For the moment, the gunfire has receded, and I am comfortable with the distance we have from the fight. Confusion floods my mind. An hour earlier, I thought I would kill Fishface without a thought, without remorse. Now she probably lives because my instinct was to help her.

Hatred for her kind still flows through me, but I couldn't watch her die in front of me.

I shake my head. I can't allow my thoughts to get muddled. I need to find out what really happened to my father, and she is going to give me the answers. I simply need a safe place to keep asking my questions. In my head, I start thinking through the streets that I remember are safe to travel. We'll find another basement or abandoned storefront to continue our conversation.

Her respirator's wheezing has slowed. "Tash'jya." She says the word as almost a whisper, though the raspy voice of her kind makes a true whisper seem impossible.

I stare at her, shaking my head in confusion.

"Tash'jya."

Shaking my head again, I hold my hands up in a shrug. "I-I don't know your language. I never learned any of it. I can't translate what you are saying."

"My name. Tash'jya."

Neural Implant Log: Entry 134
Officer: Tash'jya, daughter of Sun'tssh
Rank: Tactician

My human captor has been gifted my name. To those reviewing this log, it may seem a dishonorable choice to have made, but I cannot deny that his actions saved my life. My bonds forced my respirator loose, and he assisted in replacing it before hypoxia overtook my senses. Indeed, this would not have happened had I not been his captive, yet I do not feel that he intended this harm. If he had, my life would be ended. For reasons unknown, he assisted with replacing my breathing device.

My mission remains my priority, but escape is futile. Despite his obvious youth, my captor's tether is an effective method to keep me subdued. Since failing to follow through with his intentions to cease my life force and now rescuing me when it was happening, I am convinced that my mission may best be served to play this out.

The information I need may yet come from him, though I still have my doubts. He does not strike me as someone who would have knowledge of his father's work, much less the ability to access his most confidential work. Still, my efforts on my own have proved fruitless, and time is running short.

Honor will not allow me to take the information by force. My bonds prevent me from approaching him as an equal. Perhaps the gift of my name will be seen as a peacemaking gesture to bridge the gap between us. This is certainly the longer play, and I hope my efforts will not be in vain. Whether his father has taught him the importance of a name gift remains to be seen.

End of log.

Chapter Four

My eyes widen at the revelation. While the sharing of a name is commonplace among humans, my father had taught me enough in the rare moments he was home from his work to know that this was not the case with her kind. To tell a stranger your name was to welcome them into your circle. Even if you knew the name, and my father had known many of his fellow alien workers' names, you didn't use it until you were told. Instead, he'd referred to each of his colleagues by their title until he'd earned their trust.

Names are sacred among her people—and she'd told me hers.

"Tash-dja." I try to pronounce her name, but I struggle to mimic the sound she makes.

She bristles at the butchering of her name. Her jaw flexes several times, and I can tell I've insulted her. If names are sacred, I'm afraid I just spit on the altar with my pronunciation.

I hold my hand up, palm outward. "Sorry. Say it again, so I can get it right." *Why do I care?*

Her shoulders relax. "Tash'jya." She says it slowly this time, pronouncing each sound with emphasis.

"Tash'jya." It's still not right, but it's a much closer approximation to her pronunciation.

She nods a single time. "I am Tash'jya. I thank you for helping me with my breathing unit."

It finally clicks for me. Even though my inattention caused the problem, I chose to save her life. I could have left her to suffer and die, but I did not. My reward? Her name. Not much to a human, but everything to her kind. Maybe this is the open door I've been searching for to get my answers.

"I-I'm." I pause. "I mean, you're welcome."

She smiles. A Fishface smile is very different from a

human's. With their pursed lips, they don't exactly turn the corners of their mouth upward. Instead, all of the skin on the side of their head pulls backward creating a slight crease along the gills on either side, from the mouth to the ears. The effect is the shape of a smile, but not quite the same.

A distant blast goes off. Her smile disappears.

"My name is Theodore, but everyone calls me Ted."

Her smile returns. "I am pleassed to know your name, Theodore called Ted."

"No, just Ted."

"Just Ted." She cocks her head in confusion.

"My name—you may call me Ted."

"Ted."

I smile and nod. "I am pleased to know your name, Tash'jya." I mimic the formal language of her kind when names are shared, but I wonder if I mean what I am saying. She is my captive. She is my prisoner. She's not someone I want to get close to. Maybe I won't kill her, but that's it. No more pleasantries. Part of me wishes she was still calling me 'human.' It would make this easier. It's far more difficult to be forceful with someone whose name I've learned. Perhaps that is her plan.

Standing, I'm tempted to offer her a hand up, but I decide otherwise. Distance. That is what I need to maintain. Get my answers and get away from her. I back up a couple paces. "Get up. We're leaving this place before the battle turns in our direction."

Hands still bound, it takes her a moment to right herself and get her feet under her. She stands and studies me with her eyes. What we've exchanged means a great deal to her kind, and I can imagine her confusion as I get back to the business of moving to a new safehouse. I haven't treated this moment with the gravity she would. Maybe I could be a little gentler with her.

Instead of tugging on the rope this time, I wave my hand that we should move.

An hour passes without running into anyone. Most of the streets are vacant as anyone who is smart has cleared out from the battle area. Ducking between buildings, I lead Tash'jya to an area of the city I've visited before. There are several condos in this area that will allow us to hide again. Bombed out and falling apart, no one lives there. At least, no one did last time I was there.

Turning the corner, we spot three men. Worse, they spot us. All three wear a black handkerchief tied around their bicep. The man in the center, who must be senior to the other two, holds a baseball bat in his hand with a long nail driven through the end and out the other side. They are halfway down the alley, and while I can only see three, there are sure to be more.

In this version of the world, there are three ways to exist. I can live as a survivor on the streets, which I have. It's worked for me so far, but it is not without its risks. I can join a militia, which would provide safety and food, at least until I have to charge the enemy lines. I don't exactly want to die for a cause that I don't fully understand. The war with the aliens began so quickly after the Cataclysm that I wonder if any of the militia truly knows why they fight. The last option is to join a gang. Violent gangs litter the streets, taking advantage of everyone and everything they can. Each gang controls an area of the city, which I make a point to avoid. Still, as they seek to expand that territory, gang members can be found on streets that were once safe. I can usually see them coming and hide when necessary, but I'm distracted trying to transport my prisoner.

I should have been listening better.

"Hello, boys. Whatcha make of this?" The man with the bat elbows the guy next to him. Despite the nasal sound of his voice, he is no less menacing. "That ain't something you see every day. A boy with a Fishface on a leash. Think we should introduce ourselves?" The two thugs on either side of them grunt in response.

I hold up my free hand. "L-look. I don't want any trouble. Really. W-we'll be on our way." Glancing over at Tash'jya, I can see her slightly crouch. She knows how dangerous this group is too.

"Yeah. No good. We recently took over this block. Can't

have word gettin' 'round that anyone can stroll in and outta here. Don't worry, we'll only beat you within an inch of your life. Can't say the same about your fishy pet there."

"Well, I make a habit of avoiding everyone, so your reputation is safe. I promise." I take a step backward.

The man glances to the others on his right and left. The man on the left produces a large knife which he runs over his bald head like a comb. He licks his lips as if ready to eat us. The other hardly moves except to reach inside his jacket. Pulling his hand out, his fingers curl through a set of brass knuckles.

We're in trouble.

"Tash'jya," I whisper without moving my lips. The men are far enough away that I'm pretty sure I can't be heard. "We have to run. You have to keep up with me. If your respirator comes out, I'm going to have to leave you behind. Understand?"

Hiss. It's not an answer, but I take it as a sign she comprehends.

The men start moving in our direction, slowly at first but picking up speed.

"Now," I say in a surprisingly calm tone. Turning completely around, we take off in a sprint. I have to push myself to keep up with Tash'jya's longer strides. The cursing shouts from the men pursuing us is plenty motivation to do so. Nearing the street, I point to a set of apartments across the road. We race across a parking lot, dodging a dilapidated sign that reads, "Vacancy sale. Apply inside for special rates."

The open hallway reveals doorways on both sides. Most are broken down, raided by looters long ago. As we pass one, I swear I see a small family huddled in the corner of one of the apartments, but I can't stop to find out. Exiting the hallway, we find ourselves in a courtyard with rusted metal furniture surrounding a dried-out swimming pool.

"They went down this way." The man with the bat is not far behind.

Tash'jya points to another hallway across the courtyard. I leap over the remains of a chair as we round the pool. Reaching the hallway, I dare a glance backward. The man with the bat emerges across the pool, and we lock eyes for a moment. Brass Knuckles is beside him. Where is Baldy?

Tash'jya pulls at my arm, and we continue running. The end of the hallway is near. A man, silhouetted in the backlight, steps out into the opening. The bald head and knife tell me all I need to know. We've been penned in. In moments, we'll be trapped in this hallway.

"Upstairs." I'm already turning onto the stairwell. These lead up to the apartments on the second floor with no other exit, so I'm not sure of my plan. I simply want to put distance between me and our pursuers. Tash'jya follows. Whether because she agrees it's the right way to go or because the tether forces her to, I'm not sure. Knife Man steps in behind us, closing off the bottom of the stairwell. *Did I trap us further?*

Nearing the top of the stairwell, the door on the right opens. A large man with a graying beard steps out. I don't notice his flannel shirt or trucker's cap at first. My eyes are drawn to his shotgun.

"Duck." His words are flat and without emotion.

Somehow, Tash'jya and I both process what he is saying and fall to our stomachs at the top stair. The blast of the shotgun nearly pierces my eardrum as it echoes off the hallway walls. A scream of pain comes from behind us.

Gazing down the stairs, I see Knife Man on his back. He curses loudly as pinpricks of blood start forming around the holes in his shirt. The other two men arrive and peer up the stairs, ducking backward when they see the shotgun.

"That was birdshot. Stings like a hornet's nest but won't kill ya unless you're a grouse. Ya'll live if you leave now." The voice of the man in flannel is deep with a thick southern drawl. "Next cartridge is buck shot, which will drop you where you stand. Choice is yours. We've got armed men guardin' all four walls of this complex. The likes of you are not welcome here."

"Get me outta here, man." Knife Man waves to his fellow gang members, who seem hesitant to step into the line of fire.

"Come on, man. Help me up."

"Grab your buddy and git."

The other two men glance fearfully around the end of the stair before grabbing Knife Man. He yelps as they help him to his feet. His curses reverberate off the walls until the men pass out of the hallway and out of sight.

Slowly, Tash'jya and I stand to face the man with the shotgun. I raise my hands to either side without letting go of the tether.

"Th-thank you, sir." I barely get the words out. My eyes stay riveted on the weapon. This man saved us, but that doesn't mean he's friendly.

Flannel man drops the barrel of the shotgun toward the floor. "Don't you thank me yet. And lower them hands. I ain't going to shoot you, but we have to get you out of sight before others see."

"See what?"

He points at Tash'jya. "That."

Chapter Five

The man waves us to the door behind him. Inside the apartment, we are greeted by a small living room. The expected furnishings, couch and tables and television, have been replaced by mattresses lining the floor. A small table with too many chairs fills the dining room, next to which the sliding glass door has been covered with black trash bags. I can see a bed and a couple more mattresses through the door to the bedroom in the back. From what I can tell, at least three families are milling about the cramped space, including small children. Everyone is silent when they see Tash'jya.

"Mommy?" A tiny voice from a little boy on one of the living room mattresses breaks the tension as he retreats into his mother's arms. He is staring at Tash'jya with wide eyes. His mother, too, glares at the alien while she shushes her son gently.

"No need to worry, everyone." The man props the shotgun against the wall by the door. "They're not staying long. Chased off a couple of no-good losers. They'll be picking bird shot out of his skin until Sunday." He lets out a deep chuckle, and a few of the others in the room join him.

A woman wearing a knit sweater approaches. She smiles at me, but her pleasantness dissolves when she glances at Tash'jya. She whispers into the man's ear. I can't make out what she is saying, but her body language tells me enough. Why are we here? Or more accurately, why is Tash'jya here?

"We don't mean any harm. Please, we were running from one of the gangs, and he helped us." I hold out a hand to shake hers. "My name is Ted."

Turning back to me, her smile returns to her lips but not her eyes. She takes my hand in hers. "Name is Grace. I'm sure my husband would have introduced himself if he was more polite. His name is Gus. If you need a place to lay low for a bit, you can hide here"—she glances again at Tash'jya—"for a few minutes."

Gus places a huge hand on his wife's shoulder. "Honey, we can give them more than a few more minutes. We both know the coast won't be clear with that gang for a while. They'll be watching for them to come out." He sighs heavily, rubbing his eyes with his free hand. "Ted, you can stay for a while. But like I said, you needn't be thanking me. Don't take my kindness for acceptance. Her kind"—he juts his bearded chin at Tash'jya—"ain't welcome here."

I survey the room again, taking into account the various family units that have unconsciously retreated toward each other. "What is 'here' exactly? Do you all live here?"

Stroking his beard, Gus smiles for the first time since we've met. "This entire apartment complex is a safe haven for people who want to live their lives in peace. When their kind,"—he nods at Tash'jya again—"ruined the world for the rest of us, we wanted to create something that felt a lil' normal. See what I mean?"

I nod, though I'm not sure what normal means anymore.

Gus continues. "Grace and I brought our kids and grandkids here to stay with us where we could protect them. Lots of the apartments here are like ours. We organized and keep watches to protect the building. Second you and your—er, friend there—entered the complex, we knew. One thing we hate more than aliens who destroy our planet is the gangs who steal from their own kind. Those boys who were after you moved in across the street only days ago. I knew they'd come poking around eventually. Hoping I sent 'em a message today."

"Well, despite what you said earlier, thank you for saving us."

"We're happy to do what we can for *you*." Grace's false smile returns. "Can I offer you a glass of water? I'm afraid it's all we can spare."

"We'd like that." I glance at Tash'jya. We'd been moving since the battle started and hadn't had a drop.

Grace walks to the small kitchenette. Producing a glass, she fills it with water from one of many pitchers on the counter. "Have to fill up our water on the days when the rains come. It's been a good water week so far. All the barrels on the roof are full, so we have some to spare for now." She fills a glass—exactly one glass—and hands it to me. She does not return to the kitchen for another one. Her message is clear. Tash'jya is allowed here because she's on my leash.

The water hydrates my parched throat. I can't help but feel a pang of guilt for Tash'jya. I don't care for her or her kind, but it's hard to see a cold denial of basic needs for anyone, especially when there's plenty to go around. I marvel at how far I've come in a matter of hours. I thought I was ready to kill her. Then, I impulsively saved her life. Feeling the cool refreshment in my throat, I wish I could give her a drink of my water.

What's gotten into me? For a moment, I even think about offering her the last of what's in the glass, but I'm certain Grace would not approve.

"Is there anything else you'll be needing, young man?" Grace cocks her head and blinks several times rapidly. Interpretation? When will we be leaving?

"Gus, thanks. I realize you said they'll be watching, but we should be going." I gesture to the door with a thumb.

"I wouldn't, but if ya'll insist, I'd head out that way." He points to the south. "That end of the building has the shortest distance to cover. Besides, it's on the other side of that gang's territory. Less likely to be watching for ya there."

I hand the empty glass to Grace. "Thank you."

"Sure thing, dear."

I turn back to Gus. "Don't suppose you could tell me where we can find any food?"

Gus frowns. "Nah. That's everyone's question these days. I won't lie, if I knew I wouldn't tell you. Got plenty of mouths to feed already." He waves a hand at the various faces in the living room. "There's three different stores near here, but I can tell you now that they've been picked clean."

"Any in that southern direction you mentioned?"

"Yeah. Just a few blocks over on East."

"Cool." I reach for the door handle. Looking at Tash'jya, I can see she's ready to leave. The collective sigh in the room from Gus' family lets me know they are ready too. "Um. Thanks, again."

"Sure thing, Ted."

No sooner are we out the door, than we hear the latch thrown behind us. I've hated the Fishfaces for two years since my father's death, but my hatred had always been from afar. This felt up close and personal. Do I hate the Fishfaces? Probably. Do I hate Tash'jya? The question burns in my mind without an answer. I feel like I should hate her, but I also realize I couldn't be as cold and unfeeling as to treat her as those people had.

"I guess we go find that store. Maybe we'll get lucky and find something to eat."

Tash'jya doesn't answer. I can't blame her.

Neural Implant Log: Entry 135
Officer: Tash'jya, daughter of Sun'tssh
Rank: Tactician

Humans are a fascinating species. Their treatment of other species borders on barbaric, and yet their ability to classify and prioritize highly complex. There is a basic morality built inside of them that can usurp their base prejudices when called upon. This principled center can allow them to place members of their own species at a lower rank than other species, something we didn't think possible. I witnessed this today when a human rescuer committed violence against other humans to save me and my captor.

While this does not presuppose that they truly understand honor as we do, it does demonstrate that an innate sense of justice remains, even when they no longer sense the benefit they derive from our arrival on their planet.

My captor, especially, seems affected by our recent experience. Our rescuer, whose name was given to us without his consent—so I will not use it—and his mate known as Grace gave my captor an opportunity to see human hatred with his own eyes. I don't believe he liked what he saw as he was catered to, and I was ignored. In fact, he seems intent on finding us *both* sustenance in the wake of that display. I cannot complain. I have gone too long without sufficient hydration or caloric intake.

On another note, the gift of my name was reciprocated. My captor is known as Ted and gifted his name to me freely. His father must have taught him enough of our people that he understood the gravity of what I was giving him. I hope this connection may prove to the benefit of the completion of my mission.

End of log.

Another half-hour of slinking through the streets of the city passes without incident and without any more words exchanged between us. Standing at the end of an alley, I stare across the street. What used to be a local grocery store is located on the other side of a parking lot. Several of the front windows are shattered, one or two completely missing. The sign, which no longer illuminates, hangs loosely from the front of the building, threatening to fall at any moment. Most of these stores were picked over long ago for any remaining shelf-stable foods, but I've learned that an occasional gem could be found under the shelves, carelessly dropped by an earlier visitor.

Still, that parking lot is a large space to cross with my prisoner. I must make certain no one is watching, alien or human. We've had too many run-ins with other humans, and we need to find a place to stop so I can get answers. Amazingly, Tash'jya seems to understand and waits patiently as I scan the open area. Her kind find our food compatible with their digestive system, but their caloric need is far greater than ours. If my stomach is growling, I can only imagine how famished she is feeling.

For several minutes, I hear nothing. Not a sound, except the slightly chilly breeze that makes me shiver. I step out into the open and pause. Nothing. Motioning with my head, we tiptoe across the street. The parking lot is littered with abandoned vehicles, mostly rusty and unusable. All have their gas tank pried open as looters have siphoned any lingering drops of fuel long ago. Weaving through the lot, we arrive at the store front. I peer into the window.

Even in the dark, I can see the emptiness of the shelves. Nothing remains, and the shelves at one end were even tipped over. My stomach gurgles in disappointment, but perhaps this makes it a safer place to hide for a while. Picked over long ago, it's not a target for anyone anymore. A perfect place to lay low and finish questioning Tash'jya about what she knows.

I slip in the door which used to open automatically before the Cataclysm. Now it sits half-removed from its track, motionless. Tash'jya follows, mimicking my every move. The darkness of the store feels welcoming compared to the exposure of the lot outside. Bits of glass crunch under my feet, sounding impossibly loud in this silent space.

I cut between the registers, noting the drawers hanging open which were cleaned out when money still meant something. I choose the aisle under the surprisingly still-mounted sign saying, 'canned goods.' Stooping, I search under the shelving unit for a stray can. In the darkness, the best I can do is reach around and 'see' by feel. Layers of dust coat my fingers. I touch a rock, something that feels like an insect husk, and something soft that leaves my fingers smelling rank. I don't want to know.

That's when I find it. The magical feeling of an aluminum can against my fingertip makes my insides leap. I look at Tash'jya and waggle my eyebrows. She stoops next to me and peers into the darkness, perhaps trying to understand my expression. I reach as far as I can and manage to get enough grip to roll the can closer. I do it again, and I almost yelp with glee as the can finds its way into my palm. I mouth a silent "thank you, God" as the weight of the can tells me it still contains something. I don't allow myself to hope for canned peaches or pineapple. I'll take anything over the dry, stale crackers I've been rationing for a week.

I pull my arm free of the shelves and peer at the prize. The label is faded and dirty, but I can tell it was once green. Vegetables of some kind must be inside. Pulling my pocketknife out, I select the can-opener and begin to work on the lid. It takes time, but I'm careful not to spill anything inside. I peel the sharp aluminum aside and remove a cold, somewhat slimy green bean. I shove the salty treasure in my mouth and try to pretend it's fresh from a garden. I eat another. And then a third.

Tash'jya crouches before me, her eyes fixated on the can. I roll my eyes and hand her a bean. She turns away and cups the bean with both hands as she brings it to her mouth. With a slurp, I can hear her swallow a moment later. Turning back, I sigh and hand her another. She repeats the process. I chuckle a little and enjoy another bean. Back and forth we go until the can is empty. I swallow half the water in the can and let her have the rest. She guzzles the liquid in one huge slurp.

Without hesitation, she drops the can and begins searching under the shelves for more. I wonder if her longer arms will find something I missed. Right and left she sweeps the underside of the shelves with her slim appendage. Her expression appears child-like, as if hoping to open a present early on Christmas Eve. I have to admit that I feel the same way. She can reach things most humans cannot. If there is something under there, she'll find it.

That's when I hear the scrape of a foot behind me.

"Don't move. Stealing is a crime, stranger." The throaty voice is followed by the cold metal of a pistol touching the back of my head.

Chapter Six

I raise my hands slowly, making sure I've still got a grip on Tash'jya's tether. Having removed her arm from under the shelves, she is frozen with her arms defensively crossed in front of her face. Bending one leg under me, I push into a kneeling position. I'm relieved as I feel the pistol barrel pull away from my skull. This allows me enough maneuverability to look at the source of the voice behind me.

I'm greeted by a pair of dirty, worn work boots, and I remind myself to move cautiously as a kick from the steel toes would not be pleasant. Raising my gaze, I take in a pair of faded urban camouflage pants, an oversized belt buckle, and a gray vest covered in pockets over a formerly white T-shirt. The weathered face of the man sports a head of short graying hair and a scar that stretches from his cheekbone to the top of his scalp, leaving a hairless stripe. He is flanked by two others, who are equally tough-looking. Their forearms, which appear as big as my thighs, are crossed in front of them. Not men I want to mess with.

The barrel of the first man's .45-caliber pistol points directly between my eyes. I'm not certain I would even have time to see the flash of the muzzle before my life ended if he chose to pull the trigger. I stare silently, waiting for him to make the next move.

"On your feet, stranger." He motions twice with the pistol in an upward direction. His voice is gravelly with a slight southern drawl.

I push myself upright and get my leg directly under me. My muscles shake as I move painfully slow through the motion, not wanting to make any sudden moves. When I'm finally standing, I raise my chin to look at the man and his companions in the face. Behind me, Tash'jya still cowers on the floor.

"W-we don't mean any harm." My voice comes out as a squeak, betraying the fear inside. Who this man is or what he stands for is unclear. There are those who would be happy to see another human. There are also those who would kill anyone they considered a threat—and I've eaten a can of food that could have been theirs. Whoever this man is, he does not appear happy.

"Now, let's not begin our conversation by lying. You might mean us no harm. That remains to be determined. But that thing"—he glances at Tash'jya—"would cut all our throats without hesitation given the chance. I would have shot you both on sight had it not been in restraints."

I am reminded that Tash'jya is defenseless in her bonds. She is at the mercy of these men. Any hope we have of making it out alive is up to me.

I conjure up every bit of disdain for Tash'jya's race that I have and let it come through my voice. "This Fishface is *my* prisoner. I need information before I kill it." I can't be certain, but I think I see the corner of his mouth curl upward. His gun lowers an inch, and I allow myself to breathe.

"Prisoner, huh? And all by yourself? Not easy to catch one of these buggers. How'd you manage it?" Again, he examines Tash'jya, his eyes moving from toe to head. His lips curl in disgust.

"I got lucky." It's the truth.

He laughs. So do his companions. It's the first sound the other two have made. His laugh cuts off suddenly. "Not good enough. It's bigger and stronger than you. You didn't overpower it. For all I know, this getup is a ruse, and the Fishface is planning to jump us at any moment. How do I make certain you're not one of those peace-loving, Fishface-hugging types that still thinks they mean us no harm?"

Silence passes between us. Somehow, I have to convince this man that I despise Tash'jya as much as he does. I hate myself for what I'm about to do.

I yank on the tether.

Tash'jya's eyes bulge in panic as her respirator flies from her nose. Her throat gurgles, and her wheezes intensify like she's trying to suck air through a coffee stirrer. Her complexion deepens to a purple. Her fingers scramble to replace the respirator, which slips from her grasp repeatedly as her body trembles.

I can't help her. Not this time. I have to play the part that won't get me shot. The agonizing seconds stretch on as I silently will Tash'jya to get the device in place. Finally, she gets the clip in the correct position in her hand and replaces it under her nose. The snapping of the device as it locks in place floods me with relief, but I hold my breath lest I let out a telltale sigh. I try to appear disappointed that she was successful.

A throaty chuckle comes from behind me, followed by the robotic concert of grunts from the man's companions. "I do enjoy seeing that happen to them. It's their weakness after all. Bigger—stronger—faster—but can't breathe worth a thing in our atmosphere. Idiotic race of freaks. You'd think they'd attempt to conquer a planet they could actually live on."

"Yeah." I try to sound like I found her suffering pleasant. In truth, I want to retch. The first time I did that to her, it was an accident. This time was not. I took no joy in it. I am not a monster, but that doesn't change that I feel like one in this moment. "I make sure to do that from time to time to be certain she knows who's in charge." I force a laugh, keenly aware that his pistol is still trained on me.

"Well, well. It's nice to find a like-minded individual in our midst. Still, I cannot overlook the theft of valuable resources." Bending over, he picks up the empty can. Smelling it, he grimaces. "Nasty, but nutritious." The can clatters to the floor and rolls underneath a shelf. "Matthews, I thought you scoured this place for any remaining food when we set up camp here. How'd you miss this one?"

"Sorry, commander," the goon on the left answers in a deep voice. "I can't reach under the shelves so easily." He holds out a meaty hand. I believe he wouldn't get more than a few inches before his forearms would get caught on the edge of the shelving unit.

"Waste disposal duty tonight."

"Yes, sir." Matthews straightens, but his expression tells me that 'waste disposal duty' is not something he relishes.

"As for our thieves—"

I answer before he can finish his thought. I don't want to find out where his sentence might go. "I—I'm sorry. I didn't realize anyone was here. I w-wouldn't have taken it if-if I knew."

A long silence passes between us. Thoughts of running away or tackling him come to mind. In one moment, I think I might leave Tash'jya to her fate with these men to save my own skin, and in the next I'm prying the gun from his hands and using it. My desire for answers about my father keeps me from the first thought, and the knowledge I'd never succeed in the latter keeps me rooted in my place. My heart is racing, but I bite down to keep my face stone cold.

His grizzled face contorts into a leathered smirk. With a huff, he lowers the weapon and places it back in his waistband. His two grunts relax. This time, I allow myself a long breath of relief.

"Hear that, boys? The kid is sorry." He laughs and claps me on the shoulder with a heavy hand. His weather-worn face creases as he smiles. It's the kind of smile that sends shivers up my spine. "Truth is, we can use a resourceful young man like yourself. Hard to find those committed to the cause, much less one who can capture one of these animals all by himself. What say you?"

I realize I'm being recruited. Whoever this man is, he's obviously part of a militia. Or a gang. Or both—as sometimes one morphs into the other when someone takes charge. If his scar is any indication, he has seen his fair share of violence and war and has likely been responsible for plenty of it himself. I want no part, but I've been on the street long enough to know that declining is not an option. These street militia types see in black and white. I'm either with them or against them.

"I-I guess so."

"You guess so?" His smirk disappears. "Now don't you go showing too much gratitude. I've extended a privileged invitation to you, boy, and I don't hand those out to any youngster who crosses my path. I'm afraid you don't understand what it is you're being given here."

I swallow hard. "Uh. Sorry. I mean I'd really like to join your group."

The smirk returns. "Whoa, Rookie. Not so fast." His companions grunt in agreement. "You've been invited to apply for the position. It's not a handout. You gotta earn your place with this posse. Name is Revon, but 'commander' or 'sir' will do just fine. You got a name?"

I don't like where this is heading, but I have to play along. "Yes, Re—er—sir. Ted. My name is Ted." I bite my lip. "What do you mean earn my place?"

He extends his hand. "Well, for starters, you can hand over the reins to your Fishface there."

"Hand her over?" My grip tightens around the rope. "She's—"

"Yours. I remember. You've said so." Revon stares me down. "Still, a show of faith is in order. Besides, you won't be able to take that thing where you're going." He glances down at his extended hand.

"I'm going somewhere?" I'm certain I'm in trouble.

"A mission, boy. To prove yourself. Show that you really mean it when you say you want to join us. Then, you'll get your little prize back to do with as you wish." He waves his fingers, again asking for the rope.

I don't have a choice.

Tash'jya's eyes dart from me to Revon and back. I can feel the fear radiating from her. With me, she was in danger. With these men, she's as good as dead. If I'm going to get the information she has, I need to play my cards right. I cannot simply surrender her without conditions. For all I know, Revon's goons will take her out back for target practice.

"Okay. I'll do it. But it is *my* prisoner." I point my finger and try to harden my voice. "Commander, I expect it to be returned to me alive. The kill is mine."

Revon stares blankly. I gulp, afraid that I've overplayed my hand. Without warning, he bursts out laughing. His goons follow like automatons. Nervously, I try to join them as if I meant it as a joke all along.

"The kill is yours? That's the funniest thing I've heard in a long time. All right, Teddy Bear, you'll get your wish. Hear that, boys? Do what you wish, but she stays alive. Got it?" The two goons groan in disappointment. Revon's attention turns back to me. "Killing it would be too quick anyway. The boys could use the entertainment. It's been too quiet lately. Hand it over, and we'll take good care of it. I promise." Again, he waves his finger, but once this time. His patience is apparently running out.

I swallow hard as I slowly place the rope into Revon's hand. My gut sinks as I hear Tash'jya's panic rise to the surface.

"Yusha mei nani! Yusha mei nani ssu tani!" Tash'jya starts shouting in her own language and pulls at the rope with both hands, careful not to allow her respirator to pull free. "Yusha mei—"

Revon nods to one of his men. The man steps forward and strikes Tash'jya across the cheek. She yelps in pain, crumpling back to the floor. A kick from his boot causes her to grunt and double over.

"What are you doing? I told you she's mine!" I can't help but shout. I reach for the rope.

Revon stiff-arms my approach. "Teaching the creature to know its place."

"But-but you said you'd return it alive."

"I did. And I will. But my boys here will get to have their fun. They've all suffered under the hand of these devils, and some payback is due. That okay with you?" He's not looking for an answer to the question, so I keep my mouth shut.

The man kicks Tash'jya again, this time in the face. Blood seeps from her mouth. *What have I consigned her to?* I grit my teeth to avoid exploding. Tash'jya looks up at me, her eyes void of any emotion or trust. *She's one of them, but she doesn't deserve—this.*

"What do I have to do?" I try unsuccessfully not to sound angry.

Revon places his thumbs in his belt and turns to me. "See? That's more like it. A team player, that's all you need to be. Your mission is simple. You stole from me, so I can tell thieving is in your nature. Time to put it to use."

"You want me to steal something?"

Revon's lips spread into a devilish grin. "Not something. Someone."

Neural Implant Log: Entry 136
Officer: Tash'jya, daughter of Sun'tssh
Rank: Tactician

Stupid human. I cannot believe he handed me over to a violent militia so willingly. Does he not realize what they will do to me? Their promises to keep me alive are empty, and he leaves to save his own pink skin.

I should not have trusted him with my name. I spit on his name and will not use it. While I do not believe his desire to join with these humans is genuine, there is no honor in his abandonment of me. I was his captive, and by honor he is responsible for my safety.

I should have left my respirator on the floor and died there. Then, he would have no bargaining chip to save himself. I cannot, however, fulfill my duty if I am deceased.

My mission is doomed as long as I am in the hands of these violent creatures. I am to become the toy on which to vent their frustrations. These are the worst kinds of humans. They have convinced themselves of their just war against us and feel a sense of duty and honor by their actions. In truth, they are violent and disturbed, even by human standards. It is prejudice played out with abandon to the point of justifying evil in the name of righteousness.

I will not submit. I will not cower. I will not beg for my life. No matter what their intentions are for me, I will not play into their hand. I hope my former captor is happy with his newfound freedom. I don't believe it will be for long. These men have no intention of keeping their word. He will return to find me dead or dying and realize his error. Then, they will take from him what they want until he is no longer useful.

May my people recognize the sacrifice I have made. My mission has failed.

End of log.

Chapter Seven

I crouch against a hard brick wall. The night air is cold, awakening my senses. Two blocks away, I can see the medical center Revon described to me. Guards stand out front as survivors of the wars shuffle in and out of the building. Not even a proper hospital, the building is an old warehouse with a tent out front to admit patients. Still, it's the only medical installation for miles. Anyone needing attention in the area comes here for help.

I finger the pistol holstered inside my jacket, a gift from Revon to complete the mission. I'm not comfortable with it, and the thought of pointing it at another human being makes me ill. I hope it doesn't come to that. Had this been a simple grab for medical supplies, I would be less nervous. A simple lie to get in, and I could grab what I need and make a dash for the door. I wouldn't be the first to do so. Stealing was a way of life for me, and I'd happily grab whatever he needed to get Tash'jya back. But that is not what I was sent for.

"Westfield." I whisper the name. It's all that Revon gave me to go on. He had not been forthcoming on the details when I asked why the target was a person of interest. Whoever Westfield is, I'm supposed to deliver them alive to Revon. The question of whether a human life is worth trading for the life of a Fishface is one I can't afford to ask. I won't like the answer, and I need to find out what happened to my father. I need to know what is inside the Bubble and why no one who goes in there comes out alive.

The one solace I have is that he asked for this person 'alive.' If he wanted me to kill Westfield, I suspect he would have taken care of that himself a long time ago. Revon doesn't strike me as someone who minds getting his hands dirty.

Getting Westfield out will not be easy. Getting inside, that isn't a problem. I pull my pocketknife out and open the blade. I involuntarily suck air through my teeth as I draw the blade across my forearm. The skin opens, sending hot pain up and down my arm. I force a couple deep breaths to stay calm. The wound needs to be deep enough to require attention but not so deep to cause real injury.

I shudder as I pull the knife away and decide the cut is enough. I've dealt with cuts on my own and had even stitched my skin up once or twice when necessary. But an open wound is my ticket inside the medical center. Blood begins to trickle down my arm, and I allow it to soak into my sleeve. An abundance of blood will make it easier to get inside. Wiping the blade on my pant leg, I pocket it and begin my shuffle down the street. Holding my arm, I look as pathetic as I can.

The guards straighten as I approach, gripping their rifles.

Don't look guilty. Don't look guilty.

"State your name and business, citizen," the guard on the left says flatly.

"Theodore James. I'm cut." I hold my arm up and wince for effect.

The guard steps forward and looks at my arm. "Looks legit. Head to the tent to be admitted."

I nod. Easy. Just as I thought. What I have to do next will be much more difficult.

Inside the tent, a large woman in scrubs and tattered cardigan stands behind a folding table. She points intensely at the door to the warehouse and fusses in a Scottish accent at a young orderly. "Get that mess cleaned up. I need all the beds I can get after today's skirmish. The wounded are coming in droves, and I can't have you being lazy."

"Yes, ma'am." The boy runs off into the building, properly chastised.

Looking in my direction, she calls again to the boy, "See, here's another one. Get me more beds!" She huffs and exasperated sigh and looks me up and down. "Got yourself hurt there, young man?"

"Cut myself. Building shifted during the battle earlier. Support broke and cut me as I ran out." I give her my best 'scared out of my mind' expression. "Can you help me? It really hurts."

"Now don't be lookin' all downcast. We've dealt with worse here. Let me get you inside. We'll have you stitched up and on the mend in no time." She makes a few notes on a chart before extending one hand toward me and another toward the door.

"Is Doctor Westfield here?"

"Doctor Westfield? There's something I haven't heard before." She lets out a short laugh. "*Nurse* Westfield is quite good, but not a doctor. Doctors are in short supply these days, so I guess I can see your confusion. Is that who you'd like to see, young man? She a friend of yours?"

I have to be careful not to overreach in my lie. I don't know how well this woman knows Nurse Westfield. "Not exactly. More of an old acquaintance."

"That makes sense. All she ever does is work, the poor girl. Didn't think she had any friends. It'll be good for her to see someone she knows from the outside."

I nod. "Yeah, pretty certain she won't remember me." The woman ushers me into the warehouse which has been divided by sheets into smaller spaces. Pulling the corner of a sheet backward, she reveals a rusty bed frame with a dirty mattress. I hesitate.

"It's not the Hilton, you can be sure, but it's the best we've got. If you want to be seen, then you wait in here." She waves me in.

Nodding again, I take a seat on the bed, listening to the frame creak and groan under my weight. The woman lets go of the sheet. I can hear her call once I'm out of sight. "Nurse Westfield, I have a bleeding patient for you in exam three. Asked for you by name. Not bad looking, either, if I do say so. If I were but ten years younger…" Her voice trails off as she heads back to her table.

"Be there in a minute. Finishing up here." The feminine voice is young, but confident. It is not the voice of someone who is in over their head in this clinic. I can only guess the amount of triage experience the last couple years have brought. Injuries and illness are common enough in this version of the world, much less immediately after a battle has passed through the area.

Revon sent me for a woman? A nurse? Why?

The minutes pass, and I can hear all sorts of patients throughout the building. Some sound sick. Others sound like they are groaning from some kind of injury. Chills bolt up and down my spine as someone on the other side of the building screams for the doctors to stop whatever it is they are doing. Anesthesia is uncommon nowadays, and the clinic can sometimes resemble a Civil War field hospital. I decide right there that if I'm ever seriously injured, I'd prefer to die on the streets rather than succumb to whatever is happening to that poor man.

Feet shuffle toward my 'room.' The sheet is pulled back, revealing a woman in scrubs who can't be more than a couple years older than me. She pushes a cart of supplies next to the bed and sets up a folding chair. She wears blue scrubs bearing the stains of previous patients' ailments, either blood or fluids. Her blonde hair is pulled back in a ponytail. Even without a shred of makeup, she is beautiful despite the hardened look she wears. She has seen some things in this makeshift clinic. Grabbing a bottle of alcohol, she scrubs her hands over a bowl.

"I'm Nurse Westfield. Let's see what we have here." Pulling up the chair, she peels back my jacket sleeve to reveal my arm. I make a show of wincing. "That's an ugly cut. What happened?"

"A blast hit the building I was in during the battle earlier, and I ran into a metal support that was sticking out of a wall as I escaped."

"Mmm-hmm. Dangerous out there. Wish they'd take the war outside the city instead of putting survivors at risk each time they want to shoot at each other." She dabs at the wound with an alcohol pad. I wince for real this time. Pulling out a suture kit, she begins to stitch up the injury. I grit my teeth each time the needle pierces my skin. "You sure this was caused by a jagged support beam?"

"Yep. Got me good. Stupid of me, I know. I heard the gunfire and could only think to run."

A long silence passes as she finishes the stitching, tying it off with expert precision. Letting out a long sigh, she glares at me. "You'll need to keep that clean. Bandages are in short supply, so I won't be covering it at this time. So, before I call the guards from outside, let me guess. You're armed and taking me to Revon." Her hand darts inside my jacket and pulls the pistol from the holster before I can even react. In seconds, she removes the clip and clears the chamber.

I can't hide my surprise. *How did she figure it out? And how did she learn how to handle a pistol like that?*

She shakes her head with an exasperated sigh as she sets the gun down on the table nearby. "Thought so. That's not happening. You're not the first he's sent here to collect me."

"I-I don't know what you mean?"

Standing up, she glares down at me with her arms crossed. "Please. You were smart enough to get in here, so let's not play dumb. It doesn't help either one of us."

No point in lying now. "But how did you—"

"How did I figure it out? Easy. That cut is too clean to have been caused by a jagged piece of metal. That kind of edge would create a jagged laceration, not a clean slice." She points to my hip. "I'm guessing the bulge in your pocket is the knife you used to cut yourself and gain entrance to the clinic. Besides, you look like you've been on the streets long enough to deal with a cut like this on your own. Not a bad plan. The last guy tried to enter by faking pneumonia—which he was dumb enough to think would present as a stomachache. Where Revon finds these idiots, I'll never be able to guess."

I try not to appear hurt as I get lumped in with the other 'idiots' Revon has sent. My heart begins pounding. I'm lost and unsure what to do next. I stare. I don't know what else to do.

"Relax. I've disarmed you, so they'll likely do no more than ban you from this facility. Not enough police force to lock anyone up. Plus, you haven't really done any harm—not that I gave you a chance."

"I'm—I'm sorry."

She purses her lips and studies me. Pinching her nose with two fingers, she takes a long breath. "He put you up to this, so I'm the one who should be apologizing. What does he have on you? Withholding your food? Promising safety? What? He doesn't have your family, does he?"

"He has my prisoner." I don't know why I tell her, but the words come before I can stop them.

She glances up at me. "That's a new one. Points for creativity there. You'd risk your skin for a prisoner?"

"She has information I need. About my father. About the Bubble." I've told her this much. I might as well spill it all. "I captured her because I need to learn what happened. But she won't talk, and we've ended up on the run and ran into this militia—" I'm rambling. I hear the words spilling out of my mouth, but I can't stop them.

Nurse Westfield's eyes widen. "Your prisoner is one of them?"

"A Fishface, yes."

Her face scrunches at the use of the term. "They call themselves Skya'ja. The term you used is for ignorant imbeciles, which is possible if you're mixed up with Revon."

"Skya—Skya'ja?" The word is a mouthful. I'd heard my father use this term once or twice, but I'd never known it was the name of their race. Then again, my father didn't tell me a lot of things—or I hadn't been paying attention. Probably both.

Westfield eyes my chart. "Ted, is it?"

I nod.

"Well, Ted, if you're willing to risk your neck for one of the Skya'ja, then we need to have a different conversation. Maybe we can hold off on security for a second."

I give her no response as I am thoroughly confused.

"You see, Westfield is my mother's maiden name. When the

Cataclysm happened, I'd graduated from high school a year early and just started nursing school. Still, I wanted to help. My father, being the bigot he is, wouldn't have it, so I left home. Wish I'd done so long before it all happened." She pauses to look out the window as if seeing the memory. "I could have been far away before the Cataclysm happened. He'd never have found me then. Changing my name kept me at a distance for a while, but eventually he located me. Now I basically have to live behind these guarded walls and deal with his unfortunate gophers like you."

She pauses, probably to let me connect the dots. Slowly, the realization of what she's saying occurs to me.

She smirks. It's an expression I've seen before. "There it is. You put it together. That man you know as Commander Revon—he's my dad."

Chapter Eight

An hour passes. I sit in the makeshift office of Nurse Loren Westfield inside the clinic gently thumping the back of my head against the masonry wall as if it might help me sort out all that has transpired in the last few hours. She'd brought me here, insisting that I had only two choices—wait until the end of her shift, so we could talk, or be escorted out by the security guards. Neither are good options. The longer I stay, the greater the chance that Commander Revon will lose faith in me and harm Tash'jya, but Loren had seen right through me. My one option is to play along.

All I want are answers. I pound my fists on my thighs in frustration, wishing Tash'jya had simply answered my questions in that basement so many hours ago. I realize now that I can't kill her, not with my own hands. If she'd simply told me what I needed to know, I would have left her there and neither of us would be in this mess. Instead, I'm waiting to figure out why Revon's daughter hasn't turned me in, and Tash'jya is—experiencing whatever Revon's goons have planned for her. I shake my head at the thoughts, hoping they aren't true. My luck, they'll kill her by accident, and I'll be back to square one.

The clinic has grown quieter as the night has deepened. Fewer people arrive at this hour, except the most desperate. Patients who can do so have likely fallen asleep, and peace has fallen over the building. Still a few miserable groans, but nothing like when I first got here. I'm grateful the brutal screaming of the distant patient has ceased.

The office—if it can be called that—is nothing more than a desk in a corner of the building. In reality, the desk isn't even a desk, but rather a door lying on two filing cabinets. Still, neat stacks of patient files, a dirty coffee mug, and a picture of someone

I can only guess is her mother seem almost normal until I notice the pillow and mat rolled up under the table. She wasn't kidding. She lives here lest her father get his hands on her.

"Still here?" Loren stands at the corner, her mouth turned upward on one side in a lopsided grin. Her arms are folded, files in one hand. "I'd thought you would have taken the opportunity to get out of here. Whatever you want with your Skya'ja prisoner, it must be important."

I stare, not sure what to say. She's obviously not like her father, but I still can't predict how she'll react to my reasons for capturing Tash'jya.

"Look, if I'm going to help, you have to tell me what is going on. How did you end up with a Skya'ja prisoner? And how did that lead to my father?"

I sigh. Before I can stop myself, the story begins to pour out of my mouth. My lucky rock throw. My questioning of Tash'jya. Escaping the battle. Our run-in with the gang and Gus. Learning her name. Even our shared can of beans. As I speak, Loren turns her chair directly toward me before slowly settling into it. With her elbows on her knees, she listens to every word without interruption.

"—and that is how I ended up here with you." I swallow hard. The seconds of silence that pass between us stretch into a painful minute. She stares at the floor, either processing my story or considering calling for the guards. I'm not sure which.

Her voice startles me when it finally comes. "Ted, I'm going to tell you something, but only because of one thing you said. You've learned the name of your Skya'ja prisoner. You know they don't offer their names to simply anyone, right?"

I nod.

"Despite being her captor, she gave you hers. With what you know, doesn't that seem unusual to you?"

I scrunch my brow in thought. "I did save her life when her respirator came out."

Loren shakes her head. "No. That's not it. I mean—normally it might be—but her life was in jeopardy because of you. Your saving of her wouldn't have invoked the trust of her name. It must be something else."

"Like what?" Now I'm completely confused.

"I'm not sure. You said she was not dressed as a soldier? They do have women in their army, you know." She scratches her scalp with both hands before removing her hair band and shaking her hair behind her. Her hair is greasy and her face tired, but I note again how beautiful she is. Had we gone to the same high school, I'd have been only a year behind her and working up the courage to ask her to prom.

"I didn't realize there were even Skya'ja women until I met her. But, no, she was not wearing the armor of a soldier."

Loren straightens. "And she was by herself?"

I nod again. "What does that mean?"

She sits back in her chair, slouching a bit. Letting out a long, slow breath, she bites her lip as if contemplating telling me something. Glancing away from me, she shakes her head slightly, a silent argument with herself playing out in front of me. I remain frozen in my chair, anxious to hear whatever it is she hesitates to tell me.

"Ted, whoever Tash'jya is, she is on special assignment from her people. It's the one reason she'd be alone on the streets. The Skya'ja never go anywhere alone unless they must. It's part of their communal culture. I thought that maybe she was a soldier who got separated from her unit or the lone survivor of a battle, but she'd have been dressed like one." She pauses and looks me right in the eyes. "Whatever she was doing, it was very important—at least to her."

"How do you know that?" I lean in toward her. "How did you learn so much about their ways? My father worked with them, and I barely know anything about them."

She purses her lips to one side and chews on the inside of her cheek. Her eyes return to mine. "Because I helped them. I treated their wounded before my father found me, and I had to hide myself in here."

A curse escapes my lips. "You're a traitor?" I begin to rise out of my chair, my voice also climbing. Even I'm surprised by the flood of anger that courses through my body. "You—you treated their wounded who were hurt while trying to kill humans? What—how—why?"

In an instant, she is on her feet and shoving me back into my chair. I'm surprised by her strength. She holds a finger up in my face. "Keep your voice down, Ted. It's not like that. If you shut up long enough to let me explain, then I think I can help you. Otherwise, I'll have the guards in here to lock you up as a danger to yourself due to the raging infection I'll diagnose you with. Anything you do will be dismissed as delirium. Got it?"

I'm seething, but I sit back. My knuckles are white as I grip the arms of the chair. "They killed my father," I say through gritted teeth.

"I-I know. I'm sorry about your dad. Ted, I get your hatred of them. In a way, they took my father too. He's not the man I remember." She closes her eyes at the thought.

"At least he's still breathing." I can't even look at her.

She doesn't respond. She can't argue with that.

She reaches for the picture frame on her desk. "Ted, a couple days before the Cataclysm and the ensuing war, my mother was killed. My father's company was delivering construction materials to a building being remodeled for Skya'ja use. My mother worked in the company office, but she wanted to see the Skya'ja up close. She was so excited to accompany my father that day." She pauses, swallowing hard. Her eyes become glassy, and she blinks several times. "No one is sure what happened, but there was a collapse. My father was hurt badly. My mother—she was killed instantly. My father couldn't handle it and gave into his hatred, especially after the Cataclysm. My grief gave me clarity he didn't have and made me look at what was really happening as the war started—to ask the questions no one was asking. They are questions I still ask every day."

"Oh yeah? What would those be?" I spit the words at her.

She doesn't look at me, but rather stares off as if recounting her thoughts. "Is this war as much our fault as it is theirs? Is it still going on because we refuse to actually figure out what happened?"

"*They* destroyed our planet. *They* came here with their promises of clean energy. *They* caused the Cataclysm and the Bubble."

"I-I know, but we haven't exactly been uninvolved. After the explosion, the bullets started flying so fast that no one asked if they should."

I bite down hard and bore into her with a glare. "My father is dead. He was helping them. Are you saying he's to blame? He wouldn't have been part of anything that he thought would harm humanity. Now I can't even visit the place where he died because it's inside that cursed barrier."

She nods and glances down at the floor. "I don't question your pain, Ted. You didn't deserve to lose your father."

My anger fades a little.

"I assisted with their wounded because I don't believe that any of us deserve this. Not us. Not them. They aren't the murderers you think they are."

I roll my eyes. "That doesn't exactly stop them from shooting at us."

"No. But are they shooting? Or are they shooting back?"

I stare, not offering a response. Not offering a request to stop her explanation either. Her words gnaw at my brain. In two years, I've never heard anyone suggest that the aliens were anything but the aggressors.

She clasps her hands and leans forward in her chair again. "I've seen the fear on their faces. Took me a while to see it. Their expressions are different than ours, but I've held the hands of their dying soldiers as they wept and cried out in their own language before breathing for the last time. Do you know what I learned?"

A long silence passes between us.

"They don't want to be in this fight any more than we do. And your friend—"

"She's not my friend," I snap.

Loren sighs. "Fine. Your prisoner, then, doesn't want this fight. Whatever she was doing when you caught her, it was toward that end." She starts counting her points on her fingers. "She's not a soldier. She's alone and without her people. She treated you with respect you probably didn't deserve after what you've done to her. She's probably on a special assignment. It adds up when you think about it."

Up until now, I didn't believe what I was hearing from her. By all accounts, Loren is nothing more than a confused sympathizer. Her run-down of Tash'jya changes everything for me.

I think of the smile Tash'jya had given me. I remember the silly slurp of the beans we'd shared. I recall her gray pupils searching my face as she shared her name with me. I'm not sure if I believe Loren about the Fishfaces, but I do believe Tash'jya is different. Maybe that's why I couldn't kill her. Something inside of me realizes she's not like the rest.

My fury wilts further, leaving me exhausted. My limbs feel like lead, and I can't help but yawn.

Loren must see me relax because she reaches to touch my hand. "Ted, I want to help you get Tash'jya back."

"Why should I trust you?" I withdraw my hand, but not suddenly.

"Because you know I want no harm to come to her, and that's exactly what will happen if she stays with my father. I hate to think of what is happening to her in his hands."

"You'll come with me? Willingly?" Somehow, I might be successful in my mission.

She bites her lip before nodding. "I will."

Chapter Nine

The early morning air chills my lungs, expelling any remnants of sleep from my head. My joints ache from sleeping on the hard concrete of Loren's office floor. I wake to her dressed in a pair of jeans, boots, a flannel shirt, and leather bomber jacket. True to her word, she leaves the clinic with me. A concerned look from the guards is satiated with the explanation that I'd brought news to her that the clinic across the city had been lucky enough to get a shipment of medical supplies, and she was going to beg them to share. Now, we crouch at the corner of a building, peering at the old grocery store.

Loren pulls me back into the alley, her hand gripping a fistful of my shirt. She stares at me with an intensity that could burn the back of my skull. "You are aware he's not going to hand her to you and simply let you walk away." We've said very little on the walk over here, and her tone startles me.

I nod. "I realize that. He wants me to join up."

"So, what's your plan?" Her concern sounds genuine. She notices her hand and lets go of me, smoothing my shirt.

I look at her and shrug. "Honestly, I didn't think I'd make it this far. I thought Revon had sent me on an impossible mission, especially after you took my gun." My face flushes hot as I mentally relive the embarrassment of being disarmed so easily.

A smirk spreads across her face. Not like her father's this time. It must be her mother's smile. "Yeah, you don't exactly strike me as someone who knows his way around a gun."

"What are you talking about. Of course I am—"

She stops me with a look. "Ted, the safety was off. Seriously, I don't know how you didn't manage to shoot yourself before getting to the clinic."

I cock my head to one side. "Thanks?"

"Hey, you could have used that to get into the clinic. Would have been way more convincing than that stupid cut you gave yourself." She chuckles.

I almost laugh with her. Then, I remind myself she is a sympathizer. She might prove to be right about Tash'jya, but that doesn't mean all Fishfaces are magically good. "You're really making jokes right before we do this?"

"It's how I cope with stressful situations. Deal with it." Her words are so deadpan that I almost burst into laughter again.

"I have to admit, it's cut the tension a bit. I no longer feel like my stomach is going to crawl up my throat and out my mouth."

"Graphic." She slaps me on the shoulder. "Look at us getting along all of a sudden." I glance at her. She holds her hands up in surrender. "I know. I know. You think I'm despicable and can't wait to turn me over to my father. Still, you don't think I'm all that awful. Admit it."

I turn back and continue studying the store. No sign of movement. "I don't think you're despicable. I think you're confused. And I wouldn't wish your father on anyone. But I'm this close"—I hold up a thumb and finger close together—"to getting the answers I've been searching for two years to find. If Tash'jya really is on some kind of special mission like you say, then she definitely can tell me what's up with the Bubble and likely—what happened to my father."

Her tone turns flat. "So I'm a means to an end."

I swallow hard. "I'm sorry, but yes."

I wince at the words and the wound they obviously cause her. When did I become this person? Two years on the streets are all it took to be able to turn off my heart. In another life, I would have liked Loren. Her strength and humor are a refreshing change from the girls I've known, even before the Cataclysm. She's aware of who she is and doesn't apologize for it. Even in a world that could have hardened her to all other people, she has remained alive in spirit as much as in body. She's not wrong about what I think of her. I don't believe she's completely awful.

"Loren, I believe you can take care of yourself. I believe you have. I hate to turn you over to Revon, but I fully expect you to get away from him at your first chance. As much as I need a plan to get out of there, I hope you have one, too." I realize I'm comforting myself, but I hope the words offer her some encouragement.

Her smile returns, but only partially. She reaches into her jacket and produces the gun Revon gave me. Making a show of tapping the safety with her finger to show that it is in the on position, she hands it to me.

"Better make sure we keep up appearances. Don't want my father to think I came willingly."

I hold the weapon. It feels heavy in my hand. "You sure you trust me to have this?"

She turns to me, one eyebrow raised. "The one thing worse than showing up to Commander Revon empty-handed would be to show up with his dead daughter. No, I don't trust you with it, but not because you're *intending* to do something to me."

Once again, she's insulted my ability—or lack thereof—to handle a firearm. Yeah, I definitely would have liked her in another time.

We emerge from our corner and walk confidently across the parking lot of the grocery. I keep one step behind Loren, making a show of pointing the weapon in my hand. I whisper a prayer of thanks that she showed me the safety was on. She's right. I really don't understand guns.

Stepping inside the store, I glance over at the aisle where Tash'jya and I shared a can of beans. Straining for a sound, I listen for any sign that she's here. Somehow, I thought they'd see us coming and come out to greet us. This is Revon's daughter after all. Instead, I'm met with silence.

"Commander?" My voice echoes in the huge space.

"Welcome back, Rookie." I start at Revon's voice from behind me. Turning, I see him emerge from the corner. A shudder travels up my spine. I didn't even realize he'd been there. "I see you've succeeded in your mission. Well done. You have succeeded where others have failed miserably."

"Dad." Loren's greeting comes out sounding more like an accusation.

Revon's unshaven face contorts into a smirk. "So, she told you who she is? Her sob story has worked on more than one potential recruit I've sent to collect her. I'm impressed you didn't give into her wiles. She tell you how much she's in love with those monsters like your alien girlfriend?"

I gulp and try to sound confident. Still my voice shakes. "Okay, I've brought you your prize. So where is mine?"

Revon pats two hands downward in the air. "Whoa, slow down, Rookie. All in good time. We need to discuss your future with our gang given that you've proven yourself. Or have you already forgotten about the kind offer I extended to you?"

Loren is right. He's not going to hand her over. I straighten my spine and attempt to look him in the eye with all the fierceness I can muster. I jab the muzzle of the pistol into Loren's side, producing a grunt from her.

Revon points a scarred finger at me. "Watch yourself. You were just getting on my good side. Don't go spoiling it now. No matter what happens between you and me, she's still my little girl."

"Dad, I haven't been your little girl since—"

"Quiet. You're not helping matters, unless you want Rookie's trigger finger to twitch."

I grit my teeth and click the safety off on the gun. I hear Loren suck in a breath. I don't blame her. My hand is trembling, and I have to remind myself to keep my finger off the trigger.

Revon steps backward. Sighing, he rubs a hand down the scruff on his face. "You exasperate me, kid. I can see you won't let up about this. Your prisoner is out back. Boys are merely having some fun with her."

"What's that supposed to mean?" Loren asks the question, a clear indictment of who she knows her father to be. I'm grateful she asked, so I didn't have to. It's not breaking character for her to wonder at Tash'jya's welfare.

Revon glares at Loren, expressionless. "Exactly what you think it means, daughter."

My gut sinks. Somewhere nearby, Tash'jya is suffering at the hands of Revon's goons. I take a deep breath to calm my nerves. "You want me to join up? Then, you take me to her. She has answers I need, so she better be conscious when we arrive." One more time, I thrust the pistol into Loren's ribs, producing a pained grunt. I can only hope she understands that I am bluffing.

"Easy, hot shot." Revon holds his hands out, palms down. "Let's not get crazy. We can see her, and then you can stop threatening my daughter before I drop you where you stand. I won't tolerate this power play of yours any longer. Understood?"

"That's all I want." I wonder if he can see my hands shaking as I meet his eyes. I wiggle my finger again to make sure it's not actually on the trigger lest I accidentally hurt Loren.

Chapter Ten

The hinges of the back door to the grocery store squeak in protest as we emerge from the building. Even before seeing them, I can hear the laughter of Revon's men. Turning in the direction of their voices, I hear the scrape of feet moving behind an old dumpster.

"Not so tough when you're all tied up, are you, Fishy?" One of Revon's men chuckles. More feet scrape on the pavement, followed by a heavy thud. They've kicked her. More laughter. Rounding the corner, the same two meatheads that greeted me with Revon stand over Tash'jya slapping each other's shoulders in congratulations for their mockery.

Tash'jya lays on her side, her hands bound behind her back. Dark violet blotches cover her face and arms where the skin is exposed. Purple blood oozes from her lips. Her jumpsuit is torn at the knees and at several seams. Each tear is stained with blood.

With great effort, she worms herself onto her knees. Her shoulders slump and her head bows as if awaiting the next barrage of beatings. Amazingly, she does not make a sound. Still, the black pools of her eyes stare up at me full of accusation. I can't help thinking she's right. This is my fault. None of this would have happened if I'd let her go when the battle broke out.

One of the goons balls his fist and approaches, ready to deliver more cowardly blows. Revon holds up a hand.

"All right, Chambers. I'm going to have to put a pause on your fun here. Our rookie got a little too big for his britches and overstepped, but I can appreciate the passion." He jabs a thumb in my direction. "I intend to be a man of my word by reuniting the two of them."

Both of the men study me as if needing a moment to put together who I am. *Seriously? It's been one day.* Finally, the truth dawns on the one called Chambers when he notices Loren.

"He got her, sir?" He points at Loren with a meaty finger.

Revon nods slowly as if allowing his men time to catch up to the train of thought. "That's right. My daughter has come home. Under duress, but home nonetheless."

"Hey, boys." Loren waves at the two of them. Chambers smirks. The other guard blushes crimson and takes a step back from Tash'jya. He waves shyly at Loren, who addresses him. "Matthews, I expect this kind of brutality from Chambers, but not you. Really?" Matthews retreats another step.

Revon turns to me. Any smile he had disappears, and he points a finger at me. "Rookie, you see I've delivered on my promise. One alien beast back—mostly intact." He glances again at the wounded Tash'jya. "Now if you would kindly remove the barrel of that pistol from my daughter."

Without thinking, I lower the weapon. I hear Loren whisper a 'no' under her breath.

In a second, Revon is on me. Grabbing my wrist, he forces my gun hand down and toward him, yanking me right into his iron fist. The flash of light in my vision is followed by an explosion of pain across the left side of my face. I stumble backward as far as I can while still held by Revon's impossible grip.

"Dad!" Loren yells.

My knees feel weak. I think I might vomit. With one well-placed punch, Revon has nearly knocked me senseless. The gun clatters to the ground. Releasing his grip on me, Revon stoops to grab the pistol. He turns it on me as I fall to one knee. Then, I do vomit. Matthews and Chambers laugh and point at me.

"Enough!" Loren steps between me and her father. My vision is blurred, but I can see her turn and crouch to examine my already swelling face. "He gave you what you wanted. Just let him go, Dad. You don't need to turn every person you meet into a soldier."

"The upstart needed a lesson in obedience," Revon growls. "I may like his initiative, but we can't have him defying the way of things around here. I will not have a challenge to my authority stand unchecked, especially where you're concerned."

Her fingers gently prod the side of my face, searching for broken bones. I'm surprised she finds none. "You could have seriously hurt him."

"Good thing we have our doctor back to help." This comment produces grunts of agreement from Chambers and Matthews. "Stand him up."

"Hold a second," Loren demands. "I'm still examining him."

"Don't you try my patience, too. Stand him up." Revon nods to his men who are at my side in an instant. Their meat hooks grab me by the underarms and haul me to my feet. The world spins. I want to puke again.

Revon steps toward me and lightly slaps my face on both sides. "Stay with us, boy." He leans in, a large vein on his forehead pulsing. He places the barrel of the pistol under my chin and shoves the metal deep into my flesh. "You will come to respect me, Rookie. Is that understood?"

Nodding with a pistol pointed at your jaw is not easy. Somehow, I manage a tremble that resembles a nod. The stubble on Revon's face creases into that same smirk. I hear the safety of the gun click back into place. He marches over to Tash'jya and glances at me to make sure I'm looking. An instant later, the barrel of the pistol finds the side of her head. She yelps as she falls to the ground again, the new laceration on her scalp growing wet with blood.

"Men, take him inside. The Fishy, too. Put them in the back room. Rookie wants his private time with his captive." This comment produces chuckles from Chambers and Matthews. I'm hauled backward, my heels scraping along the ground. Revon grabs Tash'jya by the ankle and begins to drag her.

Loren seethes, her breath sucking violently between her teeth, but she remains mute, probably not wanting her words to lead to more abuse.

Moments later, I'm thrown to the floor. The concrete floor is gritty with dirt against the side of my face, but the coolness of it is comforting. A mumbling Tash'jya is hauled into the room. Footsteps leave. The door is closed and bolted.

Chambers and Matthews retreat, their waning voices debating who is going to get lunch for the two of them. Somewhere, I can hear Loren begin arguing with Revon. Tash'jya isn't moving. Neither am I for that matter.

I'm the captive now.

Chapter Eleven

I roll over, dirt and grit sticking to my cheek. Realizing I've lost consciousness for what I guess is a few minutes, I rub my eyes to wake up. My left eye feels puffy, and I have to be gentle with it. Pressing down on the concrete, I force myself into a seated position, producing an instant headache that threatens to split my head open. I curse at the pain.

Examining my surroundings, I see that I'm in a large supply closet. A single narrow transom window high above the floor allows enough light to cast long shadows everywhere. Across from me, Tash'jya lays in a heap, unmoving. Small puddles of purple blood pool beneath her body. Her face hasn't swollen—must not be part of her physiology—but the blotchy wounds have spread, leaving her face a mottled patchwork of green and violet.

I crawl over to her, my head complaining with each movement. I lay a hand on her exposed shoulder peeking out through a tear in her garment, surprised at the warmness of her skin. I'm not sure what to do. I shake her gently.

Nothing. I try again. Still nothing.

Reaching behind her, I work at the knot at her wrists. Chambers and Matthews may be brainless idiots, but they can tie a knot. It's several minutes of picking at the rope before I can pull an end loose. Releasing her bonds, I roll her to her back, laying her hands across her abdomen. On all fours, I hover over her, looking for signs of life. Pulling my face close to hers, I can hear the slight whisper of her respirator as she draws air into her lungs.

I grab a rag off the shelf that looks clean enough and dab at the bleeding cut on her head. I've never been this close to one of her kind before. The smoothness of her pale skin betrays not a single wrinkle or line, and I realize I have no idea of her age. She could be a young girl or old by human standards, and I would never know. The remarkable symmetry of her features makes me wonder if she's considered beautiful among her people.

I shake my head, dismissing the thought as weird.

Still, I can't help wondering if there is another of her kind out there who is wondering what happened to her. I think of Revon, and his desire to have his daughter close despite her hatred of him. Somewhere, I'm guessing there is someone missing Tash'jya. Would they treat me with the same vengeance the Commander did when I threatened his daughter? I shudder at the thought. What I've done to Tash'jya is far worse.

Glancing down, I see two gray pupils in the center of inky eyes staring at me. Before I can react, a piercing screech emits from Tash'jya. Her hands find my chest and thrust me backward with all her superior strength. I'm launched like a ragdoll several feet, banging my shoulder hard into the concrete.

"Sssshe-ni sssut!" She hisses what I can only guess is a curse in her language. She flips to a crouched position, her hands resting lightly on the floor. Her body is coiled, ready to spring into action. She continues her tirade in her tongue.

Whatever she is saying to me, I probably deserve it.

I hold one hand out in surrender. With the other, I rub my shoulder, which is at least distracting from my pounding head.

"I-I'm sorry. I didn't mean for you to—" I pause, unsure what to say. How do you apologize to someone, even one of her kind, for causing them to suffer abuse? It doesn't feel adequate. It strikes me how far I've come in a couple days with this alien whose name I now know.

Her people destroyed our planet.

But that doesn't mean *she* destroyed our planet. Should she have to answer for all the crimes of her people? Should I answer for the crimes committed by people like Revon?

The distinction my mind has made is not lost on me. I wish I could tell her because she glares at me with murderous eyes.

I nod in agreement with whatever thoughts about me she is having. "Yes. What they did to you was bad, and it was my fault.

If I hadn't forced you to come here with me, they never would have found you."

It's enough of an apology that her shoulders relax, and her dagger gaze softens. Her defensive posture waivers, and she slumps to one knee. Her body quivers, and it's only then that I remember she's been beaten for hours—possibly the entire time I was gone.

"Are-are you okay? Are you hurt?"

She hisses. At me or the pain, I cannot tell. "Yess, human. But my body is not as fragile as yourss. I will heal."

She called me 'human,' not Ted. It seems strange to me that, while she was my captive, she grew to trust me enough to believe I wouldn't do her malicious harm. Yet now that someone else has us both captive, the trust is gone.

"I realize that I—"

"You left me!" She hisses again. This one was clearly at me. "You handed me over like an animal for sslaughter. Then, you return with another of your kind as prissoner. I wonder, human, if your hatred is for everyone, or simply femalesss?"

The accusation stings, but I might conclude the same thing from her perspective. I handed her over to be abused at the hands of Revon's goons and brought back another person for what she can easily imagine is the same purpose.

My head hurts. My body hurts. The right words to explain won't come. "It-it's not like that."

"Then, what iss it like?" Each word bites at me.

"If we'd tried to run, we'd both be dead, or worse. The woman I brought back is the Commander's daughter. He won't harm her. I don't think so anyway."

"And yet, here we are." She gazes around the closet to make her point. "We await death, while you have brought another to an unknown fate. It seemss your efforts to save uss have only brought otherss into the way of harm, human. Perhapss, you are not intelligent."

Did she just call me stupid?

"Look, we can argue all you want when we get out of here.

For the moment, we need to figure out how to get out of this closet. They won't forget about us forever. Our best chance seems to be right now."

Apparently agreeing, Tash'jya scrambles over to the door, our shared need creating a tentative truce. She tries the handle. She examines the frame. Climbing the shelves, she examines the metal mesh over the transom window. Leaping down, she pounds her fist on the wall in frustration.

I search the room for any kind of tool that might allow us to break the door or window. Apparently, this room has been used as a cell before because anything worth wielding has been removed.

The two of us sit in silence for several minutes. Tash'jya stares at the floor as if in thought.

"It is useless, human. As they beat me, I heard the men say they've had other Skya'ja as captivess before." She touches gently a stain on the floor I hadn't noticed. Skya'ja blood? I can't be sure, but her reverence of the spot seems to indicate I'm right. "Thiss is a room where my people come to die."

Neural Implant Log: Entry 137
Officer: Tash'jya, daughter of Sun'tssh
Rank: Tactician

I remain a captive of the militia. For the honor of my people, let the record show that I have discovered the resting place of at least three Skya'ja. My cell bears the stains of their anguish. The amount of blood could only mean they spent their last moments in this room. I do not know their names. They have passed into the beyond nameless and without ceremony.

Though I cannot call out their names or perform their funeral song by myself, I record now the evidence of their passing. I pray that they will not be nameless and forgotten forever. I honor their memory through this record until their names can be known and their family be allowed to grieve.

My once human captor is far less intelligent than I'd feared. Not only did he turn me over to my new captors and assume their goodwill, but upon his return he brought his one leverage with him simply to have it removed. And his leverage? Another human—the daughter of my new captor.

What kind of species is this that would treat each other this way? What kind of father harbors such hatred that even his daughter is not immune to his toxicity? We have not proven perfect as a species, yet I have never seen a Skya'ja father place his own prejudice above the well-being of his own child. My own father, the honorable Sun'tssh, gave his life as we sought to assist the dying planet in Sector Seventeen, which is now no more. He saw the destructive rage the species of that planet carried and insisted he take my place on assignment there. It was only after the people on that planet killed every last member of the initial expedition and our mission there was cancelled that my resentment for his choice waned. Sun'tssh gave his life, not just for the honor of the Skya'ja, but to save my own. He foresaw what was coming and went anyway to save me. Let this log be another record of his honor.

Humans are different. Their level of selfishness does not boil into rage. Instead, their behavior presents a confusing set of responses. My new captor appears to love his daughter, at least to the level of not wanting to be removed from her. Yet, he is willing to force her to be with him at the end of a weapon. He may not be willing to harm her, but he is willing to feign such intention to avoid separation. The absence of logic in this dynamic baffles me.

My former captor, who is now my cellmate, is equally confusing. Though young for his people, he has managed to survive in the conditions of this planet for two years without suffering too much harm, showing a measure of adaptability that many of his kind lack. His drive has been for answers about his father, which I fear will make him all the more reckless should he ever learn the truth. I cannot share what I know. My mission is too important. And should I succeed, it won't matter anyway.

I am thankful that I have survived. On my honor, I will find a way to escape my captors and resume my mission. The world depends on it, though I wonder if these humans are worth saving.

End of log.

"There has to be a way we can get out of here." I stand again, my desire to find a way out renewed.

Footsteps approach from the other side of the door. Tash'jya rises to a crouching position, her hands at the ready to attack. She appears like a martial artist from a movie ready to engage her opponent, and I wonder what training she's been given. I, on the other hand, have no formal training to protect myself. I grab a dirty ceramic coffee mug off the shelf. It's only good for one strike, but it's better than my bare hands.

The lock jiggles as a key is inserted. Slowly, the handle turns, and I feel every muscle in my body tense for a fight. Whoever comes through that door, we have one chance to overcome them. I imagine smashing the coffee mug over the head of the intruder. My one hope is that it's a single person—and not a group. Or worse, Revon. I can't take another of his iron punches.

The handle stops turning as the latch opens, but the door doesn't move. Instead, a whisper comes from the other side.

"Ted? You and our Skya'ja friend conscious?" I note the perfect pronunciation of 'Skya'ja.' The voice is Loren's. "I realize you're probably ready to jump me when I enter, so don't. I'm here to get you out of there."

I stand straight and frantically wave my hand downward at Tash'jya to communicate that she should stand down. The door cracks and then opens fully. Loren slips in and quietly shuts the door. She flashes a quick smile at me and turns to Tash'jya, who still looks unsure how to respond to our new cellmate.

That's when Loren touches both hands to her forehead and then chest. Tash'jya cocks her head.

"Friend, I am here to help you that you may help me." Loren pauses and waits for Tash'jya's response. I notice that she doesn't use Tash'jya's name, though she knows it. Loren has clearly spent a lot more time with the Skya'ja than anyone I've met besides my father.

Tash'jya's body relaxes, and she straightens. Returning the gesture, she asks, "And how may we help each other, daughter of my captor?"

"Truly, I am sorry about what my father and his men did to you. We can get out of here if we leave right now. Chambers and Matthews are too preoccupied drinking themselves stupid, and my father believes I went to lay down." She glances at the door as if listening for anyone approaching. "He knows I'd never leave while he could hurt you. That's why you're not dead already—to keep me obedient. I swiped his keys, but it won't be long before he realizes what's happened. My father is a lot of things, but stupid is not one of them. Besides, the rest of his men are returning in an hour, and then there's going to be a lot more eyes in this place."

Tash'jya steps closer to Loren. "That iss how you help me, but how do I help you?"

"I need you to take me someplace safe. Someplace he won't find me or want to look for me. I can't go back to the clinic. It's clear he's determined to get me out of there, and it won't be long before another one of them succeeds at bringing me back here." She glances at me, and I feel my face grow hot. "I need to disappear beyond his reach. Got someplace like that?"

Tash'jya studies Loren for a long moment. Then, without a word, she touches her forehead and her chest with her hands. Then, she points to me.

"And thiss human?"

"He comes with us."

I don't recognize Skya'ja expressions well, but my best interpretation of Tash'jya's is annoyance.

Loren nods. "I know. But we can't leave him here."

Chapter Twelve

Senses on high alert, I follow Loren and Tash'jya out of the room. The door latches behind us, and Loren quietly turns the lock back into place. Her eyes meet mine, and she places a finger over her lips to remind me to be silent. I nod.

Tiptoeing down the dark hallway, I wince at every miniscule scrape of our feet on the concrete floor. We pass doors of what used to be manager's offices and employee lounges. Surely, if Revon's men were back, these spaces would be swarming, and we'd have no hope of leaving unnoticed. So far, no one is around. At any moment, I expect Chambers or Matthews to come around the corner and discover us. Or worse, Revon. Incredibly, we get to the end of the hallway without being noticed.

I hold my breath as we sneak out into the open part of the old store, dashing into one of the many empty aisles. A few rows over, the inebriated voice of Chambers guffaws at some stupid joke Matthews has made. A glass bottle rattles across the floor as, no doubt, the two men continue to consume more of the alcohol stores than Revon probably has authorized.

Making our way down the aisle, my heart leaps at the sunshine pouring in through the front windows. We are so close to freedom. A few more steps, and we can bolt across the street and get lost in the city.

Loren holds a hand up, and we pause. The chuckling behemoths have gone silent. Crouching, we listen for any sound. Footsteps. Breaths. I hear nothing.

The breathless moment stretches, and my quads begin to ache from my position. Reaching out, I grab the metal shelf next to me to steady my balance. To my horror, the end of the shelf bracket unhooks from the vertical support. In the silent grocery store, the crash of metal on metal as the shelf falls to meet the one below it is deafening.

Heavy footfalls.

We straighten to make a run for it.

One step into the open, and a huge hand grabs Loren by the hair. She yelps at the pain as Chambers yanks her backward. Another set of arms wraps me from behind, choking the breath from my lungs in the giant bear hug. I squirm to free myself, but Matthew's grip is locked. That leaves only Tash'jya free.

The two meatheads don't have time to realize their mistake.

"Shya-sii!" A sharp cry from Tash'jya escapes her lips as she leaps into the air, higher than any human would be capable of from a standing position. In an instant, she lands on the back of Chambers, who lets out a confused 'huh?' Tash'jya's fingers jam into Chambers' neck. Letting go of Loren, he instinctively reaches for his throat, gasping for air. Twisting her back to his, Tash'jya's feet land on the floor, her arm wrapped around Chamber's neck. Sinking in her stance, she hurls Chambers into the shelves in a massive hip throw.

I've obviously underestimated Tash'jya's strength and realize how incredible it was I got the jump on her in the first place.

Whirling, she turns to Matthews. His grip on my chest loosens, and he shoves me to the floor. Balling his fists, he squares off against Tash'jya, who circles slowly with her hands at the ready.

Lunging, Matthews throws a wild punch. Tash'jya is unfazed. Almost lazily, she steps to the side of the lumbering man, her foot connecting with his stomach. Matthews expels a grunt as he doubles over. Not hesitating, Tash'jya grabs his head in both hands and hurls him into the shelves. His huge body slumps to the floor in an unconscious heap.

Tash'jya straightens slowly, muttering what I can imagine is another of her native curses and letting her guard down slowly.

Loren lets out a breathy laugh. "That was incredible!"

I stand dumbfounded, unsure if I should be impressed or nervous. I am keenly aware that I had bound her and could have easily been the recipient of her wrath had she ever gotten loose.

Tash'jya stares me down. "Ssee, human. We are not sso helpless when the fight iss fair."

I swallow hard and send a silent prayer that I never had to face off against her one-on-one. "I-I don't doubt it."

A door slams at the other end of the store. Revon's voice comes into range, muttering about *two idiots* and the *stash of liquor*.

"We have to go. Now!" Loren whispers sharply.

Bolting for the store window, we ease out through a missing pane. Loren squirms through last as Revon nears.

"What in the—"

We don't stick around to hear the rest of his sentence. Abandoning stealth, the three of us sprint for the corner of the building to get out of sight. Moments later, we find ourselves ducking between the buildings.

"Rookie!" Revon's voice startles me from behind. I dare a glance backward.

Revon is standing out in the middle of the parking lot staring at me. No pursuit. No reaching for his pistol. Just two piercing eyes boring holes into mine. The message is clear.

As far as he is concerned, this isn't finished.

Message received. I sprint into the shadows to catch up to Loren and Tash'jya. All we can do for the moment is put distance between us and Revon. When his men return, he's coming for us.

Several blocks later, Loren waves us into a doorway alcove. She throws her back up against the brick wall, her hands on her knees, as she gasps for air. I collapse to the ground, my lungs burning from running. Even Tash'jya seems winded as her respirator wheezes louder than usual.

"Okay—friend—your—turn." Loren speaks between breaths. "Take us—someplace—safe."

I sit up and scoot over to the wall. I gaze at Tash'jya. She is unbound. She is stronger than the two of us combined. She has no reason to help us. Actually, she has every reason to leave us behind to get caught. It's what I would do. I expect any moment that she will take off running, and I decide that I won't even bother giving chase. There is no way I could catch her.

Slowly, her respirator quiets, and Tash'jya straightens to look at both of us. Turning to me, she cocks her head slightly to the side. "You think I will run, human?"

There's the lack of my name again. I don't respond.

"We are not as disloyal to our promisses as your people." She glances at Loren and makes the head-chest gesture. Loren nods and returns it. "Thank you for releassing me. You may call me Tash'jya."

Loren, still catching her breath, whispers. "I am pleased to know your name, Tash'jya. And you may call me Loren."

"I am pleased to know your name, Lor-en," Tash'jya bows slightly, emphasizing the second syllable of Loren's name. "There iss a place we may go, but thiss human may not approve." She points to me, still looking in Loren's direction.

Loren glances at me. "The human will not be a problem. Will you, Ted?"

I shake my head. They both seem to realize what Tash'jya is talking about, and I can't help feeling like the third wheel of our group.

Tash'jya lets out a slight hiss that sounds like annoyance. "Very well. Eyess open, human. You may learn ssomething."

I have no idea what they're talking about.

***

Neural Implant Log: Entry 138
Officer: Tash'jya, daughter of Sun'tssh
Rank: Tactician

The human known as Loren, whose name I know, gives me hope for this species. Before today, I have not encountered any human during my mission who learns and respects our ways. I had come to believe the days of benevolent relations between our peoples were a thing of the past. The daughter of the militia leader, however, has obviously spent a lot of time with Skya'ja. She approached me with respect and did not dishonor my name, though I suspect the other human carelessly shared it with her.

We have arranged a mutual deal. She has offered me my freedom in exchange for safety. I will deliver her to such a place on my honor. Perhaps there are more like her in this world. I can only hope. If I am successful in my mission, it will be those like Loren who make this world worth saving. She has honor and a sense of morality.

I am no longer captive. The other human may still wish to get his answers, but my mission cannot delay. Once rested, I will resume my search.

End of log.

Chapter Thirteen

An hour later, we stand outside a ruined coliseum. The venue, once the site of professional sporting events, has collapsed in on itself. A couple of red letters, which used to be the illuminated name of the fast-food sponsor of the building, still cling to the side of the structure. The walls, which mostly still stand, are jagged across the top where the roof has caved in.

I gaze into the distance, where downtown used to be visible about a mile away. An opaque bubble covers downtown Charlotte. The outside shimmers as with a light of its own. Swirls move in blue-green waves across the exterior like the surface of one of the gas giant planets.

I think of my father, who was there at the epicenter when the Cataclysm happened. The Bubble appeared, and the world died. I can only assume my father did, too. I have so many questions for Tash'jya, but I no longer have the advantage over her. Now, I am at her mercy. Somewhere inside this coliseum, she claims we'll find a safe place to hide from Revon's inevitable pursuit.

I can't imagine what could be inside the dilapidated structure.

Tash'jya emits a sound I've never heard one of her kind make. It sounds like she is whistling, but the tone is far more musical than that of a human whistle. A few moments later, a similar note comes from inside the ruins. Turning to Loren, she waves her inside. I guess I'm included, but she ignores me.

Carefully, we climb over the concrete rubble and twisted steel that rings the building. Tash'jya moves with surprising grace over the debris, whether because of her natural agility or because she's been here before, I'm not sure. Maybe both. Ducking through an opening, my eyes need a moment to adjust to the darkness. A few rays of the limited sunlight pour in through cracks and holes, illuminating particles that float in the air and create a patchwork of shadows on the floor.

The atmosphere feels cold and thick with dust, and I silently coach myself not to sneeze. While the building seems to have stood like this for some time, I can't help but feel that any sudden noise might bring the whole place down on us. On one side, rows of counters that used to sell concessions to fans sit vacant. Here and there, a piece of old sports merchandise litters the floor. I remember when places like this used to be hotbeds of entertainment for huge crowds. Survival has replaced all other impulses.

We travel farther into the structure to what used to be the arena. The upper floors are covered in bits of debris and metal from the caved-in ceiling. The center of the room is no longer a basketball court or hockey arena but has been replaced by a pile of rubble on which the overcast skies light up the faces of the concrete pieces. Particles of dust hang suspended in the air, giving the room a hazy appearance like something from a dream.

Going from light outside to the darkness of the building and back to the light of the arena, I blink hard trying to get my vision to adjust. I scan the room around me in the sections that used to be for spectators. Slowly, shapes start to appear in the shadows. Blobs of movement begin to sharpen as I see more clearly.

The giant room is filled with Skya'ja. Hundreds and hundreds of Skya'ja.

Many of the creatures look worse for the wear. Some bear scars. Others have missing limbs or eyes. Some simply look malnourished and unable to get up.

Out of the shadows, a Skya'ja steps forward. I guess that this one is male. He approaches Tash'jya and holds his hand as if offering a high five. Tash'jya places her palm on his and holds it for a second completing the greeting.

A conversation ensues in the Skya'ja language. The male gestures to Loren and me, his expression and movements angry. The interpretation isn't hard—why have you brought these humans here? Tash'jya hurriedly explains herself. I have no idea what she's saying, but Loren occasionally nods as though picking up a word here and there. I do notice Tash'jya making an abbreviated form of the forehead to chest sign. The male stops and turns to Loren. He touches his head and chest, apparently accepting Tash'jya's respect for her. Loren responds in kind.

Well, that's something. At least one of us is accepted.

"Tsh yat?" The male points at me. I guess that means "and what about this guy?"

Tash'jya's face darkens. At least I think it does. She slowly speaks, pointing to her chafed wrists and her respirator. The male's gray pupils look me up and down. I don't think I've won any points. If he decides to take out any frustration on me, I'm toast.

I open my mouth to explain myself and my need for answers about my father, but I'm interrupted by the male. I can't translate what he is saying, but the meaning is clear. "Shut up. You don't speak here." He produces a thin strap as he steps toward me. Grabbing my arm, the strap self-tightens around my wrist. With a jerk, he forces my arms together, so the strap can wind itself around my other wrist.

I pull against the restraint, but it won't budge. I glance at Loren, and she shakes her head to let me know to go with it. I'm not sure, but I think I see her grin as she turns away. Glad she finds this funny. I sure don't.

Roles officially reversed, I gaze at Tash'jya. She doesn't say anything, but her eyes appear to turn downward slightly. She almost looks apologetic. Then again, reading the expression of the Skya'ja is not my forte. Is it possible that this is not what she wanted? Again, I wonder if Loren is right. Is Tash'jya different from her people?

More conversation in hushed tones, and the male tugs at my bonds as he waves the group toward a huddle of aliens in the corner. The male shoves me hard onto a chunk of concrete, the irregular shape of the block striking my tailbone. That's going to hurt for a while. Loren and Tash'jya settle in on the floor next to me.

The circle of creatures around me stare. A small circular

device in the center glows dimly red, providing heat to the group. Now that I'm closer, I can see there are both males and females. One male in the corner, appears older—the lines on his face deeper than others in the group. He sits silently, fixing his eyes upon me. For a long moment, we stare at each other, the sourness of my stomach increasing with each moment. I can't help but notice the stub of an arm where his hand used to be.

Another male sits with a bandage across his head, through which blood seeps from a fresh wound. A female kneels nearby, preparing a fresh bandage with one hand. The other is in a sling. A final female stands, whispering with the male who greeted us.

"What happened here?" I dare a whisper to Loren. "Who are these Skya'ja? They look like they've been through hell."

Loren bites her lip as she scans the group. "Got me. I've heard of camps of Skya'ja, but this group seems to have suffered more than most."

I study the room. "None of them are wearing battle armor. These aren't wounded soldiers."

"I noticed that too. These are not fighters, merely civilians." She turns to Tash'jya. "What happened to these people?"

"Humans happened, Lor-en." Tash'jya says flatly, her eyes never leaving the warming device in the center of the circle.

"Humans did this? You mean from the battles?"

"Not in battle. Not from soldierss. Just humans hurting Skya'ja. Taking what they want. Hurting who they wish."

I scan the room, my gut twisting as I do. Everywhere I look, scenes of pain and suffering are taking place in circles like ours. A few circles away, a quiet moaning emanates from the group as they kneel around a member laying on the ground. His breathing appears labored. A minute later, it stops. One of the group members solemnly removes his respirator. Gently, several members turn the deceased Skya'ja on his side and curl his body into a fetal position before covering him with a blanket.

Stepping forward, a tall male touches his head and chest. "Sut-shi." He kneels and places his hand on the head of the deceased Skya'ja. Each member of the circle repeats the ceremony.

The word 'Sut-shi' repeated each time.

"What are they doing?" Loren asks, following my gaze.

"They are honoring their dead family member." Tash'jya's voice is somber and hushed, as if not wanting to disrupt the ceremony. "They honor the name of the fallen member. The last rite for any Skya'ja is to be known, to not pass on nameless."

The members of the group place their right hand on the shoulder of the Skya'ja to their right. Together, their moans change from a dissonant chord to a single unison. The note is held, the intensity growing, echoing through the cavernous space. All at once, they stop. The tall one resumes speaking in his own language to the group.

I believe I've witnessed the beginning of a Skya'ja funeral. It is strangely haunting.

The urge to say something swells inside of me. These refugees, for lack of a better term, have suffered at human hands, and the need to speak—to apologize—to explain that not all humans are capable of this overwhelms me. Turning to Tash'jya, I dare to speak. "I-I don't know what to say. I don't understand why this is happening."

Tash'jya turns her slate pupils in my direction. "And that, human, is why I do not answer your questionss. You do not understand your own people, so how could you ever understand mine?"

She's right. I don't deserve an explanation if this is what humans represent to her. I can't blame her for not explaining to me, even during our short-lived trust. War rages around us with neither side gaining ground since the Cataclysm, but this is different. These Skya'ja have done nothing to us except simply be here. My father is dead because of them, but the Skya'ja man, whose death I witnessed, fell at the hands of humans.

For the first time I understand. There are no innocent species in this war.

Glancing at Loren, I see the glint of light reflect off the tears clinging to her cheeks. Her closed eyelids flutter as if she cannot take the sight anymore. The grief of it all must hit far too close to home for her. She may have compassion for the Skya'ja, but people like her father do not.

I reach my bound hands and take her hand. Her eyes lift to meet mine. For a long moment, we gaze at each other as I do my best to silently communicate my empathy.

"Loren, I can see why you helped the Skya'ja. Seeing them this way—" My words cut off, and I swallow to avoid the swell of emotion that threatens to overwhelm me. "I-I don't know what to say. It's horrible."

"They may not look like us. They may not talk like us or act like us, but they are people. They live and breathe and feel and hurt—just like we do." She sniffs and wipes her eyes with her free hand. "I've seen Skya'ja celebrate. I've seen more than a few cry. I've even seen one laugh."

"They do laugh?" I straighten, taken aback by the notion. I imagine the moment in the basement when I heard what I thought was Tash-jya's laughter.

Loren chuckles softly. "I didn't realize what it was at first. Doesn't quite sound like your laugh or mine, but it was laughter." She glances back at the mourning group who continue their ceremony. "Now we've both seen them grieve."

The entire group has their hands on the body at the center of the circle as if they don't want to let their family member leave the Earth. Their hushed words and chants are melodic, showing the full range of their language.

"It's beautiful, isn't it?" Loren asks, squeezing my hand.

It's not the word I would have chosen, but the more I consider it, the more it fits. These creatures whom I have hated and blamed for everything—and they may still not be innocent—are beings, not automatons. They have culture and grace. I've never seen it. Perhaps it was there, and I didn't want to. Before the Cataclysm, I was too disinterested in it all, finding my father's work dull and idealistic. After, I was blinded by grief and rage.

"Yeah, I guess it is beautiful." I return the grip on her hand. "To be honest, I'm not sure how to process it all. My father is gone, and I need to find out why." Out of the corner of my eye, I can see

Tash'jya's body straighten slightly at my words. She knows something that she isn't telling me. For a moment, I consider asking her again. Perhaps with the tables turned, she will not believe I'm forcing her to respond but truly asking.

"Ted, there may be a reason she won't share. Or she may know less than you hope. It—" She hesitates. "It won't bring your father back."

I hang my head in defeat. "I realize that. I can't help being bothered by all the mystery of it."

She smiles at me, her eyes sad with compassion. "Trust me. I am fully aware of how hard it is to let go of a father."

Silently, I chastise myself. Here I am making the entire conversation about me, when she is hours removed from having escaped from her crazed father. "Um, yeah. I bet you do. Thank you by the way—for getting us out."

"I knew he'd lock you guys up the second we got there. I only went along with it to make sure you two had a chance."

"It wasn't my finest hour, but then again I've managed to avoid the militias until this point." I pause, wondering how to ask. "What are you going to do now? I mean, you said you can't return to the clinic, so what's next?"

Loren lets out a long sigh, letting go of my hand and covering her face. For a moment, she rests her head in her hands with her elbows on her thighs. She turns back to me. "All I've wanted to do is help in my own little way. Humans and Skya'ja alike. The clinic was the obvious choice, but after all that's happened, I don't know. Maybe here"—she scans the room around us—"I could do some good if it wasn't for my father."

"What about him?"

"He will never leave it alone. These people are suffering, but if I stay, I set a target on this place. Even at this moment, he's probably mustering his boys to get ready to start looking for me again. He won't stop, which puts all these Skya'ja in more danger than they already are. I'm not sure who did this to them, but can you imagine if my father found this place?"

I shudder at the thought.

"There's a whole world I can help. If I can make it to Asheville or even Raleigh, maybe it'll be far enough away that I don't have to hide."

Some part of me aches at the talk of her leaving. I don't want her to go. Since the Cataclysm, I have not met anyone like her. Someone who is doing more than surviving. Someone who is actually attempting to find their place in this version of the world.

"Whatever it is, Loren, I hope you find it."

"Thanks, Ted." She laughs. "You're not so bad when you aren't trying to kidnap me or handing me over to psychos or forcing me to run for my life."

I shrug as best I can with bound hands. "I like to keep things exciting, I guess."

We both laugh.

I think about reaching out and taking her hand in mine again when a clamor begins to rise at the other end of the arena. Voices rise in inhuman wails. Light flashes followed by the ear-piercing report of guns being fired in the echoey room. Gruff shouts issue orders in words I can understand.

Humans have arrived.

Chapter Fourteen

"Back off, Fishface, before I put a bullet in your gut." The unshaven man in camo pants and jacket strikes the Skya'ja male with the butt of his rifle. The alien stumbles clutching his forehead, purple blood dripping between his fingers. All three men laugh as the Skya'ja loses his balance and tilts backward over a stool.

Loren and I lay still, peering from under the blanket Tash'jya threw over us. These humans have no hesitation about harming Skya'ja, and finding two humans among them would not be received well. Especially with one having their wrists restrained. The three men point rifles at the group across the arena as they search the area. Canned goods, tools, anything of value is taken. Anyone found with something of worth is kicked or beaten.

"Just go away. Just go away." Loren is whispering to herself, willing the men to find what they came for and leave.

Gradually, the men make their way from circle to circle, plundering mercilessly. In their wake, the Skya'ja speak in hushed tones tending to their wounded as best they can without drawing attention. None of the Skya'ja fight back. No one rushes to harm the men.

"What do we have here?" Camo pants growls at the group as he kicks aside the blanket covering the dead Skya'ja. "Ha. Riley, this your handiwork?"

A second man in jeans, a trucker cap, and a battered t-shirt, presumably Riley, steps close and examines the deceased Skya'ja man. Shifting his half-gone cigar to the other corner of his mouth, he laughs hoarsely. "Now that's funny. I think this is the one that gave me some trouble last time we were here. Tried to hide a stash of batteries." Turning to the closest living member of the circle, he nudges the Skya'ja woman with the barrel of his rifle. "See what resistance gets you, you filth? It's our planet. Our stuff."

The woman glares at the man, but she does not move.

Riley's lips curl slowly as a sinister grin spreads across his face. "Ah. I see. A fighter?" He leans over to look at her closely. "Go ahead. Take a swing. You know you want to." He taps his chin several times. "Come on. Right here. Tempting, isn't it?"

I suck in a short breath as I see the woman's hands twitch slightly. She is resisting the urge to give into Riley's temptation, and I silently mutter a prayer that she will remain still. Riley is searching for any excuse to harm her.

"Tsk ya!" The woman's cry pierces the tense silence. Her hand flies across her body, aiming for Riley's left cheek. She only finds air as Riley fades backward. Her Skya'ja curses continue as she falls forward onto all fours, taking a second futile swing with her other hand.

"That's what I thought." Standing over the woman, Riley chews the end of his cigar silently a couple seconds before nodding to the two others. They step forward and yank the woman to her feet. Camo pants begins binding her wrists with a cord. Riley reaches a hand and brushes the woman's cheek with the back of his fingers. "This one has some scrap in her, boys! She'll make some good entertainment for us, don't you think?"

Grunts of approval come from the other men.

Sufficiently bound, camo pants shoves the Skya'ja woman forward. She stumbles but catches herself as she begins her march with Riley and his men. Her head hangs in defeat, the last shreds of fight appearing to vaporize as her fate becomes apparent.

I tense as the men approach our circle. My legs ache in my crouched position, and I steady my breathing to keep from moving the blanket that covers us.

Camo pants and the other man shove the woman ahead of them. Bringing up the rear, Riley eyes our group, quietly chuckling to himself and shouldering his rifle. He scans the group, and I hold my breath as his gaze passes over our hiding spot. In the dark room, I pray we look like nothing more than a bundle of cloth.

All at once, the old Skya'ja man rises from his seat, meeting

Riley face-to-face. Riley's grin melts into a frown.

"Leave her here." The Skya'ja man's throaty voice issues the command, pointing to the bound woman with one hand. "She stays. Take anything else you want and leave."

Camo pants pauses and looks to Riley, raising a brow.

The end of Riley's cigar glows red as he inhales deeply. The air is thick with tension as the two men face off in a silent showdown. With one more puff, Riley pulls the cigar from his mouth.

"That right, grandpa? And how is an old bag of bones Fishface like you going to stop me?" Flipping the cigar in his fingers, he drives the lit end into the Skya'ja man's skin. The man grimaces as the cigar singes his shoulder. Still, he does not move.

Recovering, he straightens. Resolve washes over his face. "She stays. You go."

Riley spits on the ground, shaking his head in disbelief. "If that's how it's going to be—" He steps backward and pulls a pistol from his belt, aiming the barrel inches from the Skya'ja man's face.

The rest of the group stirs slightly, whispered pleas from the other Skya'ja are spoken. One woman lets out a quiet whimper. Still, the old man stares down Riley. My heart races as I expect the ear-shattering report of the pistol to punish my ears at any moment.

A jolt of adrenaline surges through my body as my legs thrust me up and forward. I'm caught off-guard by my own attack, so I can barely think to tuck my chin as I barrel into Riley's side. I hear the expulsion of air as the wind is knocked from his lungs. We both topple to the ground, and I yelp in pain as my elbow strikes the concrete.

A clatter to my right draws my attention, and the glint of black metal catches my eye. Scrambling with all four limbs, I grab Riley's pistol with my bound hands and spin in a kneeling position to aim the weapon at the fallen man. The maneuver is something out of an action cop movie, and I can hardly believe I am capable of it.

"What the—" Riley cuts off seeing the pistol pointed at him.

Camo pants spins, pointing his rifle at me. "Boss?"

I have to say something. My voice cracks as I speak. "D-drop your weapon, or he gets it." The line sounds so cheesy to me that I immediately follow up. "I'm not kidding. Rifles on the floor."

Camo pants glances at Riley, who nods silently. Both he and the third man place their rifles on the ground. Emerging from our hiding spot, Loren scoops them up, handing them to two Skya'ja nearby. She then rips the rifle off Riley's shoulder and points it at the other men.

"Okay, now get up." I wave the end of the pistol upward, trying hard to disguise how much I'm shaking.

Riley curses as he pushes up from the floor. I stand and nod that he should join his buddies. Slowly, he raises his hands in surrender. "Look, kid, I don't know what you think—"

"Shut up!" My voice cracks again, and I clear my throat. "Unbind her." I nod at camo pants, who turns to untie the Skya'ja woman. Stepping away from the men, she retreats to the older Skya'ja man who still stands resolutely in his place.

Riley rolls his eyes and angles his jaw to one side. "A couple of filthy sympathizers?" Seeing my bound wrists, he cocks his head. "Or maybe not? You seem a little confused, kid."

I hesitate. Loren speaks up for me. "No confusion here. We have the guns. You don't. That's all we need to be clear about for the moment."

Riley turns to Loren, not hiding his annoyance. "You look familiar."

"I-I'm not sure what you mean."

"You're Revon's girl, aren't you." He pauses. "Yeah, word on the street is he's been wanting to get you home for some time. It's not often he puts out a call for someone to be brought in alive." He licks his lower lip as he looks Loren up and down. "Didn't say his little girl was a sympathizer."

Loren straightens her posture. "Yeah. Well, doesn't mean he wouldn't waste you if you did anything to me, sympathizer or not."

Riley laughs. "I don't doubt it. A man like Revon? I have no desire to mess with him. I'm aware of my place in the pecking order."

Loren glances over at me. "So, cowboy, what do you want to do now?"

My jaw hangs open. I hadn't thought that far. I hadn't really thought at all about what I was doing. Yet again, I find myself in a situation where I'm required to be proficient with a firearm, and I'm severely lacking. I make a show of checking to see the safety is off on the pistol.

A warm, pale green hand rests on my forearm. I turn to Tash'jya whose dark eyes meet mine. "Let them go." Her words are a barely audible whisper, and I take a second to register what she's said. I give her a questioning look.

"But—if they tell Revon—"

"It's not our way. As much as we can, we do not hurt humanss, Ted." She turns gracefully to look at Riley and his men. "Even when they hurt uss."

She called me Ted, not Human.

Chapter Fifteen

Neural Implant Log: Entry 139
Officer: Tash'jya, daughter of Sun'tssh
Rank: Tactician

This report is to enter a correction to previous logs. The human known as Ted, whose name I know again, has shown signs that he may have more understanding than I considered. Observance of Skya'ja funeral rites prompted curiosity and a desire to understand our people. I bore witness to his conversation with the human known as Loren, whose name I know, who honors our people with her respectful wonder at our ways. Ted shows empathy for the grief and loss our people experience at the hands of lesser humans who revel in doing us harm.

I am not certain from where this new sensibility has arisen. Perhaps the cessation of my role as captive and his as captor has allowed both of us to see more clearly. Any doubt about his renewed sense of our people was dispelled when he intervened against his own kind who desecrated a funeral ceremony and threatened one of our own. Placing himself between us and our abusers, he defended Skya'ja with whom he had no relationship. I believe it was only my own personal intervention which prevented him from taking the life of our intruders.

It has never been the Skya'ja way to hurt humans. We indeed fight them in battle, but only when provoked. We defend, but we do not attack. We have culpability in this war, but we honor our desire not to cause more harm than necessary to this planet. We have done great harm already, and it would serve no purpose to subdue the population by force, though we could.

Each hostile interaction we have with humans damages the

word we gave them that we have come to benefit their civilization. It docs not matter that we are not the aggressors. Violence is violence. Today I find myself among the most honorable of my people. They are Skya'ja who have suffered abuse at the hands of humans, but even in their defiance refuse to raise a hand against them. That is our way. Let this record show that the actions of this refugee camp are to be honored.

Now free, I have the chance to change the course of this planet. My mission can resume. But what to do with my human companions? I cannot leave them with my people. They pose too great a risk to themselves and our kind. After today, they will be targeted. Yet, I cannot be slowed down in my quest. Do I involve them? What will Ted's reaction be to the knowledge I carry?

Let this record show I do not take this decision lightly. The fate of my mission may very well depend on the choice I make.

End of log.

Loren sits down next to my right and lets out a huff. "Took my time out there to make sure those losers didn't double back on us. Riley may look tough, but that man can run off like a chicken with the best of them." She laughs.

She's right. I laugh at the image of Riley and his men scampering off as fast as their legs would take them the instant they believed we were seriously letting them go. Riley might have run track in high school with the speed he showed getting out of there.

"That doesn't mean they won't be off to tell Revon everything they've seen." I let out a long sigh. The adrenaline of our encounter is slowly draining from my body, leaving me shaky and impossibly tired. "I expect a bottom-feeder like Riley won't hesitate to trade our location for any good grace he can get from your father."

"And that means,"—Loren turns to Tash'jya—"everyone here is in danger. If my father finds out I am here, he will come for me."

Tash'jya nods and turns to the Skya'ja who'd bound my wrists. After a few words in their language, he stands and begins to make his way around the arena. Warning everyone to pack up to move on, no doubt. My thoughts are confirmed when each circle of Skya'ja begin standing and collecting what they can carry.

I rub at the chaffed skin on my wrists, which Tash'jya unbound immediately after she stopped me from shooting Riley. Across the circle, the old Skya'ja sits stoically, the young woman he stood up for sitting to his left. His expression is hard and unmoving. The young woman rests her head on his shoulder and holds his hand. Both stare at me without a word.

Tash'jya sits to my left and leans in toward me. "She is hiss niece. Her father was the one who died before the men arrived."

"Why did he not attend the funeral? I mean, it was his brother."

"Funeral ritess are performed by the children. Other family grieve privately unless there is no other family present to name the dead."

I nod to the old Skya'ja and his niece. While the old man shows no recognition of my gesture, the daughter smiles. "I am Shoi'tu. Thank you for ssaving my uncle. And me."

I think for a moment about how to respond. "I am pleased to know your name, Shoi'tu. I am Ted."

"I am pleased to know your name, Ted."

"Not *Just Ted*?" Tash'jya smiles at me. It takes me a second to realize she's telling a joke, and I laugh, feeling awkward at my delayed reaction. I have an inside joke with a Skya'ja?

"Tash'jya, I am pleased to know your name again." It is the first time we've spoken of it since she used my name, and I hope I have the protocol correct.

"And I am pleased to know yours, Ted."

Relief washes over me. Somehow my actions with Shoi'tu and the old man have won over Tash'jya. I have her trust again.

She fills in the explanation I'm lacking. "Ted, I have not before sseen a human harm another to save one of uss."

"Yeah, well, I guess." I rub my neck embarrassed. "He was

an awful excuse for a human, and I couldn't let him harm anyone. It's not how I want to be."

"And you were in no position to harm Revon to ssave me." It's not a question, but rather a statement of fact. She has put the pieces together of why I abandoned her at the grocery store.

I let out a long shaky breath, surprised at how much I care that she judges me rightly.

"I hated leaving you there. I hated more what his men did to you because I put you in that position. I hate that I caught, bound, and threatened you. I never should have done that. It was ignorance. I still want answers because my questions are that important to me, but I never should have done that to you. I-I'm sorry. I ask your forgiveness." I touch my head and chest with my hands.

Tash'jya returns the gesture without a word, but I can swear I see a tear at the edge of her eyelid.

Suddenly, the old Skya'ja stands and approaches me. Startled, I shrink backward in my seat. He looks down at me, his features unreadable. A long minute passes without a word before he speaks. "You, human, apologize to one of our people? You beg her forgiveness?"

I stammer, thrown off by his gaze. "I-I guess. Yeah. I didn't want her to be harmed by those men, and I am responsible for what happened to her."

Without moving his head, the old man glances at Tash'jya. I can't be sure, but I think I see her nod slightly out of the corner of my eye, but I don't dare turn to find out. Somehow, I recognize this Skya'ja man is not to be ignored. His gaze returns to me. To my shock, he touches his head and chest. His movements are fluid and intentional, adding a dignity to his gesture. "I am Tsstk."

I gulp, sensing the gravity of a Skya'ja his age accepting me in this way. "I-I am pleased to know your name, T-T-Tsstk." The name is barely pronounceable, but I force my tongue to approximate the sound. "I am Ted." I mimic the head and chest motion.

"I am pleased to know your name, Ted."

With that, he returns to his seat, once again comforting his niece. I glance around the circle. All eyes are on me. Whatever just happened, it was significant to everyone present. Even Loren seems to understand its importance.

Tash'jya breaks the silence. "Ted, you are the firsst human Tsstk has offered his name to. He iss an elder among uss. He does not trusst humans." She pauses, glancing at Tsstk's missing hand. "They have done much harm to him."

"Which is why my apology meant so much to him?" I bite my lip, hoping I've deduced correctly.

"Yes." Tsstk affirms my guess.

Loren raises a brow in my direction and playfully elbows my ribs. "Look who's getting in good with the Skya'ja. Not what you thought you'd be doing when you woke up this morning."

That morning feels so long ago, and so much has happened since waking up in Loren's office at the clinic. We've literally escaped death twice today. Suddenly, I feel exhausted and everything in me wishes to lay down.

"No rest for us I'm afraid." Loren motions to the Skya'ja around the room who are hurriedly packing what little they have. "If I know my father, he will be here in a couple of hours if Riley has reached him. My father's men are certainly back by now, and they will come in force. They won't wait until morning."

I turn to Tash'jya. "Where will your people go?"

"They are used to moving. They will be ssafe."

"I assume you will be going with them. We should separate from your people. It is probably safer that way." My heart sinks as I realize what I'm doing. I will not get the answers I am looking for by letting her go, but she is not my captive anymore. I don't want her to be my captive. It is my next thought that catches me.

I want her to be my friend.

Tash'jya touches my hand. "Ted, I will stay with you and Loren."

I look up to meet her obsidian eyes. Still hard to read, I would guess they look compassionate. I search her face for answers, but I shake my head to let her see I don't understand.

"I will remain with you, not as your prisoner. I would like your help."

"My help? How can I help you? With what?"

Tash'jya glances away. Her mouth purses tightly as if she is struggling with her next words. "I was ssent on a mission by Kenneth James—your father."

Chapter Sixteen

"My father? Wait. You knew my dad?" I stammer as the words come out. How can this be? What are the chances that the Skya'ja I captured to get answers actually knew my father personally?

Tash'jya holds up a hand. "Ted, we musst begin to move. We do not have long. Then, I will answer your questionss. Skya'ja do not break their promisess. I promise to share my knowledge."

I nod, pushing down the rising bubble inside of me that is somewhere between relief that I will finally learn what happened to him and anger at having to wait another minute to get my answers. I feel my face grow hot and take a deep breath. Despite my feelings, I realize she is right. We must move before Revon arrives. Any delay could mean disaster for them and us.

Neural Implant Log: Entry 140
Officer: Tash'jya, daughter of Sun'tssh
Rank: Tactician

Ted, whose name I know, will learn the truth. I do not understand the full wisdom of this decision. I cannot ignore that he has become the first human to receive the name of Tsstk, whose name I know. I do not need to record the honor of elder Tsstk, for his story is well told among our people. He was the first among us to explore new worlds and to suggest that our discovery might benefit other civilizations.

To the great honor of our people, he has shepherded countless worlds to cease their warring over limited resources and instead find the common good. What has happened here on this planet is not enough to dishonor his legacy, yet I fear it is the reason he has chosen to live among the refugees. His suffering is deeper than the physical affliction caused by humans. His is a silent, self-prescribed penance for our failure to usher this world into a time of great peace.

I ache to see his honor restored in his own eyes so that he may lead our people once again. My vigor for my mission is renewed, so I will inform Ted of the truth—all of it. Some of the details will be to my shame, but if he is to assist in my mission, then I must tell him everything.

Let this record show that Tsstk is worthy of the full honor due to him.

End of log.

Twenty minutes later, the dilapidated coliseum is behind the three of us as we cross the ruins of Highway 74. The central artery through the southern portion of the city is motionless. Burned out cars and gashes in the pavement stand testament to the two years of war between humans and the aliens. Buildings in this business district are vacant, abandoned in the conflict.

Yet, I am traveling with one of those aliens. Not as captor or prisoner, but as equals. A couple days ago, I would have never imagined being in this close proximity to a Skya'ja without one of us attacking the other. In fact, it was not long ago that we found ourselves clashing ever so briefly in the basement before the recent battle. That Tash'jya wants my help and that I'm offering it freely today—well, it's been a long couple of days.

The Skya'ja are not what I thought. They are not the conquering, arrogant species I'd imagined. I had thought them mindless invaders who'd taken what little was left of our planet, leaving the rest of us to starve. To see so many of their kind homeless and struggling as much as me to survive at the coliseum raises questions, instead of providing answers.

I glance at Loren and realize how little she has said in the last hours. "Did you know?" I motion with my head back toward the coliseum. "That they live like that?"

She presses her lips together as if considering what to say. "I knew." She pauses. "But I've never seen it."

"And what Riley and his guys did? I've never seen people be so cruel. I mean, there's the war, but that is—different. Somehow it seems less cruel when both sides are firing at each other. Those in the coliseum, they did nothing to those men."

This time, she glances away. A blush of what I interpret as shame flushes her skin crimson. "Ted, I've seen my father do horrible things. He's hated Tash'jya's people from the day they arrived, and he's not alone. No, I'm not surprised by Riley. Humanity has made a poor showing of itself in people like him and my father."

Out of the corner of my eye, I can see Tash'jya straighten at Loren's words, and I wonder if she's heard an admission like that out of the mouth of a human before. The three of us proceed in silence as businesses give way to neighborhoods. Quiet streets of historic homes line the block in front of us. This area had been a trendy place to live prior to the Cataclysm, with more and more people attracted to revitalized neighborhoods close to downtown. The appearance of the Bubble and the ensuing war had forced everyone in this area from their homes.

I nod to one of the houses that seems in better shape than the others. The yellow paint is peeling and several of the windows are broken. Still, the roof is intact having somehow dodged the debris from the fighting. In silent agreement, the three of us plod our way toward the home. Walking up the covered porch, I try the handle of the solid oak doorway. The heavy wooden door swings inward. Stale air greets our noses. Stepping inside, the hardwood floors creak under our steps. Uncarpeted steps rise to the second floor next to a hallway leading straight back to the kitchen. To the left, the living room sits almost untouched. A couch and two chairs bracket the fireplace above which protruding wires indicate where a television once hung on the wall. Early looting focused on valuables until everyone began to realize that they couldn't eat televisions and jewelry.

Walking back to the kitchen, we find all the faded white cabinets open. A mouse scurries away on the counter, abandoning whatever crumb it had been feasting on. I check the pantry. It's picked clean. Picking up a fallen chair, I return it to the kitchen table, and the three of us sit.

"Think we can stay here tonight?" I glance at the window to the fading light. "I don't exactly want to be outside in the dark, especially if Revon is on the hunt."

Tash'jya scans the room nervously. "Too many entry pointss. Humans build large spacess to live. It is so unnecessary and inefficient."

I cock my head at her comment. Having the Skya'ja on Earth has become a part of life, and I hadn't stopped to think that it probably still feels foreign for them to be here. I wonder what a Skya'ja home would look like. I'm reminded again how little I know about Tash'jya's people.

Loren shrugs. "Safer than the streets."

Tash'jya gazes out the window. "I would rather be able to see my enemy coming, but perhapss it iss safer than the street."

It's settled, then. We're spending the night here. I can't help but be a little relieved. It's been a long time since I've slept in a real home. The living room couch or a mattress from upstairs sounds inviting. Suddenly, my body grows heavy with weariness. I straighten with a cleansing breath. I can't rest yet. I have questions.

"Tash'jya, about my father—"

"Ted, it's late." Loren places her hand on mine, cutting me off. "Can't it wait until morning?"

"No." Tash'jya's voice is sharp, and it startles me. Loren sucks in a breath, also surprised. "Ted has waited long enough to learn of his father."

My heart skips a beat. It's been two years since I lost my father. Two years of living on the streets and fending for myself. Two years of wondering what happened to create the Bubble and take my father from me. It has been the reason for my survival.

Otherwise, I would have joined a militia, succumbed to a gang, or died of starvation long before now. But not knowing—that kept me going even through the worst of times.

Am I ready for the answers?

I lean forward and place my elbows on the table in front of me. "H-how did you know my father?"

Tash'jya stares blankly at me. A long minute passes in silence. My heart pounds in my chest waiting for the answer, and I can't imagine what gives her pause. My father is dead. She realizes I am aware of that already.

I hear her respirator wheeze deeply as she takes a long breath.

"Ted." She pauses. Another wheezy breath. "I know your father."

"Yes. You said that you knew him already."

"No. I *know* your father. He iss alive."

Chapter Seventeen

All the breath leaves my lungs. It's as if I'm floating in the vacuum of space, and all the life is being sucked from my body. I can't breathe or move or say anything.

My hands tremble on the table, and my eyes begin to burn. Alive? How can he be alive?

Part of me is leaping for joy at the revelation. I want to run and shout. I want to leave now and find him. If she knows my father, she can tell me where he is. I can be with him tonight. Certainly, he's nearby. He wouldn't leave the city without me. I can find him. I can see him again. I can—

My smile falls flat as the excitement drains from my body. The immense joy of learning my father has somehow survived the apocalypse we live in begins a metamorphosis. Inside me, a ball of rage begins to grow in my stomach. My skin becomes hot. My hands ball into fists. If I wanted to take a wall out with a single strike at that moment, I almost believe I could.

"He's alive?" My words escape through gritted teeth. "You knew this and said nothing? All that we've been through in the last two days, and you knew this the whole time? You could have told me at any moment. And what harm would have come to you? None, that's what. This could have been over long before the battle or Revon or—" I lose my words to the boiling anger inside me.

Loren squeezes my hand. "Ted, I'm sure there's an explanation that—"

I rip my hand away. "No, there's not! She-she knew. This whole time." My face feels wet with tears that I can't contain any longer. Am I angry? Am I sad? Am I in disbelief? Yes. All of it. "For two years I've been on my own. Two years! And she couldn't tell me?" I glare at Tash'jya, whose gray pupils stare back at me without betraying any emotion. "It's all you had to tell me, and I would have let you go. Nothing we've been through would have been necessary. I could be looking for him at this very moment." My angry words begin to take on sobs. I can't control it. My stomach seems to be crawling up my insides, and I fear I might vomit.

Tash'jya glances down before returning her gaze. Loren looks from me to her and back. She bites her lower lip like she wants to interject but thinks better of it.

I swallow hard. There is one more thing I need to learn before I storm out of the room. "Where is he?"

A long wheeze. The two inky pools of her eyes remain motionless across the table.

I repeat myself, slowly this time. "Where is he?"

Tash'jya's gaze drops. Her expression appears to be sorrowful, but I don't care. All I want are her next words. She wheezes in another long breath. "Your father iss inside what you call the Bubble."

Neural Implant Log: Entry 141
Officer: Tash'jya, daughter of Sun'tssh
Rank: Tactician

Everything I have feared about involving the son of Kenneth James has come to pass. Instead of accepting the revelation of his father's survival as worthy of relief or even joy, he views my withholding of this knowledge as a breach of trust. He is not wrong. I cannot accept that keeping Ted James from his father is anything less than dishonorable.

I seek to save this world. My mission is paramount to the greater good. And yet, until this moment it has required the utmost secrecy to prevent Ted from leaving me dead or bound, and thus keeping me from finishing the task. And there is the matter of the trust we have built. Would he have believed me before today? I am ashamed to have wounded him. Is it possible that an act of dishonor can be done in the name of something honorable? It is the struggle I will likely take to my grave. Even if my mission succeeds, I will bear this dishonor—for I don't imagine Ted James will release me from it. In my observation, even the best of humans struggle to forgive. It is not in their nature.

What grieves me even more is that I have not finished my explanation. There is more to tell, yet he will not listen. He is blinded by his rage, for which I do not blame him. There is a righteousness to his indignation. I may try to justify my actions in the name of my mission, but that cannot change that I have wronged another human who did not need to be wronged. Merely hours ago, I informed him that injuring another is not our way, and yet I have done so. The wound may not be visible, but it cuts deeper than any physical injury might. I am dishonored yet again.

Should the day come when all that is left of me is this record, please understand that I deeply regret what I have done to this young human. He did not deserve this. His world did not deserve what happened. I hope that the completion of my mission will allow me to, in some measure, right this wrong.

I am sorry, Ted James.

End of log.

I don't use foul language. It's something my father insisted on from a young age. "Young men don't speak like that," he told me on countless occasions. That lesson was lost to me the moment I stood up and stormed out of the kitchen. Now I sit on a dusty bed upstairs, as far as I can get away from her.

I know your father. Her words repeat themselves countless times in my mind until my head hurts. Tears stream from the corners of my eyes, and I make no effort to wipe them away. I rest my head in my hands and allow the flow of sadness to course through me.

No one who's attempted to enter the Bubble has been seen

again. All evidence is that they die. Vaporized. Or absorbed. And yet, somehow Tash'jya believes he is inside, living and breathing. In other words, he might be right up the road, but I cannot get to him. It is a sick irony to be so close and unable to travel any farther.

The cruelty of her words courses through me, and my body trembles. To tell me my father is alive but is in the one place I cannot go is too much. My brain aches as though it's being pulled in several directions. No matter how hard I try to process what I've learned, I can't focus on any one part of it. The more I try, the more I fail. The more I fail, the angrier I get. And that simply makes it worse.

"Dad? Are you really out there?" I whisper to the darkness of the bedroom. The sun has fully set. The one answer to my pleas is the creaks and groans of the old house as the evening cools.

Laying down, I allow my eyes to close. The rush of energy that my outburst gave me seeps out of my body. My limbs grow heavy. Letting out a long yawn, I allow myself to succumb to sleep. At least it will numb the pain of it all. It's a relief, however temporary, that I welcome at this point. I don't want to feel anything, and unconsciousness sounds good to me.

Instead, I dream that I'm pounding on the outside of the Bubble and shouting my father's name.

I awaken to a gentle rapping on the door to the room. My eyelids crack, and I can see the sunlight creeping through the broken window blinds. I've slept like the dead and can barely move. The rapping comes again, and I let out a croaky "come in." I close my eyes again, but I can hear the creak of the old door hinges as someone enters. I have a good guess as to who it is.

"Ted?" The voice is Loren's and sounds almost apologetic. "You awake?"

"No."

She lets out a breathy chuckle as she cracks open the door farther. I watch as she pokes her head in through the gap. Our eyes meet, and she smiles softly. "Mind if we talk?"

"Yes."

She purses her lips. "Then, mind if I talk?"

I sigh, pushing up to a seated position on the edge of the bed. "I guess not." I'm being a jerk with my short answers, and I offer her a smile. "Sorry. Just not all here yet."

She sits next to me and grabs my hand. It feels warm and soft in mine, and I find it remarkable she feels so comfortable with me. We only met two days ago. Then again, she's helped hundreds of patients, and a comforting touch is probably something she's practiced well. I don't mind it. In fact, something inside me flutters, and I allow my gaze to linger on her.

Neither of us has bathed in any form since we met at the clinic. Her blonde locks, though dirty and slightly unkempt, fall in natural waves to her shoulders. It's the first time I've seen her hair down like this. Her eyes find mine, and she offers me a smile. The flutter comes again. This time, I don't stop it.

We stare in silence for a long moment. My brain is exploding with a dozen thoughts, and I am desperate to understand what she is thinking. Instead, we share silence. It is a gift after two long days of running. My soul, amped and ready for a fight hours earlier, melts in the quiet. I return her smile.

"Ted, what you learned last night is good news. I hope you can see that." She pauses, gauging my reaction. My smile fades, but I offer her a nod to keep going. "If Tash is right, and your father is alive inside the Bubble, then there's hope."

"But how? No one can get in there. If there are people inside, why has there been no sign of them?" It's a logical question, but not the one that I really want answered. "Why wait to tell me?"

Loren sighs. Not the kind that conveys annoyance but understanding. "I think Tash has more answers for us on how it's possible and why she hasn't said anything until now. You didn't exactly give her a chance to explain last night. When I asked, she said she knew more but wanted you to hear it from her."

There's more? I'm not certain I want to hear it.

"As for your other question,"—Loren hesitates—"I think you

should cut her some slack. Imagine what it's been like from her perspective. She gets hit in the head with a rock. Wakes up the tied prisoner of a human. Is dragged through the streets during a battle, to then be handed over to my father. Locked up with her captor, only to run for her life. Finally, to see her people abused and forced to relocate." She pauses to smile at me again. "She hasn't had much opportunity to tell you all this, much less any reason to. She's been surrounded by nothing but hostility for two days."

The ball of anger threatens to rise inside of me, still aching for the supposed justice I demanded last night. I take a deep breath to release it. Loren is right. If I were Tash'jya, I'd have felt no obligation to reveal my knowledge. Empathy is winning inside me, and for the moment, I hate it. I want to be angry. Anger makes me feel powerful. Without it, I will need to face my sadness, and it will leave me weak.

I double over and cross my arms over my knees. Knowing Loren is right doesn't help me feel better. The anger is dissipating, but that leaves me tired. It was easier to lash out and mentally burn the world to the ground than to accept the truth. That's the way with truth sometimes—we don't like it. That doesn't change the fact that it is truth.

"Where is she?" I ask.

"She's downstairs. She hasn't moved from her chair, like she's waiting for you to come around. I'm not aware of everything about her people, but I have learned they can be patient when they need to be. I believe Tash still wants to tell you what she knows. I think you should go to her and listen—really listen."

I nod. She's right. She usually is. Annoying, but it makes me like her all the more. "Tash? When did you start calling her that?"

Loren chuckles, her eyes sparkling as she looks up, probably recalling the memory. "Last night. I've called her that in my head from the beginning, and I let the nickname slip last night. I freaked out and blurted an apology. Sort of yelled actually." Loren gently smacks her forehead, her face blushing with the embarrassment of the story. "Names are so important to her people, and I was terrified I'd insulted her. One of us had to stay on her good side."

She pokes my shoulder playfully with her free hand.

I laugh. "Yeah, I suppose so. What did she say?"

"She stared at me a long time in silence. It was terrible. I thought she was about to bite my head off. Then, she smiled—and laughed. I told you that I've heard a Skya'ja laugh exactly one other time in my life."

"She laughs? Not Tash'jya. Not possible." The thought seems so foreign to me, and I find myself wanting to hear what a Skya'ja laugh sounded like.

Loren chuckles. "Yeah. She actually laughed. Said it was what her sister called her for most of her life, and she likes the sound of someone calling her by that name."

"She has a sister?"

Loren's smile fades. "She does. Like I said, there is more to the story, and she wants to tell you. Ted, you're not the only one who lost someone in the Cataclysm. Tash's sister is inside the Bubble, too."

Chapter Eighteen

Tash'jya straightens in her chair as I enter the kitchen. True to what Loren said, Tash'jya hasn't moved. Same chair. Same position. I offer an apologetic smile and slide into my seat from the previous night, leaning backward onto the rear feet of the chair. I let out a long, breathy sigh and rap my fingers on the table. Loren takes a seat next to mine.

This is awkward.

I'm not able to take the silence any longer. "Tash'jya, I am sorry. I shouldn't have gotten so angry. Finding out that my dad is alive got me so—"

Tash'jya cuts me off with a raised hand. "No, Ted. It iss I who should be apologizing to you. For it iss I who have wronged you."

I swallow hard. "Tash'jya, come on. I hit you over the head with a rock. Tied you up. Interrogated you for hours. Called you a 'Fishface.' Left you with Revon and his goons who beat you the entire time I was gone. Everything you have suffered has been because of me."

"I appreciate that you would attempt to own such behavior, but it is not the truth. I am done with the deception. I suffer because of myself!"

The outburst is so unexpected that I tip backward in my chair, nearly toppling over. I catch myself with one hand on the table. Loren places a hand on my shoulder, assisting in catching me. Tash'jya's respirator wheezes loudly as she breathes deeply, trying to calm herself. To my surprise, a tear gathers at the edge of her eye, clinging to the lid for a moment before tumbling down her cheek.

She can laugh. She can cry.

"I am ssorry, Ted." Her voice is raspy, almost choked. Her dark eyes seem to gaze right through me. "I wass angry—at your father. He sent me away from the energy project. He knew what wass to happen and sent me away. Now I am outside the Bubble."

I finish her thought. "And your sister is inside. Loren mentioned her."

She nods.

"Tash." Loren whispers her name sympathetically.

I close my eyes and take a deep breath. The details aren't coming together for me. "Tash'jya, I think I need you to explain from the beginning. What did my father know, and why did he send you away?"

Tash'jya's eyes find a spot on the wall and fix there, as if she were watching the replay of her thoughts. "The clean energy my people promised is something we have offered to other worldss. It iss our gift to bring peace to others who war over the resources of their planet. Time and again, we have helped civilizationss transition from warring, selfish peopless to speciess that serve each other. In our successes, we have become arrogant, believing we cannot make mistakess. When we came to your planet, we assumed the process would be the same as before, but your world iss different. We should have studied more, but we thought we fully understood the kind of planet that can sustain life. Despite objectionss from humans like your father, my people chose to move forward with the project. They activated the device. The project overloaded, and—" Her voice trails off. Her lips form words, but no sound comes from them.

"The Cataclysm." I complete the thought.

"And the resulting electromagnetic pulse destroyed all electric devices followed by the explosion that launched particles in the air that ultimately destroyed any usable farmland." Loren recites the events of the Cataclysm flatly, as if to indicate there's no point in getting emotional since we all are aware of what happened. "Worldwide starvation and quarrelling over the remaining scraps are then simply made worse by the war of revenge on the Skya'ja."

Tash'jya nods. "Our arrogance destroyed your home. Instead of launching your speciess into the next great stage of your development, we have given you a death sentence."

"My father knew this would happen?" I have to be certain if I heard her correctly.

"Guessed iss more accurate. He kept saying 'the numberss don't add themselves up.'" She stops to look at me. I nod. I'd heard my father use that phrase on more than one occasion when he was working. "He wanted more testss and data, but my people assured those above him that all was well. He sent me to find his creation. He believed it would help contain the overload."

"Creation? What do you mean?"

"His capacitor prototype."

Images of countless hours of my father working in our garage, which he'd converted to a clean room laboratory, flooded my mind. Clean energy had always been his passion. It was the reason he'd been selected to work with the Skya'ja when they'd arrived. Always on the verge of a breakthrough, I'd assumed it was more of a coping mechanism after my mother died. Had he actually finished one of his designs?

"My father sent you to find his prototype. Why not pause the project and get it himself?" I'm worried my expression appears angry instead of confused. I make myself soften my features.

"Our leaderss wanted to meet their promised deadline and felt his concernss unwarranted. He needed to stay to assist, so he sent me momentss before—as you humans say—it 'blew up in our facess.' He had time only to tell me to find his laboratory. Nothing more."

The three of us sit in silence, mourning the truth of what happened.

"Tash," Loren speaks in a hush, "how can anyone be alive inside the Bubble, then?" The question makes me shiver. It's one I've been avoiding, and I'm grateful she finally asked for me. "Ted's father? Your sister?"

"The Bubble is not impenetrable as iss assumed among humans. It is a barrier between timess."

I raise an eyebrow. No, I'll be honest. On the outside, I'm still, but inside my brain is exploding. I'm not sure I heard her correctly. "Times?"

"The reason our people have become technologically advanced so quickly iss that our first discovery was the ability to slow time."

"You can travel through time?" My face contorts as it swaps between disbelief and shock. "So you're from the future or something?"

"No. Not time travel. We cannot go places in the past or future, but we can slow time down. We call it what would translate to your language as 'time expansion.' The effect iss not permanent or global but works in a small, localized area. Inside, time would pass at a fraction of the speed, while outside time would resume as it normally would, given the conditions before time expansion was activated. This gave our best scientistss the ability to work several lifetimess in length. When the effect is turned off, the expansion would collapse, and the rest of our world would adjust as if all the technology discovered inside had always existed."

"So you're saying—" Loren begins.

"Inside the Bubble, it is still two yearss ago. The time expansion devicess activated automatically as a safety mechanism the instant something went wrong—in this case, the overload. To those inside, the overload is only beginning. And they are trying to fix it."

"And out here? Why is the world destroyed out here if the explosion hasn't happened in there?"

"Because out here the world existss as if events had proceeded at the Cataclysm. Unless they can fix the problem and turn off the Bubble, nothing will change. But time iss not at a standstill inside. Eventually, the explosion will begin, and they won't be able to stop it."

Loren sucks in a breath. "And why hasn't anyone emerged from the Bubble to tell everyone this? To prevent the war that is going on? Or better, to mobilize the effort to help?"

Tash'jya's face darkens. "The barrier cannot be crossed that way. We may pass inside to the past, but traveling forward would rip the fragile lining of the time expansion. It iss why none of your people, who have entered the Bubble, have emerged. They are trapped.

"And to tell the world would not have the effect you believe it would. What would happen if everyone discovered that the Bubble contained the world from two yearss ago?"

Loren nods. "Refugees would flock inside."

"And that would disrupt all efforts to fix the overload," I say.

Tash'jya wheezes. "For more than a year, I searched for your father's laboratory. I found it, but I could not find the prototype. I believed he lied to me. I grew angry that he sent me on thiss mission. Separated me from my sister. All for something that did not exist. So—I came looking for you."

"For me?" I point to myself.

"I planned to see my sister again, if only for a while. They have what will feel to them like two dayss before the explosion begins inside their time. But—I would bring you, so your father would be forced to face you as they ran out of time. He would have to watch as the explosion slowly made itss way close to the time expansion device, knowing it was his failure that killed uss all. He would watch you die. That iss how you came to find me, Ted. It was no coincidence. I was following you. You were going to be my captive, but I ended up as yourss. I hated you—but then you saved me when my respirator detached. You risked your safety to return to Re-von. You helped my people in the camp when you didn't need to.

"I have dishonored myself all the while convincing myself that my actions are just. I have even doctored my logss to make myself seem noble, so when the remainder of our people come to investigate, they will not leave me nameless."

"Logs? What logs?" I glance at her clothes, expecting to see a journal or tablet sticking out somewhere. "I've never seen you write anything down."

"It is a neural log." She taps the side of her head. "It is an implant that allowss me to record a journal simply by thinking about it.”

“Crazy.” At first, I’m fascinated by the idea of recording thoughts, but then I consider what kind of surgery would be required to install such a device. I think I’ll pass.

“If you were to learn nothing of me these last few months other than what I have logged, you would believe me a martyr when the explosion becomes unstoppable, and the fate of this world is sealed. My very legacy will be a lie.” She lowers her head. “I should die nameless for what I’ve done and what I planned to do.”

Loren’s hand finds mine and squeezes gently. A single tear escapes my eye. Running down my cheek, it drops to my lap.

I breathe in, not fully sure what to say. “It seems we’ve both made mistakes we regret. And we’ve come a long way in our opinion of each other.”

“So where does that leave us?” Loren breathes a heavy sigh.

“With no capacitor. And without hope.” Tash’jya won’t meet our gaze. “I will confess in my log what I have done. It is the one truly honorable choice I have left. Then, I will leave you both to return to my sister. To spend what time I can with her.”

Her words stab at my heart. I don’t want her to go, but I can’t stop her from seeing her sister. She’s right. If my father was wrong about his capacitor, then there is no plan. My mind scrambles for a solution. “You said you found my father’s lab?”

“Yess. I found many thingss, but no capacitor.”

Then, it occurs to me. “Did you check the floor safe?”

Tash’jya’s head jerks up with a penetrating stare. “I did not see a floor safe. There iss a safe?”

All the breath escapes my lungs for a moment. I nod excitedly until able to speak. “In the corner of the room, under the worktable. Half the time dad even forgets it’s there. Much of what is in there is probably forgotten.”

“That means—” Loren says, bolting upright in her chair.

“That means we leave now. We have a capacitor to find and deliver.”

Chapter Nineteen

Neural Implant Log: Entry 142
Officer: Tash'jya, daughter of Sun'tssh
Rank: Tactician

This report will not be like those before. This one will be honest. I confess that I have not been forthcoming in my intentions. I have presented myself in a dishonorable way, and I wish to make that right.

I abandoned my mission months ago and have falsified my records to appear otherwise. I came to the conclusion that the capacitor I was sent to retrieve was imaginary or was unfindable. In the first moments of searching the home of Kenneth James, whose name I know, my hope became desperation. Nothing matching the description he gave me could be found there. That frantic search soon became anger as I felt robbed of my remaining time with my sister. Instead of sifting through the rubble of this world for false hope, I could have had two years with her inside the Bubble.

My longing to see her before she died overwhelmed me, and I discarded my mission to return to her. My anger, however, would not let me simply come back to her in defeat. I would make the man who sent me on this fool's errand pay for what he took from me. He would live out his remaining days knowing his son would be trapped inside the Bubble and not survive the explosion. He took me from my family, so I would take his.

I am dishonored, and I make no excuses.

But now, by some miracle of grace, I have renewed hope that my mission may yet be complete. The son of Kenneth James is aware of a hidden floor safe in the laboratory. In the hasty moments before the Bubble came to be, the knowledge of this safe was not divulged. Whether Dr. James considered it obvious, or it simply slipped his mind in the chaos of trying to get me to leave before the overload, I'm not sure.

Let the record show that I have accepted my dishonor and seek to right my wrong. I have wasted too much time avenging a wrong that was not actually committed. There is still time to complete the mission, and I intend to. If I fail, I hope my people will see this confession as a return to honor and not leave me nameless. If I succeed, perhaps that is my proper recompense.

The understanding between the human known as Ted James, whose name I know, and me has grown a great deal. In this we share common ground, we make mistakes. We are flawed to our core. Yet grace is found when the flaws are recognized, owned, and atoned for in humility. Ted has atoned for his and even received the name of one of our respected elders. It is my turn.

My people want to restore this world to its former glory, and my chance to facilitate this is renewed. Millions of lives are on the line. We are returning to the laboratory as I make this entry. I must not fail.

End of log.

My heart leaps inside of me as we make our way down the remains of Highway 24, heading east out of the city center. We've been walking for hours, but I can barely feel my feet underneath me. The thought of showing up inside the Bubble, seeing my father, and presenting his capacitor to him fills me with a dangerous hope. I temper the flutter in my stomach as best I can, but I cannot prevent the bounce in my step.

Could all this really come to an end?

Could it all really be undone?

My home is not in one of the glamourous parts of the city, but my mother made it a nice place to grow up. She'd always kept it neat and well-decorated. After she passed, my father refused to relocate to something smaller and easier to care for despite his busy schedule. He'd obsessed over the thought of creating a clean energy solution, and most of the finances went into his lab work, leaving our home in desperate need of updating. Still, it was home for the two of us for a long time.

I haven't been back since the first days after the Cataclysm.

Turning into the neighborhood, I am reminded why.

The burned husks of homes stand on either side of the road. Blackened beams jut upward where rooftops once stood. Much of the neighborhood is gone. Several of the remains have fallen over. Here and there, a house stands intact, a miraculous survivor of the fire that broke out. These homes appear frozen in time with children's toys and abandoned cars still in their driveways. Still, the encroachment of mold and overgrown lawns stand as testament to their neglect. Without rescue to put out the flames, the entire block was obliterated, and families who lived here left long ago.

Turning onto Eagle Lane, we approach the dilapidated ruins of my home. The left side of the house is charred, and the roof on that side has collapsed. The right side still stands untouched, the work of a torrential thunderstorm that finally put out the flames before the entire home could be destroyed completely. Still, it is unlivable, and the streets have been my home for two years.

I breathe in a lungful of hopeful air at the sight of the garage on the right side of the home. Intact. Untouched. Mildew covers what used to be a white garage door. Loren tries the handle to see if it will lift.

"You can't get in that way. My father sealed the room to create his lab. That door is a façade now. Only one way in." I point to the front door—or rather, where it used to be.

Stepping inside the home, I gaze around silently. A scorched frame in the corner is all that remains of my father's favorite chair. The carpet is moldy, exposed to the elements. My mother's piano remains near the wall, warped and peeling from the rain that has destroyed it. Despite the destruction, there is a faint odor that floods my mind with childhood memories.

In that moment, I sense images of the past. The ruins of the home transform in my mind to days when this was a home. Christmas morning with my mother's homecooked feast and presents by the tree in the corner. Spraining my ankle as a boy as I jumped off the couch with a blanket around my neck for a cape. Watching my mother's declining health as her disease overtook her. The flood of emotion hits me at the door, and I stop.

"You okay?" Loren asks, placing a hand on my shoulder.

"Yeah. I'll be fine. Just—just haven't been here in a while. Sometimes I forget that it wasn't that long ago that everything felt normal."

"Well, we're here to make that happen again."

I nod. It's hard to imagine that all this could be undone, but the memories fill me with resolve to see it happen. I wave the group to the right through the kitchen. Loren points to the cabinets. "Got anything?"

"Sorry. Picked it clean before I left."

Tash'jya hasn't said a word. Her expression is somber as she scans the remains of my home. She's been here before, but not with me. I wonder what's going through her mind and what happened when she believed she'd been deceived. What memories does this place have for her?

The door on the other side of the kitchen is cracked, evidence of Tash'jya's previous visit. I pull open the creaky entrance to the garage. It's dark inside, but enough light spills in through the door for me to make out the lab. Plastic sheeting hangs loosely, once suspended neatly from the ceiling. The air filtration unit sits in the corner. Inside the plastic 'tent,' a table with various equipment still sits. Moisture and dust cling to every surface.

Turning to the left, I pull against the weight of the workbench in the corner. It slides with a grating screech across the concrete. Kneeling, I blow on the dusty floor. A cloud of particles wafts into the air, forcing me to wave a hand in the air as I cough. The thinnest line in the concrete is revealed.

"As promised, a floor safe."

Tash'jya wheezes loudly in her respirator, the one sign she shares my excitement.

"Can we open it?" Loren asks.

"That—is the only problem." I point to the lock near the wall. Sunken into the floor is a metal latch, a large padlock holding it closed. "That's not exactly going to snip with bolt cutters—not that we have any."

The three of us scan around the room as if asking it for answers. Something has to be here to give us access. Suddenly, Tash'jya bolts to the other side of the room. She rips open a cabinet and begins tossing tools behind her, creating an echoing clatter as the metal objects skitter across the floor. Seconds later, she rounds the corner of the plastic pulling a small cart on which sits a tank. In her other hand is a hose and cutting torch.

"You know how to use that?" I ask.

"Working with your father did not mean paperwork, Ted. I learned many of your human toolss." She smiles at us. "I can use thiss."

Loren bounces on her feet in excitement.

This is really happening.

"Please, give me space to work." Tash'jya waves a hand. "This will take some time." Attaching the hose, she opens the nozzle of the tank, producing a slight hiss as pressure fills the line. Holding an ignitor near the tip, a flame bursts from the nozzle. Turning the adjustment, the fire transitions from a loose orange flame to a scorching blue inferno. Grabbing the welder's mask off the top of the cart, she slips it over her head, smiling again before pulling it down over her face.

Loren grabs my hand, and we return to the kitchen. We hear the torch go to work on the massive lock.

Wandering around the home, Loren stops in front of a series of photos on the wall. She gazes at the pictures of my childhood. Laughing at a picture of me in a swimsuit and snorkel gear from my childhood, she points to my gangly arms and legs.

"At what age did you finally fill out and not look like such a nerd?"

"Very funny," I say.

She moves on to a picture of the whole family from a vacation many years ago. Three of us stand on a beach. My father, wearing a smile I haven't seen since childhood, stands with his arm around my mother. Her hands rest on my shoulders. I squint against the sunlight behind the camera. We look happy.

"What happened to your mother?" Loren asks. Her voice is soft, like she's afraid she's overstepping with the question. When I don't answer, she adds, "I'm sorry. You don't have to—"

"No, it's okay." I interrupt. "She died not long after that picture. Cancer." Saying the word makes my stomach sink. Reexamining the picture, I can see the slight gauntness in my mother's cheeks from weight loss. It had been our last vacation before she was too sick to do anything but endure her treatments. The days and months following that vacation were filled with her decline. That daily pain and the treatment-induced illness were almost too much to witness. All for a battle she lost in the end.

"I'm sorry. She was beautiful."

"My father was never the same afterward." I let out a long sigh. "He and I still had each other, but he was never as happy again. That's when his work became so important. He poured himself into it."

Loren turns to me. "What about you?"

I shake my head. "It's not what you think. He didn't neglect me. We became—disconnected. I've always been pretty independent and didn't need much from him. It was easy for us to drift apart. We've never had a bad relationship. Still—" I pause, choking up.

Loren gazes into my eyes, patiently waiting for me to continue.

"—I guess I needed him more than I realized. Since the Cataclysm, all I've been able to think about is him. Now that I learn he's alive, I—I—" I run out of words.

Loren places a gentle hand on my cheek. It's warm and comforting. "Hey, we'll get you back to him, okay? Tash will have that safe open, and we'll be on our way. You could be seeing him in a matter of hours."

I nod, the odd mix of despair and hope threatening to

overcome me. I place my hand over hers on my cheek and wrap my fingers around hers. Our hands drop until I'm clutching hers against my chest. Her eyes search mine, glistening with empathy.

I lean in and kiss her.

I'm not sure why. For a second, I think she will pull away. I feel her suck in a breath in surprise, and I almost break contact. Then, her grip on my hand closes tighter, and she leans into me. Our lips press for a long moment before we part.

I smile and breathe a sigh of relief when she does the same.

"I'm not sure where that came from," I offer. "Hope it was okay."

"Definitely." She leans in and kisses me again. Stepping forward, she wraps her arms around me and rests her head on my chest. We hold each other in silence before she lets out a breathy laugh. "You know what this means, don't you?"

I raise my eyebrows. "What does it mean?"

"My father has another reason to hate you." A clang of metal from the garage signals the lock has been sprung and cast aside. Loren grabs my hand again. "Come on. Let's get you back to your father."

Chapter Twenty

Our noses sting as we enter the garage from the metallic burn left in the air from the cutting torch. Tash'jya stands over the floor safe, the lock cut and thrown open. The three of us pause as if afraid to open the safe and find the capacitor missing. I've dared to hope that it will be in there, and I'm not sure what I will do if we're wrong. There is only one way to find out.

Loren gestures toward the latch with a hand. "Care to do the honors, Ted?"

I nod, glancing at Tash'jya. Her hands are folded tightly in front of her, something I've come to recognize as anxiousness from her. Stepping over to the far end of the door, I reach down and grasp the handle, which is sunken into the floor. Wrapping my fingers around the metal bar, I pull.

Nothing. It doesn't even budge.

Repositioning my feet, I gather my strength to get better leverage. Grabbing with both hands this time, I pull upward. I feel my face grow crimson under the strain as the safe begins to open. The door screeches a complaint, and the disused hinges fight my efforts. The tiny movement of the bar provides enough momentum, and the force of my pull finally overcomes the resistance. The door flies open. I stumble at the sudden shift, barely catching my feet before I'm pulled over.

The heavy door clangs to the floor next to the safe. A cloud of dust rises into the air, obscuring our vision for a moment. Inside the safe, several objects lay, covered in microfiber cloth. I pull a few away, each revealing a new device of my father's invention. None of which I am familiar with.

"Anyone have an idea what a capacitor looks like?" I ask.

"It could look like a soda can or be shaped like a small

rectangular box," Loren says. I raise a questioning eyebrow. "My father worked on air conditioning units, and I once had a boyfriend who worked on hybrid cars. Those are the capacitors I've seen them work with."

"Boyfriend?" I raise an eyebrow at her.

Loren rolls her eyes. "Former. Long time ago."

"Thiss one is not shaped like that." Tash'jya draws in the air with two fingers. "Your father described it as two cylinderss attached along their long side by a box in-between. His own design for the prototype."

Pulling back a few more of the cloths, a ball of fear rises in my gut as I begin to wonder if the prototype is elsewhere. I push back any thoughts that he may have stored it in the part of the house that is now a burned husk. Cloth after cloth reveal objects, the functions of which I can barely guess. Grabbing the final covering, I pull.

Two cylinders attached on their long side by a box in-between.

I almost don't want to ask the question. "Tash'jya, is that what he described?"

"Yess." Her voice is nearly a whisper.

I hold my breath as I gently remove the object from the safe. It's not much larger than a thick encyclopedic volume, but the surprising weight hints at the materials inside. For a long moment, I stare at the object in disbelief. Could this little device save the world? Had my father really invented something that could improve upon alien tech?

Grabbing one of the larger cloths, I carefully wrap the capacitor and hand it to Tash'jya. She stares at it in awe, her eyes dancing over the wrapped package. It occurs to me that this means a reunion with her sister as much as it means my return to my father. We've found her ticket back to her family. She cradles it in her arms as if afraid to drop it.

Loren disappears into the kitchen, reappearing with a backpack from the closet. Gently, Tash'jya lowers the capacitor into the bag and zips it up. Slipping her arms through the straps,

Loren tightens them to fit and lets out a long sigh.

"So, what are we waiting for?" she asks, a slight chuckle to her voice.

"We can simply walk to the Bubble now? To give this to my father?" I glance at Tash'jya. "It feels unreal that we are on our way."

She nods. "Yess."

I stand, and the three of us file out of the garage. It seems far too unceremonious. This incredible discovery. The fate of the world is at stake. I feel like I should say something memorable. Part of me wishes this moment felt bigger than it is.

We arrive at the front of the house. I curse myself for wanting something bigger to happen.

Revon stands out on the street, flanked by eight men.

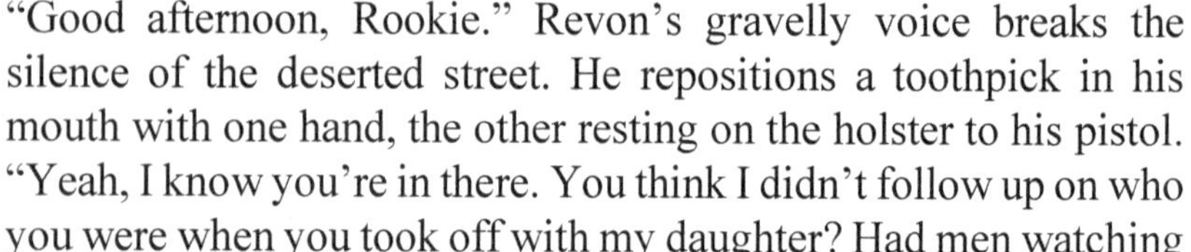

"Good afternoon, Rookie." Revon's gravelly voice breaks the silence of the deserted street. He repositions a toothpick in his mouth with one hand, the other resting on the holster to his pistol. "Yeah, I know you're in there. You think I didn't follow up on who you were when you took off with my daughter? Had men watching this place from the moment you left us. Saw you, my daughter, and the beast enter an hour ago."

I remind myself that I'm still in the shadows of the house interior. He may have figured out I'm here, but there's a good chance he hasn't actually seen us. Waving a hand, I motion Loren and Tash'jya back into the hallway. I retreat with them and peer out from around the corner.

Among Revon's men, I recognize Matthews and Chambers, both of them sporting bandages on their heads from Tash'jya's beating. Both of them look ready for some payback. On Revon's other side, I also see Riley and Camo Pants, who have apparently been adopted into the clan thanks to the intel they brought. The other men are unfamiliar, but each appears as though they would be comfortable killing without a thought.

Revon stands unmoving. The man brims with confidence. His smirk reveals he knows we cannot overpower him with this show of force.

"We just want to be left alone." I shout the words toward the back of the house, so the direction of the sound is indistinct for Revon. "Please, we're not wanting trouble."

Riley mutters a curse, and Revon casually turns to him with a raised brow. Riley cuts himself off, retreating a step from Revon. Revon returns his gaze in our direction. "That's not what I hear. My new friends here say you got the drop on them with the help of some Fishfaces. They say you're in league with the enemy and prevented them from claiming what rightfully belongs to humanity. In my book, Rookie, that sounds like *wanting trouble.*" A long pause. "To be honest, I'm impressed. You escaped my men and got the better of two armed men. You belong with us and not with that Fishface. Now, I can send my men in there with a single command. You wouldn't stand a chance, but I don't trust you with my little girl. So, why don't we end this peacefully, and we can talk man-to-man. Come out, and we can discuss if my generous offer still stands. You won't get this chance again."

I glance at Loren. She's biting her lip and not looking at me. I can guess what she's thinking.

"No. Don't even think about it." I whisper. "You're not going out there. Not alone."

"I have to." Her eyes find mine. "It's me he really wants. If I go out there, I might be able to get him to leave you two to finish what we've started."

"Or he might open fire knowing you're out of harm's way." My words give her pause. "You know I'm right. You are the reason he's hunting me, but you're also the reason he hasn't killed me."

She shakes her head in frustration. "What do we do then?"

Tash'jya wheezes as she studies the group outside. "I cannot overpower so many. Not by myself."

"I wouldn't ask you to." I peer back around the corner. Revon is unmoved. This is not his first standoff. "Besides, they would gun you down before you made it halfway across the lawn."

"I would make it closer than that, Ted." Tash'jya's voice carries an edge, and I wonder how fast and fierce she really can be when pressed. Her expression is stoic, but I can feel the anger coming from her. This is a delay. This is keeping her from her sister.

And me from my father.

Revon shakes his head impatiently. "Rookie, you have five minutes to decide. Man up or face the business end of my sidearm. Your choice."

"He's bluffing." Loren's voice is flat. "He won't shoot while I'm with you."

"I don't exactly want to use you as a human shield." I grab her hand.

"I don't exactly want to be a human shield, but it's our best chance. If we can make a break for it, we might have a chance. Is there another way out of here on this side of the house? We step out into the open, and they'll surround us."

I scan the hallway. My eyes rest on the door to my bedroom. More than once, I'd managed to break curfew by sneaking into the window of my room. Right outside, a large shrub obscured any view from the street. From there, it was merely a short sprint to the trees. We might be able to get lost in the woods.

"Right there." I nod to the door. "We can get out that way. They wouldn't see until we were almost beyond the tree line."

Loren sighs. "It's running then. You good, Tash?"

"I will be fine. You will need to keep up with me, Lo-ren." Tash'jya's tone is determined. She is already shifting her weight from one foot to the other, readying herself to flee.

Loren begins to slip the backpack off. "Maybe you should carry this, then? If you're going to be so much faster than the rest of us, then—"

"No." Tash'jya grabs her arm. "They will not shoot at you. They will shoot at me. The capacitor is safer with you. If something happens to me, please get the capacitor to Dr. James…and tell my sister to remember my name."

"It's not going to come to that." The words are as much for

me as for Tash'jya. "So that's it? We run?" I'm already breathless at the thought.

Loren shakes her head. "In a second. One more thing—just in case." She pulls on my hand and plants a firm kiss on my lips. We linger for a moment, drinking in each other's touch before slowly pulling away.

Tash'jya glances at both of us, silently asking 'when did this happen?' "Humanss," she says flatly. I almost think I see her roll her eyes.

"Yeah," Loren chuckles, "humans."

My face grows hot with embarrassment. I point to the door. "Let's go before Revon decides five minutes is four minutes too long."

Chapter Twenty-One

Carefully, I slide the bedroom window open. Sticking my head outside, I confirm the obscured view I'd counted on so many times when I was younger. Pulling back inside, I motion for Tash'jya to exit first. With inhuman adeptness, she contorts herself silently through the opening. Turning to Loren, I motion for her to go next.

She is scanning my old room. Turning to me, she points with a thumb at the concert poster still pinned to the wall. "I never took you for a metalhead. Kinda surprised."

I let out a breathy laugh. "Believe it or not—it was my mom's. She always said Gen-Xers like her were the 'angry generation' and the music was an outlet. After she died, I kept it. It reminds me of her and all the things she likes. Not my style of music, though."

Loren smiles as she ties her hair back. "I think I would have liked your mom. Seems like she knew who she was and didn't apologize for it." Swinging a leg out the window, she drops silently to the ground below. Seconds later, I'm out the window, the muscle memory of countless trips sneaking out coming back to me.

"One minute left, Rookie!" Revon's shout echoes in the empty neighborhood.

He hasn't seen us. Good.

Silently, I point to the spot in the trees that kept me most hidden for years from Mrs. Winston, our nosy neighbor across the street. I'm struck for a moment with the realization that I have no idea what happened to Mrs. Winston after the fire. I gesture that we'll be hidden for half the distance before we're exposed to Revon and his men.

Tash'jya and Loren nod. Loren holds up three fingers and begins a countdown.

At the drop of the third finger, we bolt for the trees.

Panic sends shockwaves through my body, making me feel stiff and clumsy. My feet slip on the overgrown grass, and I clench my jaw as I will my body to move. Loren is right beside me, pumping her arms with each step. Tash'jya is several steps ahead of us, her alien physique besting us in our sprint.

Shouts come from the street as we burst into full view. A shot rings out and the bark of a tree at the edge of the woods explodes as the bullet strikes, missing us. Then, another. Instinctively, I duck my head as I run.

"Riley, you,"—Revon's voice sounds off into a string of curses—"that is my daughter out there!"

Steps from the trees, I dare a glance at the street. Revon's face is crimson, and his teeth are bared. He raises his sidearm at Riley, who drops his rifle and holds both hands up in surrender. The pistol flashes. Riley's head snaps violently as his body hurls backward onto the street. He doesn't move. When it comes to his daughter, Revon is not a man with any mercy. I don't want to find out what he'll do if he ever catches me.

The rest of the men begin their pursuit after us. It's the last thing I see before disappearing into the trees.

Making no effort to hide our footsteps, we scramble from the edge of the woods into the deeper, denser parts. Twigs snap under our feet. Branches swipe at my face, leaving stinging scratches. My lungs burn as I push my body harder and faster than it's normally capable of moving. Loren's heaving breaths sound next to me.

Behind us, Revon's men come crashing into the woods. I hear one trip and fall to the ground, followed by his cursing. We follow Tash'jya, who seems able to navigate a clear path through the brush, though I can't see one. The heavy footfalls begin to sound more distant.

"I think—we're losing them—keep running." My voice is a wheeze between breaths. Loren nods, wincing as her hair snags on a branch. She runs through the snare, the twig snapping off and remaining entangled in her locks.

Ahead, the trees open to a road cut through the woods. Without stopping, we burst into the clearing. The roar of an engine startles me, and my feet tangle as I stutter-step out of the way of the pickup. Hitting the ground, the air expels from my lungs. The tires of the truck cross inches from my head.

"Ted!" Loren screams.

The truck slams on its brakes, dirt and gravel scraping under the locked tires. The pickup skids to a near stop before the wheels begin to spin on the loose roadway, turning the vehicle back in our direction.

"It's my father!" Loren shouts loud enough to cause her voice to crack.

Sure enough, Revon's face appears in the window over the wheel, his lips curled into a snarl. The engine roars as he floors the pedal. The tires shoot dirt and rocks behind as they search for traction. My brain screams at my body to stand up and keep running, but I am frozen—helpless before the approaching truck.

Pop! Hiss!

The tire of the truck explodes with a rush of air, a sharp end of a rusty piece of rebar protruding briefly from the rubber tire wall before the blowout. Unbalanced, the truck veers to the side of the road. In an instant, Tash'jya appears, landing on the hood of the vehicle. She raises her arm, a large stone in her hand. "Shya-sii!" Bringing the rock down, the windshield of the truck spiderwebs, leaving it nearly impossible to see through.

The truck swerves as Revon unsuccessfully tries to compensate for the blown tire. Tash'jya leaps from the hood, landing in a roll on the ground, which she uses to transition into a defensive stance. With a large thud, the truck strikes the trunk of a tree, buckling the hood into an upside-down V.

The woods become silent, except for the approaching footfalls of Revon's men. Smoke and fumes rise from the ruined engine of the truck. Inside, a dazed Revon mutters and swipes at the deflating airbag.

Two hands grip under my armpits. "Ted, we have to go. Now!" Loren pulls me upward. Lungs still burning, my body finally obeys, and my legs find purchase on the ground. We resume our flight into the woods on the other side of the road.

"Commander, you okay?" The voice of one of Revon's men gives me hope that they will give up the chase in favor of checking on their boss. I don't look back to make sure.

Minutes pass, without any sign of our pursuers. Still, we do not stop. Distance is our ally. The more we have between us and Revon, the better. As the threat recedes behind us, my mind begins to transition from flight-mode to our surroundings. I try to get my bearings and figure out where we are. I've traveled in these woods so many times since childhood, but everything looks different. Overgrown.

Tash'jya gallops between tight gaps and leaps over fallen trees. Her prowess amazes me, and I'm struck with wonder at how humans ever fought successfully against her people for so long. Even the force with which she would have needed to hurl the rebar from a distance to pierce a tire is well beyond human strength. Speed, agility, and strength are all on her side in a fight. Toe-to-toe, no human could stand up to a Skya'ja.

How has the battle between our people lasted for two years? How have the Skya'ja not bested humans in every battle they've faced? *It's not our way. As much as we can, we do not hurt humanss, Ted.* Tash'jya's words come to mind. Could it be that the war is at a stalemate simply because the Skya'ja refuse to conquer us?

I wave a hand to signal the other two as we break out into a light industrial area. "Slow down for a moment. I need to breathe." We duck behind the corner of a trucking facility. Dozens of truck bays line the two buildings on either side of us. We slip over the edge of one of the ramps by a loading bay to get out of sight. Collapsing, the three of us fall into a heap, our lungs sucking at the air to feed our oxygen-starved muscles.

Finally able to breathe, I wait a good ten minutes before I emerge to try the door to one of the loading bays. To my relief, the handle turns, and the door swings open. Poking my head inside the dark space, I glance around. No movement. Inside, a heavy layer of dust coats everything in the room. Cardboard boxes containing air conditioners lay on pallets ready to be loaded. A stack of shipping orders lay clipped together atop one of the boxes. A Styrofoam cup with a straw still sits on a shelf.

It's a moment frozen in time from the Cataclysm. Men and women going about their work and dropping everything to return home to their families when the world began to die.

Loren and Tash'jya slip in behind me.

"I always forget how normal life was two years ago." I gesture to the room. "Workers were here loading trucks like any other day. And then the world ended."

Loren picks up the clipboard of orders and absently flips through them. "My father worked at a place like this. He was a supervisor."

"You mean he wasn't always the charismatic leader of a violent militia?" I let out a laugh, which I stifle immediately when I see the hurt on Loren's face. "Sorry. I—"

She shakes her head. "No. You're not wrong." She replaces the clipboard and sits down with her back against a large box. She swallows hard, and I can see her attempt to hide the emotions welling up inside her.

Quietly, I approach her side and slide down next to her. Tash'jya squats in front of us. I grab Loren's hand, which trembles in my grip.

"That—that man out there"—her voice quavers—"is not the man who raised me. Believe it or not, he was a kind father once." She sniffs and looks at Tash'jya. "Everything changed when your people arrived, Tash. I was in nursing school but living at home to save money. My father began talking about how everything would be ruined. Clean energy would destroy the shipping company he worked for, which, of course, relied upon traditional trucking."

Tash'jya's head droops. "Fossil fuelss will not last forever, Lo-ren. Our people wanted to help you."

"I know that." Loren offers Tash'jya an apologetic smile. "I didn't mean to imply anything. My father was merely scared. He saw the arrival of the Skya'ja as a threat to his ability to provide for us. Rational thought would have given him the chance to adjust and come up with a plan for the inevitable change, but he gave into his fear instead. Fear became hate."

Loren bites her lip for a long moment. She blinks hard to control the dampness in her eyes and looks at us. "Sorry. Seeing him so crazed like that reminds me of how far he's slipped. He and his workers would go out drinking after work to complain about it all. One night, they'd had too much, and one of his friends struck a Skya'ja man in the parking lot with a beer bottle in a drunken rage. When he was arrested for assault, my father couldn't believe it. Came home shouting about the injustice of a world that would favor an alien over the native race. He hated your people for coming here."

Loren takes Tash'jya's hand in hers. Together we sit for a silent moment, broken only by Loren's sniffs. Her tears flow down her cheeks, leaving clean paths through the dirt and sweat that coat her skin.

"And that's why he formed his little army?" The question feels dumb as I ask it, but I sense that Loren needs to get this out, as though it were a confession that alleviates a sin burning against her soul.

She shakes her head. "No. He was all talk at first. He wanted to protect mom and me from the 'invaders' as he called them. He made plans to leave the city as soon as he could transfer to another branch of the company—to stay away from them."

I sigh. "But then your mother was killed? Like you told me back at the clinic?"

She nods and sniffs again. Swallowing hard, I can see the pain of the memory on her face. "Something in my father broke when they found her body in the rubble of the collapsed building. He blamed the Skya'ja for her death. When the Cataclysm happened and everyone was looking for someone to blame, my father went into a rage. The war started, and he wanted to be part of it. It was a few days later that he and his buddies killed a Skya'ja man they cornered. That's when I knew I had to leave."

Her eyes find mine, searching my face. "That's when I knew

my father had died, too. That man out there—he's not my father." The sobs overtake her, and I release her hand so I can wrap her in my arms. She leans into me, and I can feel her body quake as she allows the sadness to pour out freely, perhaps for the first time.

The three of us stay like that for several minutes until Tash'jya shifts on her feet to get closer to Loren. She places her other hand over Loren's and speaks in a low tone. "Lo-ren, you are not your father. His sinss are not yourss. His hatred is not yourss. You have proven that to me more than once."

Loren unburies her head from my chest to turn to Tash'jya.

"Lo-ren, you are my friend. You saved my life. You show compassion for my people. And now you seek to save them by helping uss. You are not your father."

Loren lets out a long shuddering breath, and I can feel her relax in my arms. She sits up and pulls away from me, throwing her arms around Tash'jya's neck. The Skya'ja woman straightens, obviously uncomfortable with the hug, but she slowly brings her arms up to embrace Loren. Finally letting go, Loren sniffs again. "I'm sorry. I'm aware your people do not hug each other like we do."

"It is okay, Lo-ren. I am honored that you would see me as no different than a human friend."

Pulling the backpack off Loren, I open the zipper to carefully remove the cloth covered device. I hold my breath, unable to stop my hands from shaking, as layer after layer peels back. Finally, the glint of metal shows, and I pull back the final cloth.

Not a scratch.

Loren and I breathe a collective sigh of relief. Even Tash'jya's respirator wheezes a long airy expulsion.

Rewrapping the capacitor, I return it to the backpack. "So, what now?"

"My father recognizes what direction we headed." Loren runs a hand through her hair. "He will regroup and be out looking for us. How long did you say we had, Tash?"

"Two dayss from thiss morning. But we must arrive with time for the capacitor to be installed by Ted's father."

"Still, I think we should wait. Even if my father and his goons trace us here, there are a million exits from this huge facility. They can't guard all of it. We can slip away if necessary."

Tash'jya wrings her hands and glances around as if Revon might burst in at any moment. "We cannot delay long, Lo-ren. We must go soon."

I tap my chin with my finger. "Just until nightfall, then. We stand a better chance of getting away unnoticed after dark. From there, we can be at the Bubble in a few hours. That will still leave my dad about a day to install his capacitor."

"We'd better rest, then. Might be the last we get for a while." Loren yawns.

Tash'jya's shoulders slump, and she rubs her shoulders with one hand. It occurs to me that she sat at the table at the house waiting for me all night and hadn't slept a wink. She has to be exhausted.

"Tash'jya?" I say. She glances up at me from her stooped posture. "You rest first. We'll stay up and watch."

Tash'jya offers the tiniest perceptible smile. She touches her head and chest. I return the motion. Without another word, she retreats to the corner where she lays down. In a minute, her wheezing slows, and she appears to fall asleep.

Neural Implant Log: Entry 143
Officer: Tash'jya, daughter of Sun'tssh
Rank: Tactician

We have succeeded in securing Dr. Kenneth James' invention. The intel provided by his son, Ted James, proved invaluable as the capacitor was in the floor safe previously not detected. To think that the moments that kept Dr. James from sharing the existence of the safe have led to years of suffering and death for this world leaves me crushed. I am responsible for the devastation around me. The pain and death around me were not necessary had I simply discovered the safe a year ago.

I hurt for my friend, Ted, whose name I know. He has been separated from his father, believing his life to have ended. I see the cruelty that I inflicted by not sharing the knowledge of his father's survival earlier. He suffers as one who has lost everything. I am aware of the story of this mother. His has been a life of loss and grief.

I ache for my friend, Loren, whose name I know. She suffers under the hands of her father, who bears the burden of hatred for our kind. While I am not the creator of his prejudice, my delay has exacerbated his venom for our kind. My fellow Skya'ja have died because he has been allowed to roam free to follow his abhorrence of our kind.

Ours is a friendship that was birthed in trauma and misunderstanding, to then experience the healing balm of honest confession and forgiveness. I am grateful for my friends.

Let the record show that my inaction—my willingness to put my own pursuits ahead of my mission—has led to a literal world of suffering. I am dishonored. I am guilty of the worst offense— placing myself above the needs of the greater good. I am barely a Skya'ja. This is not our way.

Yet, I dare to hope that my honor may be restored. We have the capacitor. We leave for the Bubble in a matter of hours. I yearn to see my sister, Tash'jyi, whose name I know, with my honor restored.

The father of Loren, whose name I spit upon, pursues us. His intentions are murderous and could spell disaster for the mission. We have evaded him twice now, and I am afraid we may be unsuccessful a third time. I am unaware if he knows our intentions. I cannot let him thwart our opportunity to rescue this world. On what honor I have left, I will not allow him to harm my friends.

For the moment, I must get what rest I can.

End of log.

Resting my back against the box, I slide closer to Loren. She grabs my hand, intertwining our fingers and rests her head on my shoulders. The minutes crawl by, and I feel my eyes begin to droop. I'm spent after all this running.

"We can't fall asleep." Even as I remind Loren, my will wants to give up and fall unconscious.

She sighs heavily, sleep attempting to take her. "I know. We need to keep talking then."

"What do you want to talk about?"

Loren lifts her head to look at me. "Tell me more about your mother. All I've learned about her is that she was beautiful, liked heavy metal music, and passed when you were young."

"For starters, she didn't only like heavy metal music. She liked all kinds, really. It always seemed like she had a tune in her head. It wasn't uncommon to find her singing whatever song she had stuck in her brain when she thought I wasn't looking."

"Even the metal tunes?"

"Nothing like finding your mom headbanging while making dinner." I let out a chuckle at the memory. "She also played guitar. She used to tell me about her dreams of playing in a band when she was a teenager."

"She sounds like a fun person."

I sigh. "She was. She was sort of the glue that held us together. My father was so alive around her. When she died, some part of him died, too." I stop, unsure if I want to continue.

"That's why you felt so disconnected from your dad after she was gone?"

I nod. "In truth, we were never really connected to begin with. I've always believed he loves me, but mom was the one that made us all feel close to each other. Once she was missing from the picture, it was easy for dad and me to drift apart. He did his own thing, and I did mine. It's how we dealt with it—my mom's death, I mean. It wasn't until he started working with the Skya'ja that I ever saw him happy."

Loren looks up to meet my eyes. "I'm sure he misses you,

Ted. He's probably in the Bubble right now worried sick about you being out here."

I press my lips together. I'm not sure I agree with her. "I love my dad. I really do. And I need to get back to him to make certain he's okay. I just—"

She leans into me closer. "What is it?"

"I sometimes wonder if he is as desperate to get to me as I am to him. I've realized how much he means to me, even if we weren't that close. But what if he's still closed off? What if he doesn't really need me?"

Loren pulls away and grabs my face in her hands to turn my gaze toward her. "You can't think like that. I've obviously never met your father, but I can't imagine that you aren't on his mind every second of each minute that passes."

"How can you be certain of that?" Dampness threatens to escape my eyelids and my breath shudders.

"No one has a more dysfunctional relationship with their father than I do. I want to help people and respect the Skya'ja, and he wants to kill every last one of them. We couldn't be further apart from each other. And yet—" She pauses and takes a long breath. I search her eyes, hopeful that what she says next might breathe some life into my soul. "As crazy as he is and as much as I've made it clear I want nothing to do with his crusade, my father still won't stop fighting to get me back. It's why he sent you to find me. It's why he's hunting us. If my father can be both insane with hatred and love me in whatever way that he's able, I have no doubt your father loves you. He's on the other side of the Bubble waiting for you. Worried sick probably. Scared he'll never see you again."

For a moment, her thoughts penetrate my soul and almost take root there, allowing a glimmer of hope to emerge. Then, it's gone…tamped down by the despair that I've lived with for two years. My quest had been for answers, fueled by anger. I was not prepared to find out he was alive. Now that I have, I am both excited to see him again and terrified he will still be the closed-off man I've known since my mother left us.

My conflict must be written all over my face because the

corners of her eyes crease with concern. She caresses my face with her hand and pulls me toward her. Our lips meet, their soft warmth mixed with the saltiness of tears, mine and hers. We lean into each other as though frightened this moment of connection will be torn away by the chaos that has defined the last couple days. I gasp for air, the kiss having stolen my breath, as we embrace.

My life has become so different from the reality I knew. Two days ago, I was on my own on the streets, living to get to the end of each day. My one goal was to obtain some truth about what happened to my father, maybe for closure. I can't be sure. Today, I'm on the run with a woman I could have only dreamed of meeting in the midst of the decaying world and my former captive Skya'ja who has challenged everything I thought I knew about our extra-terrestrial visitors.

Pulling away, I smile, taking in her features one by one. "I want to hope you're right."

"I know. And I am." She returns my smile.

"Besides, if my mother were here, she would be turning the city upside down to get this capacitor inside the Bubble. If I have nothing else, it's what she would do."

"She sounds like a determined woman. And cool on top of that."

"More than you'll ever realize."

Loren scrunches her brow, a mischievous smile on her lips. "How did she and your dad end up together anyway? I mean, you have a rocker guitarist on one hand and the green, tech-inventing scientist on the other."

"Honestly, I have no idea. But they definitely loved each other. Goes to show that any two people can meet and connect, I guess."

She playfully punches my shoulder with one eyebrow raised. "Kind of like the daughter of a militia commander and a street-dwelling, alien-capturing survivor?"

"Street-dwelling?" I feign offense.

"What do you prefer? Homeless guy? Down and out drifter? Hobo?" She sucks in her lips, trying to contain her laughter.

I smirk at her. "Hobo? Really?"

"I'm not sure. I can sort of see you heating up a can of beans over a small fire as you ride a freight train across the country." She bites her lip to contain the giggle welling up inside her.

"Nice to learn that's what you think of me."

At that, she can no longer contain her laughter. She bursts into a guffaw that she stifles immediately with a hand across her mouth, not wanting to wake Tash'jya. She doubles over, and I can feel her body shake with mirth. After a moment, she returns upright, and we chuckle silently.

We gaze at each other, enjoying the quiet moment. Loren's smile suddenly melts into a frown. Her eyes start looking behind me, searching for something she can't see. That's when I pick up on what she's hearing. The low rumble of an engine—no, two engines. Someone is slowly driving through the industrial yard at barely more than an idle.

I lock eyes with Loren, who seems short of breath. We both realize there is exactly one person who would have any need to search this facility on this night.

Revon.

Chapter Twenty-Two

I shoot a glance at the door and whisper a prayer of thanks that we fully closed it behind us, leaving no obvious sign of our entry. Loren scurries over to Tash'jya, shaking her awake. Tash'jya is up and on her feet in a moment. Whether it is the Skya'ja equivalent of adrenaline or yet another advantage of her physiology, she shows no signs of her weariness.

Bolting to the door, I place my ear against the metal to listen. The drone of the two truck engines is near, but not right outside. I gesture to Loren and Tash'jya that they are approaching. Grabbing the backpack, Loren waves us to a door on the backside of the room.

The door reveals a narrow hallway. A window, looking into a small office space stands to the left. The right contains solid doors marked for storage or restrooms. At the end of the hall stands a lone door with a slim vertical window. Fading grey light from the setting sun pours through the glass. Scrambling down the hallway, I peer out the window to the left and right. All seems quiet, but I cannot get a good angle to see everything.

Gently pushing the crash bar on the door, I wince as the hinges complain from disuse. I listen for movement on this side of the building. Nothing. Just silence.

Waving a hand for the others to follow, I creep out into the open. Loren turns to gently shut the door after us. Only a small parking area separates us from the trees where we can disappear. I turn to scramble into the darkness of the trees.

"That's far enough, Rookie."

A shiver travels the length of my spine at the sound of Revon's voice. I turn slowly to see the commander step out of the shadows along the building, a spot blind to the doorway we'd exited. I take a step toward the trees. Revon's hand raises in a flash, the barrel of his pistol pointed squarely at my chest. Slowly, I raise my hands.

"I said that's far enough." Revon's voice is calm in a way that unnerves me.

I glance back at Tash'jya and Loren, who are frozen in place. Loren shakes her head slightly.

"You want to find out how I caught you here, don't you? You think I'm stupid enough to come barreling in here with two trucks to warn you that we're coming?" We don't answer, and he smiles. "Nah. I've been here for half an hour doing recon. No one's been in this place for months, maybe years. Wasn't hard to find your steps in the dirt and dust outside the door you entered. I knew you'd come running out the back when you heard my men arrive."

"Dad, please," Loren pleads. "Let them go. I'll leave with you. I'm the one you came for." She begins to slide the backpack off. My heart skips a beat as I realize she really intends to leave with him. She creeps close to Tash'jya and me, setting the bag at my feet. "Let them go, and I won't fight you."

Revon frowns. "Now as much as I'd like to believe that, I'm not blind. Rookie, here, thinks himself a hero after your dramatic escape from his house. That tells me all I need to know about what is going on between you two."

"Please. They've done nothing to you."

"Nothing? I extend a warm welcome to this boy, who repays my kindness by beating up two of my men, ruining my truck, and most of all…stealing my daughter away from me." Revon's brow lowers. "I don't call that *nothing*."

"So what? Are you going to shoot them? Is that it? It's your answer to everything these days. Shoot it dead if it doesn't agree with you." Loren shouts as she lowers her hands. She steps toward Revon, daring him to harm her. "Is that supposed to win my approval? Newsflash, *I* don't agree with you. You're consumed by hate, Dad. Don't you see it?"

Revon jabs the pistol in the direction of Tash'jya. "And why shouldn't I hate them? After what those monsters did?"

"They didn't kill Mom." Loren's tone lowers to almost a whisper. "When will you finally figure that out?"

Revon visibly winces at the mention of his late wife. For a moment, I wonder if Loren has broken through to him until his face darkens again. "Don't you bring her up. How could you love these demons after what they did?"

"They didn't kill Mom." Louder this time. "Humans did."

Revon bares his teeth at her words. I try to hide my trembling, scared she's pushing him too far. "Loren, I don't think—"

She silences me with a hand. She straightens and turns to her father. "No, he needs to hear this. Not that I haven't said it before, but he never listened. Well, listen now, commander! Mom died because humans killed her. It was an accident. All you see is a murderous red for their kind, and you are using the memory of my mother—your wife—as justification for your actions. That's not fair to her. No more, Dad. It's time to face the truth. The Skya'ja didn't kill her, and you know it."

Revon shakes his head and raises his hands as though he wants to cover his ears. Then, just as quickly, he returns the pistol in the direction of Tash'jya. "The building would never have collapsed if their kind hadn't come here. The company *had* to have the construction contract with these animals. We never would have been on that construction site if they hadn't required facilities to work in the first place. Your mother was so excited and couldn't be kept away from the action. She wanted to see them up close. I wish she'd remained in the office. Why did she have to come with me?" He mutters a few curses and racial slurs about 'Fishfaces.' He faces Tash'jya. "Why did you have to come here? Why couldn't you leave well enough alone? Our planet was fine without you poisoning it."

"Dad, that's not what they came to do. You have to believe—"

"No more. I don't want to hear it. Your mother is dead because of them. And I have to suffer with this." Lifting a hand, he pulls the hair around his scalp backward, revealing the full length of his scar. At the top of the scar, the skin is stained murky green. "See that? Grows more every day. Those demons didn't even have the courtesy to let me die when I was wounded. Gave me a blood transfusion right there on the site *with their own blood.*"

The sight of the murky green scar produces a gasp out of Loren. Tash'jya straightens, gazing at Revon's wound somberly.

"Dad, they saved you," Loren whispers. "How could you hate someone who saved your life?"

Revon speaks through gritted teeth. "They didn't save her. I tried to tell them to help her first, but instead they poisoned me." He swallows hard and lowers his voice to an almost inaudible whisper. "I will never forgive them for that." The finality of his words gives Loren pause. She retreats back a half-step, her resolution faltering. If Revon cannot see what the Skya'ja did for him as anything other than mercy, then his hatred is too deep to overcome with words.

"My father is gone, then." Loren's voice catches, and she swallows to regain it. "I don't recognize you anymore. Nor would Mom. She loved you, but I'm not sure she would recognize you now. Goodbye, Dad. I can't—I won't come with you." Turning, she walks back the couple steps toward us. She glances at me and then the trees. Her message is clear. *We're getting out of here.*

Revon snaps the pistol in her direction. "Don't you turn your back on me, girl. Don't you *ever* turn your back on me."

Loren doesn't turn around. She stares into the distance behind us, her expression flat. "I turned my back on you a long time ago. I'd hoped it would be different—that you would come around one day. I realize that's not possible anymore."

"I can't let you leave. You are my daughter, and you are coming with me whether you understand my reasons or not." Revon's voice shakes, and I realize how desperate he is. In his own twisted way, he loves Loren.

Loren finally turns to Revon. "I'll never understand. I offered to stay with you if you'd simply let my friends leave, and you couldn't even do that. If you really wanted me with you, that would be a small price to pay."

"You would run again."

I swallow hard at Revon's words, which are said with finality.

He doesn't intend to leave without Loren. But more than that, he doesn't mean to give her any option of leaving again.

"Well, I'm not going with you. You'll have to shoot me, Dad."

"Don't force my hand."

Loren's face flushes red with anger. "I'm not forcing you to do anything other than look at the monster you have become. What would Mom think about you pointing a weapon at her daughter and the people she loves?"

For a moment, Revon falters. His lips tremble, and the barrel of the pistol drops almost imperceptibly. I swear I see his eyes glass over, and his defenses drop.

He straightens, and the moment is gone.

"Loren, you are coming with me. I see you won't go willingly, so I'll need assurances of your cooperation. Your friends, here, are all the insurance that I need that you won't run again." Revon stands silently, letting the words hang in the air between us. His jaw muscles pulse. His forearms flex, the tendons rippling under his weathered skin, as he readjusts his grip on the gun.

Loren sucks in a breath as if anticipating what is coming. "Dad, you don't have to—"

"No, I do. I need them so you will come with me." He pauses. "But I don't need both of them." In an instant, he redirects the pistol toward Tash'jya.

"No!" Loren reaches for Tash'jya.

The flash of the muzzle blinds my vision as I hear the pistol fire.

Chapter Twenty-Three

Turning to Tash'jya, I expect to see her laying on the ground, thrown backward by the impact of the bullet. Instead, Loren hangs like a ragdoll in her arms having stepped into the path of the bullet. Loren's eyes are wide, and her mouth hangs open with a scream that won't come. She clutches on to Tash'jya, her arms trembling with any attempt to stand.

A stain of blood begins to spread across her back.

A shuddering breath escapes her mouth as her knees finally give way. Clutching Loren, Tash'jya gently lowers her to the ground.

"Loren, no!" Revon screams. "What have you done?" The pistol falls from his hands and clatters to the ground.

I race to the other side of Loren and kneel beside her. Violent shakes overtake her body. Turning her gaze to me, her saucer eyes meet mine. A tear leaks from the corner of her eye and falls to the pavement. With a quivering hand, she caresses my cheek. I place mine over it, and we stare at each other silently.

"My girl. My baby. No." Revon steps toward us, his face twitching from shock like it can't decide how to react.

Somewhere in my gut, a flame ignites. Rage fills me, and I can feel my face grow hot. As Revon takes another step, I rise to meet him. I no longer care that he is a deadly leader of a militia. If I had the strength, I would rip him to shreds in that moment.

"Are you happy now? Look at what your hate got you!" The words erupt between my gritted teeth. "How could you? To your own daughter."

"I-I didn't mean—" Revon can't finish his thought. He stares at Loren on the ground.

I take another step toward Revon, no longer intimidated by his size. I'm going to make this man pay for what he's done. I ball my hands into fists.

A cry of pain from Loren snaps me back to reality. Unbearable grief floods over me, cooling my anger at Revon. The world spins in my view for a moment, and my vision blurs as salty dampness fills my eyes. I rub them with my palm as I turn back to Loren. Tash'jya kneels beside her, cradling her head in her lap. With one hand, she clutches Loren's hand.

Kneeling, I swipe a sweaty hair from Loren's face. She gazes at me, her bluing lips quivering. Taking her hand from Tash'jya's grip, I kiss the back of Loren's fingers. Her fingers curl around mine but with a weakness that betrays her declining state.

"Please don't leave me." I whisper in part to Loren and in part as a prayer. "We just found each other."

Loren swallows hard and smiles feebly. "I-I'm sorry, but I th-think the next time you stupidly cut yourself, you'll n-need to take care of it yourself."

I return her smile and let out a breathy laugh. So does she.

"Ted, we can save her." Tash'jya's words sound muffled in my ears like they are out of a dream.

"W-what?" My words sound more like a breath than my voice.

"We can save her." Tash'jya's voice is louder this time. The world goes silent around me as the words push through my sorrow and into my mind. Even Revon pauses, dumbstruck by the statement.

"Save her? How? There's no field hospital for miles, and the clinic isn't prepared for this kind of wound." I swallow, trying in vain to moisten my dry mouth. I don't want to hope. I don't want to allow myself to believe she might be okay simply to have my heart crushed when Tash'jya's words come up empty.

"No, Ted. *We* can save her. My people."

I stumble backward as I attempt to stand, my knees shaking

as if the words nailed me between the eyes. "Y-your people. Can save her?"

"In the Bubble. My people would have everything we need to help her."

I shake my head. "It's too far. We could never carry her there in time." Another cry of pain from Loren punctuates my words.

"No, we cannot. But he hass a truck." Tash'jya's obsidian eyes snap in the direction of Revon, who still stands there riveted by the sight of his daughter bleeding out on the ground.

An electric surge courses through my body as I am suddenly hyper-aware. The cloudiness of my brain clears as though Tash'jya's words breathe new life into me. This time, I am able to stand. Sorrow, grief, and even anger are pushed aside to one thought—save Loren.

"She's right," I say, turning to Revon. "You can help. Where are your men?"

Revon finally peels his eyes away from his dying daughter. I can't tell if his expression is fear for her safety or anger at me. "You want to give her to—to them? Those monsters?"

"It's our only option to save her."

His breaths come in quick succession like he is about to hyperventilate. "No. No. No! Not them. They can't poison her, too. I won't let them."

"Take her to my people, or she will die." Tash'jya's voice is in a tone I've never heard, almost regal—her willingness to help shining light on the darkness of Revon's hatred.

"You can't get to them anyway. The Bubble kills those who enter. You can't get in there." Revon grips his head in his hands. "I won't do it."

I shake my head, stupefied by his stubbornness. "You have to trust us."

"No. I won't."

Loren doubles over in a fit of pain. The boiling anger reignites inside me, but instead of throwing me into a hot rage, I am filled with a deadly calm. As if controlled from the outside, my body begins to move. Two strides later, I bend over and pick up Revon's pistol. Days before, I'd never held a firearm before. Now, I confidently grip the handle and flick the safety to make sure it's off. The weight of it surprises me and then fills me with power. Righteous anger forces my arm to extend, and I glare at Revon over the black barrel of the weapon.

Revon grits his teeth and steps once in my direction. His eyes meet mine, and he pauses. He can see my determination. My willingness to do whatever is necessary. This is not like before. I'm not shaking. I'm not scared. He is going to do what I say.

"Call your men, Commander. We are taking her to the Bubble."

Chapter Twenty-Four

A minute later, a dirty pickup rolls up to our location. Revon's goons, Matthews and Chambers, emerge from either side of the truck with expressions of confusion, their eyes glancing repeatedly at Revon for answers that don't come. Loren, their target, lies bleeding on the ground, and it is me who holds the pistol instead of Revon. I can see their faces contort as they try to put together what has happened to lead to this scenario.

I flick the barrel of the pistol in the direction of Chambers and Matthews. "Tell your men to drop any weapons they have, Commander, before they both hurt themselves trying to figure this out." My voice is flat.

"Boy, I don't think—" Revon begins.

I extend my pistol-wielding arm out an inch farther, while I interrupt. "No. You don't get to think right now. Your thinking put a bullet in your daughter. No, you will do what I say, and nothing more."

Revon grits his teeth. It's clear he doesn't like his men to see him in this position.

I don't have time for this. I turn my gaze to the two men by the truck. "Drop your weapons, or your commander gets shot. Is that too hard to figure out?"

Matthews and Chambers glance at Revon, who offers the slightest of nods. Both of them pull their guns from their waistband and toss them to the ground.

"Kick them well away from yourselves."

They comply, the guns skittering across the pavement out of reach.

"Okay, put those gargantuan bodies to good use and help get

Loren in the backseat of the truck." I lower my brow and my voice. "And be gentle."

Approaching Loren, while keeping one eye on me, Matthews takes Loren's upper body from Tash'jya. Chambers places his hands under Loren's knees. The two men lift her, almost effortlessly. I wince as Loren cries out in pain and remind myself we are getting her help. Moments later, they slide her into the backseat. Tash'jya crawls in the other side with the backpack in hand to hold Loren for the ride.

"Good. Leave your radios in the truck and stand over there." I wave the barrel of the pistol toward the wall. Both men toss their radios in the windows of the vehicle and walk slowly as if waiting for Revon to contradict my orders. He does not. "Face the wall and kneel. Hands on your head."

Once both men are in position, I turn back to Revon. "Commander, you'll be driving. Get in."

He doesn't budge. "You're going to kill her."

"Actually, I believe that was your move. Get in the driver's seat."

Revon's shoulders slump at the reminder of his actions. Hesitantly, he walks toward the driver's side of the truck. Glancing at his men who still face the wall, he lets out an elongated sigh. I circle the truck, never removing my eyes or aim from Revon. Climbing in the passenger side, I buckle in so I can remain steady should Revon try anything evasive.

"Now drive."

Revon throws the shift into gear and pulls away. In my periphery, I can see Matthews and Chambers scramble to their feet and run toward their pistols. "No one can enter the Bubble, Rookie. We're better off trying to get to a hospital."

"She'll die before we get there. You know that. The Bubble is her only chance."

"You really think the Fishface is worth trusting? Her kind wants our kind dead so they can take our planet. They poisoned me. They will poison her. Fishface is enjoying this, I assure you."

I curl my lip in disgust at his spewing venom even when his daughter lies in peril right behind him. "Just drive. Hit Trade Street."

The truck winds its way down silent streets. On open roads, we could be there in a couple minutes, but we are forced to drive serpentine through the abandoned cars and rubble from partially destroyed buildings. In the distance, I can see the shimmering Bubble approaching.

"Hold on, Loren. We're almost there."

"Lo-ren, keep breathing, my friend." Tash'jya's voice whispers from the back of the vehicle.

"Friend?" Revon sneers. "I didn't realize your species knew that word."

Tash'jya pauses as if considering whether to dignify his words with a response. "We know far more than you will ever accept we do, human."

Quietly, I smile a little that Tash'jya refuses to use Revon's name.

Neural Implant Log: Entry 144
Officer: Tash'jya, daughter of Sun'tssh
Rank: Tactician

My mistake has brought disaster on my friend, Loren, whose name I know. Under the violent hand of her own father, she placed herself between his hatred and me. Now we race to the Bubble as her life bleeds out of the projectile wound.

A human offered her life for mine. An action made necessary because I allowed my judgment to be clouded by my anger. Abandoning my mission has led to this moment. As a result, one of the few humans who shows honor to my people lies dying in my arms.

I am responsible for the life of Loren. If she dies, it shall ultimately be from my inaction, and not simply from the hand of the one who pulled the trigger. On my honor, I will see her to my people. Her life is worth far more than mine as she has spent it healing human and Skya'ja alike.

My regret is that entering the Bubble will not allow me to take my vengeance upon the man who shot her. May justice find him.

End of log.

Bits of rubble crunch under the truck tires as we pull to a stop. Merely twenty yards away, the swirling surface of the Bubble glistens with its own blue-green light. Two years ago, downtown disappeared behind its haze, and the rest of the world has fallen into decay. What will it be like to see what the city looked like two years ago? Do I even remember what it looked like?

I shake my head. It is not the time for curiosity. Saving Loren is the priority.

I turn to Revon. "Get out, Commander."

He shakes his head. "You think I'm going to leave my daughter with you? Think again, Rookie."

I twitch the end of the pistol in my hand to remind him I have it. "I don't think you are in a position to negotiate. Now get out."

With another sigh, Revon throws his door open and slides out of the truck. I do the same and wheel around the front of the vehicle. "Turn and start walking."

Placing his hands on his head, his jaw flexes. "You're not taking my daughter from me."

"You heard her earlier. Her father is gone. She doesn't recognize you anymore. So, yeah, *we're* taking her. Turn and start walking."

Revon spins in place and begins to plod away from the Bubble. "This isn't done, Rookie. If you don't die by that Bubble, then you can be sure you'll die by my hand." Despite the threat, he continues to walk away. I exhale in relief. No matter how terrible he is, I have no desire to actually use the gun. I wait until he is far away before I am comfortable enough to move.

I climb into the truck and take the wheel. "Now what? I drive at the Bubble?" My fear rises to the surface. All the stories of those who have tried to cross this barrier come to mind, and here I am about to attempt the same—on the word of a Skya'ja.

"Ted, I promisse you. You will see your father today. We must hurry. Lo-ren doess not have much time."

As if on cue, Loren emits a whimper of pain. She is growing weaker by the minute. Resolve washes over me like a wave, and I throw the truck in drive. Gently pressing the accelerator, the surface of the Bubble approaches. Not knowing what I'll encounter on the other side, I elect to drive slowly. Either that, or I'm simply terrified.

My breath quickens. The veins in my temples pulse with anticipation. Ten yards. Five yards. I instinctively brace for impact as the nose of the truck reaches the barrier. Instead of a jolt, the hood of the truck slides into the haze with ease. The surface approaches, swallowing the vehicle like glittering vertical quicksand. Hood gone. Engine gone. Windshield gone.

I hold my breath as my world fades to a blur of blues and greens.

Chapter Twenty-Five

Describing what passing through the Bubble feels like is no different than trying to explain a dream to a friend. All the details can be there, but the sensory and emotional experience is inevitably missing.

What should be a few feet of travel from one side of the Bubble to the other feels instead like traveling miles. My body buzzes with energy with each heartbeat. Blue-green haze surrounds us, so thick that I can barely see my hands in front of me. Each breath makes me feel like I am drowning as I inhale the almost-gelatinous mist, yet I am strangely still—almost paralyzed.

I have not moved my hands from the wheel of the truck nor taken my foot off the accelerator, but it no longer feels like we are moving. Floating. That would be the more accurate description.

"Tash'jya?" My voice sounds echoey and distant like it is coming from someone else. "Tash'jya, is this normal?" Minutes pass with no answer and no sense that we are going to escape this place.

A ball of fear ignites in my gut. We are going to die. Everyone who has entered the Bubble has disappeared—probably absorbed into this thick goo and floating around somewhere nearby. My breaths quicken, and I reach for the handle of my door. My movements are slow and laborious.

"Do not be afraid, Ted." Tash'jya's tone is soothing like that of my mother. Her voice sounds far away, and I wonder if I really heard her. "It will be over soon."

Do I trust her?

I could leap out. I could try to run—or swim—or fly—back to where we came in. Maybe she can take this, but my body cannot.

I am going to die in here.

Loren.

Somewhere behind me in the truck—though seeing in the mirror in this haze is hopeless—is Loren. Wounded. Dying. Her one hope of recovery is for me to stay put and keep the truck moving forward, if that is what it is still doing. I can no longer tell.

I close my eyes and grip the wheel tightly. I will stay. If I die, it's for her.

Cool air rushes over my face, and I dare to peek with one eye. Brilliant sunshine warms my skin. The air feels damp like it is morning. I move my foot to the brake and feel the truck slow to a stop. Opening my other eye, I fill my lungs with fresh air, which produces a fit of coughing. Each wheezy cough tastes like the milky vapor of the Bubble.

The Bubble. Are we inside? Did we make it?

I blink hard to look around me. Shadows begin to take hard edges as my eyes adjust to the light. Buildings. Trees. The skyline of Uptown Charlotte, at least a few square blocks as it existed two years ago before the Cataclysm, stretches before me.

Tap. Tap. Tap.

Glancing to my right, I am startled by a face. A balding man with round glasses smiles at me through the window. He is wearing a powder-blue button-up shirt and maroon bow tie. He also wears what appears to be a lab coat.

"Young man." His voice sounds slightly muffled from the closed window. I hit the control to roll it down. "Young man, welcome to the past version of our city."

I look behind him and realize he is surrounded by several others. Some are human. Others are Skya'ja. All wear lab coats. All are smiling.

I must look terrified because his expression morphs into one of concern. "I realize you must be disoriented. All reports from those who have passed through the barrier say it is a confusing sensation to say the least." No longer muffled, I pick up his British accent. He reaches a hand in the window. "I am Dr. Geoffrey

Smythe. We detected an anomaly in the barrier and suspected someone may be crossing over. We've had others, soldiers and such, but must say I didn't expect a young chap such as yourself in a truck. What brings you inside the—erm, I guess you outsiders would call it the Bubble?"

The reality of why I am here washes over me with electricity that wakens all my nerves. Confusion gives way to focus, and I point to the back seat. "Sh-she's hurt. We need help."

Smythe follows my finger, and he straightens as if noticing Tash'jya and Loren for the first time. "Oh my. A Skya'ja and humans arriving together?" Loren lets out a cry of pain, and Smythe repeats his exclamation. "Oh my."

"Shstuk shii tassi twoah." Tash'jya's voice startles me from the back seat. Her tone carries an authority I have not heard before. Immediately, the Skya'ja present snap to attention and rush the vehicle. Opening the doors, the first to arrive see Loren's condition. Calls in the Skya'ja language are voiced over radios. In seconds, a gurney is brought.

I step out of the truck as Loren is gently moved to the gurney. My legs wobble beneath me, still adjusting from the sensation of traveling through the Bubble. I walk, or rather stumble, over to Loren. Reaching out, I take her hand in mine. Her grip is feeble and none of the strength I've known from her seems to be there. Still, the fact that she is alive is testament to her fortitude.

"They're going to take care of you." I look to Tash'jya. "She's going to be okay, right?"

"My people are skilled at medicine, Ted." Tash'jya smiles at me. "She will survive." Another of the Skya'ja says something I do not understand to Tash'jya. She turns back to me. "They must take her now, Ted. I will be notified when we can see her again."

Loren's fingers wrap a little tighter in mine. "Be here when I get out, okay?" Her words are barely a whisper. Not the kind of whisper that wants to keep a secret, but the kind that is managing all the volume it can but still hushes out in breathy sighs.

I return the squeeze of her hand. "I'm not going anywhere. I promise." I feel a tear at the edge of my eyelid, and I do nothing to swipe it away as it falls. "I—" I want to tell her that I love her, but the notion seems so forward. We've only known each other for a couple days. Love seems so unlikely, yet I cannot deny the flutter of my heart to be near her and the ache in my soul to see her healed. Again, I try to say it, but the words get caught in my throat. Instead, I stand there like an idiot with my mouth hanging open.

Loren smiles weakly at me. "I know. Me too."

Our hands pull apart as the gurney is rolled away. I keep my eyes locked on hers as they enter the double doors of what used to be a corporate building. The doors swing closed, and I'm left with a sinking feeling in my stomach.

Tash'jya's hand finds my shoulder.

"It will be okay, Ted. You got her here in time to ssave her. Do not fear."

I nod, taking a deep breath. I turn to Tash'jya. I'm not sure why, but I lunge at her wrapping my arms around her. I can feel her hesitancy at my embrace until slowly her strong arms curl around me. Her touch is tentative and unsure. A ball of sorrow grows in my stomach and rises to my throat. I choke on an involuntary sob, and my lip begins to quiver. "Th-thank you for bringing us here. I'm s-sorry for everything I did to you and for everything that happened because I didn't prevent it from being done to you."

I'm acutely aware of the eyes of all standing around, especially the Skya'ja. Their faces bear expressions of confusion at the very human display of emotion. The gravity of this moment is bigger than my apology, and I realize I must make it so.

I take a half step backward, releasing my embrace without breaking contact with Tash'jya. I gaze into her gray pupils for a long moment, searching for the right words. Then they come to me. "Tash'jya, I am pleased to know your name. I ask you for forgiveness. I was ignorant and hateful. I assumed the worst of you and your people. I was wrong." Pulling my hands back, I touch my forehead and my chest, adding a slight bow for good measure.

All faces turn to Tash'jya.

Her eyes study mine, slate islands on inky pools that cross left and right over my face. A long, slow breath wheezes through her respirator. Her hands rise, and I can see a slight tremble in them. She touches her forehead and slowly drops her fingers to her chest.

I let out a sigh and smile. Before I can complete the breath, she throws her arms around me. This time, there is no caution or lack of certainty. Her strength crushes me in an embrace. Audible sounds of disbelief emanate from humans and Skya'ja alike. Still, she clutches me, and I return the hug. "Ted, I am pleassed to know your name." Her voice is a whisper, yet loud enough for others to hear. "You are forgiven. And I am ssorry for not telling you about your father sooner. I should have known the son of Kenneth James was a man of honor. I ask for your forgiveness in return."

"Forgiven. One hundred percent." I can't help but smile from ear to ear. Here I am, hugging a Skya'ja I wanted dead merely days ago. My doubt has morphed into absolute trust. My enemy has become my friend.

"Excuse me." Dr. Smythe's voice breaks into our moment. "I hate to disturb this. And to be honest—it raises so many questions. I mean—a human and a Skya'ja." His thoughts are disjointed as if the whole scene has thrown him off his guard. "To tell you the truth, there are plenty of interspecies friendships here, but to scc— well—initiated by her—you see—"

I let go of Tash'jya and turn to Dr. Smythe. "Easy, doc. You're not making sense."

"Yes—well, um—you're right. Erm." He pauses to collect himself. Raising one finger, he points at me. "Did she say you were the son of-of Kenneth James?"

I nod.

"Dr. Kenneth James?"

I nod again, raising my eyebrows to make the point.

"You're Teddy?"

I smirk. "Teddy? Dad's been telling stories about me, I see.

He's the only one who calls me Teddy. I prefer Ted."

Dr. Smythe retreats a step. "Yes, Ted. Sorry about that. What I mean to say is that if you are Ted James, then you"—he points to Tash'jya—"are the one he sent to find his capacitor that could stop the reaction. Am I right?"

"You are right." Walking over to the truck, the slowness of her steps adds to the weight of the moment as if the urge to rush would cheapen the gift we bring. Tash'jya reaches inside. Grasping the backpack in one hand, she unzips the back in one smooth movement with her other hand. Pulling out our carefully wrapped package, she begins to peel the layers aside. The moment feels stretched in my consciousness over hours as the shiny metal of the capacitor is unveiled, a little at first until the last layer reveals the entire device.

A gasp ripples through the gathered crowd.

"Doctor, I present to you, Dr. Kenneth James' prototype capacitor."

Dr. Smythe steps forward, his hands extended toward the object. His fingers tremble slightly as he touches the capacitor, as if afraid it might disappear before him. His eyes grow wet. Others in the crowd share hugs or quiet expressions of joy.

"W-we were starting to lose hope. We don't have long before the overload takes place, and then the world will be—" His voice chokes on the words.

"Lost," I say. "Trust me. We are aware of what would happen."

Dr. Smythe smiles gently with a tiny nod. His lips curve into an expression of gratefulness, as if he's glad he didn't have to say the word. "The others that have passed through the barrier have told us about the world outside. I cannot imagine the horrors you three have experienced."

Tash'jya replaces the wrapping over the capacitor and returns it to the bag. "Then, let uss see to it that devastation never happenss. Tell me, doctor, where is Dr. James? My mission wass for him, and I would like to see it to itss completion."

The notion snaps Dr. Smythe back to the present. He straightens, smoothing his lab coat with both hands. "W-what? Oh, yes. Dr. James. The two of us should go see him at once."

"Do you not mean the three of uss. Ted iss his son."

Dr. Smythe raps himself on the side of his head. "My, my. What is wrong with me? Of course, lad! You'll want to see your father. It's been—what—a year and a half on your side?"

"Two years." My voice croaks, the reality hitting me that I may see my father soon.

"Two years? The slowing of time really does a number on one's perception of the passing of days. Come, come. It's time to see your father, Teddy."

Neural Implant Log: Entry 145
Officer: Tash'jya, daughter of Sun'tssh
Rank: Tactician

My mission is nearly complete. Despite my own shameful abandonment of my duties, I have managed to find the capacitor and deliver it inside the Bubble. I will not be content until I place it personally in the hands of Dr. Kenneth James, whose name I know. Only then will my honor be restored. Only then can I truly breathe free of the pain I have brought upon my legacy.

Though there is great joy and hope in this moment, my heart is drawn to find my sister. I have missed her. To see her with the knowledge I have restored honor to our family will heal the wounds that have formed on my soul. I long to hear my name from her lips that I may learn I am still her family.

And what of my companions? Loren, whose name I know, is severely injured. I have confidence in the medical abilities of my people, but I pray I have not overstated my confidence to my friends. I have given them assurance that she will be fine, but I am not as sure as I present to them. And Ted, whose name I know, will be restored to his own father. I cannot believe I allowed myself to sink so deeply into despair as to have hoped this reunion would have been tragic. I am grateful that circumstances have not allowed the hollowness of my former actions to have ruined this moment. Reuniting father and son further replaces my lost honor.

As to the task of installing the capacitor, time is short. I realize that Dr. James will want to proceed with caution, but I hope that the previous overreach of my people to start the energy project will not cause him to overcompensate and proceed with too much fear. The world depends upon the success of this installation, yet I cannot imagine allowing the world outside to suffer more than it has. And I do not trust the one who shot Loren. He has seen us pass into the Bubble.

It is time to right the timeline.

End of log.

Chapter Twenty-Six

Dr. Smythe leads us a block away to a building on Trade Street. The mirrored glass on the side of the building reflects the sunlight into our eyes, and I realize how long it has been since I've felt its warmth. The doors open automatically at our approach, and an icy blast of air conditioning hits me in the face. A chill travels from my feet to my neck. Conditioned air hasn't existed in my world for well over a year. Goosebumps spread over the surface of my arms and neck. I breathe in the air, feeling the cool sensation in my lungs.

Dr. Smythe smiles as he turns to me. "You think that's something. Check out the restroom. We have running water, young man."

"R-running water? How?" I make no effort to lift my jaw, which hangs open.

"My boy, I have no idea. Time expansion is a wonderful mystery, but not one we've had a chance to discuss with the Skya'ja. All efforts have been to contain this overload. All I know is that somehow our world is—two years did you say?—two years in the past when public water and sewer were still in operation."

I shake my head in disbelief. Our world had been so comfortable before the Cataclysm, and I had taken it for granted.

Stepping aboard an elevator, Dr. Smythe presses the button for the top floor. My knees weaken as the lift lurches upward, and I throw my hand against the wall to brace myself. To my surprise, Tash'jya laughs slightly. I'm not sure I've heard her laugh before.

"Something funny, Tash'jya?" I throw a smirk in her direction.

"Ted, your legss seem to have forgotten the world they came from."

We laugh together. Dr. Smythe shakes his head watching the two of us. "How long have you two known each other? Months? A year?"

"Just a couple of days."

Dr. Smythe returns his slipped glasses to the bridge of his nose with one finger. "Remarkable. To build such trust and companionship in so little time across species. We must discuss this after seeing your father, Teddy."

My stomach drops as the elevator slows to a halt as it reaches its destination. The doors part with a melodic dinging sound.

The room we enter is surrounded by windows on all sides. Outside, the tops of a few buildings can be seen. Mostly, the blue-green glow of the Bubble fills the area around the few blocks it covers. Tables litter the room with feats of engineering in various stages of construction. While a few of the projects seem fresh and connected to computers, which scroll data, many of the projects seem abandoned. Dust has begun to coat their services.

"Smythe, don't tell me another set of soldiers has crossed the barrier." The voice comes from a man hunched over a table. Fumes rise from the tip of his soldering iron, which hovers over a component on an electrical board. His glasses rest on the end of his nose as he stares down at his project. His movements are steady as if handling the delicate electrical board a million times before. "We don't need protection—we need minds to help us. Soldiers are simply more mouths to feed."

"Actually, sir, it's not soldiers this time." Dr. Smythe shakes, barely able to contain his excitement to deliver the news. "Our visitors are quite unexpected."

The man picks up another component and begins to solder it in place. "Tell them I'll be down to greet them as soon as I'm finished here. I've been staring at this thing all day, and my eyes need a break anyway. We're going to recreate that capacitor today, friend. I can feel it. This one is going to work."

"Well—erm—that may not be necessary. You see—"

"Dad?" My voice is nearly a whisper as I speak his name.

The man pauses, and I can see a tremble in his once steady

hand. He glances upward at me. Our eyes meet. His hand slips, and the soldering iron sears his skin. He yelps as he straightens, shaking his hand. Placing the burned flesh in his mouth, he stares at me. Slowly, his hand drops to his side.

"Teddy?"

"Hi, Dad."

He pulls his glasses from his face with fumbling fingers. "My boy? You're here. I'm not—seeing things?"

No more words are exchanged. I leap forward as he rounds the table. Seconds later, I'm wrapped in the folds of his lab coat. We embrace, each of us seemingly trying to out-squeeze the other. It has been years since I've hugged my father, more than the two years we've been separated. My soul melts into contentment inside me, and I don't want to let go.

My father steps backward and grasps my face in both hands. His eyes study my face several times over. Tears rim his eyelids.

"Son? How long has it been for you?"

"Two years, Dad."

"Dear, God. Two years? And you've survived that long on your own?" He grabs me again, crushing me in his arms. "I'm so sorry, Son. I should have brought you with me that day. You should have been there. You never should have had to endure—"

I can't stop the shuddering of my shoulders as emotion pours out of me. Relief floods my body. I never thought I'd get this moment. I thought he was dead. And here I am hugging him in the flesh. "It's okay, Dad. We made it."

"We?" Pulling away again, he looks behind me. As if for the first time, he notices Tash'jya. "Tash? You've returned?"

I note his shortened use of her name, like Loren. "We did more than that, Dad. We brought you something."

Tash'jya opens the backpack and retrieves the capacitor. My father's breath catches as he sees the layers fall away revealing his prototype. Tash'jya touches her head and chest with her free hand. "Dr. Kenneth Jamess, I have brought you the prototype capacitor you needed. I found it with the help of your son, who showed me the safe in your lab."

My dad runs both of his hands through his hair, leaving it a floppy mess. A shudder explodes from his lips, and he falls to his knees. Still grasping my arm, he looks up at me and Tash'jya. "You brought me my son and my invention. When you left, I realized I hadn't been able to share about the safe in the floor. And I feared—I feared the worst." His voice catches and, for a moment, he covers his trembling lips with his hand to keep his composure. "Tash'jya, I am pleased to know your name." He taps his forehead and chest in return.

"Tash'jya suii sussani! Est tuss?" A desperate Skya'ja voice comes from behind us. We turn to the elevator in unison. Had I not known that Tash'jya was standing beside me, I would have thought the woman to be her, except for the lab coat. Her features are so similar that I recognize instantly this is Tash'jya's sister. She swipes a tear from her eye. "Est tuss?"

I hear Tash'jya's respirator wheeze as she sucks in a sudden breath. "T-T-Tash'jyi?" For the first moment in the time I've known her, I see the strength drain from Tash'jya. Stepping forward, she stumbles toward her sister, arms extended. Tash'jyi runs forward, and the two meet. Hands on each other's shoulders, they touch their foreheads together. Remaining in that position, I can hear whispered words between the two of them.

My breath shudders as I realize how much anxiety has begun to drain out of me. Gratitude warms me from the inside, and I want to stay in this moment.

Dr. Smythe steps forward, a wide smile across his face as he glances at the sisters and then me. "Dr. James, this truly is an exciting day. And yet"—he frowns—"I must put a damper on this moment. We have much to do."

My father's expression transforms into resolve. He nods and stands, his legs finding their strength again. "As you often are, my friend, you are right." He turns to me and places his hand on my shoulders. "For too long my work has kept me from you, and I have every intention of making up for lost time. And yet, my son, I have to ask you to be patient a little while longer."

I smile and grab his forearm in my hand. "I get it, Dad. Go get to work. Save the world."

Chapter Twenty-Seven

An hour later, I'm sitting on a chair with an actual cushion eating a sandwich. The bread is a little stale and gummy. The cheese is warm but not the good kind. And the meat is definitely not freshly sliced at the deli. Still, it's the most delicious thing I've tasted in years. I relish every bite as if it will be the last one.

Tash'jya sits across from me. Her meal sits before her untouched.

I point to it, not bothering to swallow before I speak. "You going to eat that?"

She glances away without answering. Her hands rest on the table, but I can see that she is clasping them tightly.

"Something bothering you, Tash'jya?" I place the last couple bites of my sandwich on the plate and wipe my lips with a paper napkin. "One way humans and Skya'ja act alike is we lose our appetite when we've got something on our minds. Out with it." I wave a hand to encourage her to speak.

Her respirator wheezes loudly. Did she just sigh? "Ted, I am pleased that you are reunited with your father. I am pleased that we have been able to deliver the capacitor to your father."

Where is she going with this?

"Tash'jya, I am pleased that you and your sister have found each other again. This is a good day."

She pauses, her stare boring into my forehead. "I am also able to tell you that Loren is expected to recover fully."

I blink hard. "What? That's great news! We need to go see her…like now." I start to get up out of my chair, but Tash'jya catches my arm.

"Wait."

I slowly sink to my seat. "Tash'jya, that's great news, isn't it?"

Despite everything, she appears forlorn. "Ted, if all happenss as we hope it will—if the capacitor is the means to curb the overload, the time expansion will be turned off."

"Well, yeah. Isn't that what we want?" I am so confused.

She shakes her head with her eyes closed. "When the time expansion iss turned off, time will correct itself. The world will change to become what it would have been without the explosion."

"I don't understand. That's what we've been trying to do this whole time." I scratch my head.

"You and Lo-ren are coupling?"

"Coupling? What do you mean? I mean we aren't—"

"You are together in a romantic relationship as humanss do?"

I swallow hard. We've never voiced it in the short life of our relationship. "I suppose you're right. We are together. I mean—there's definitely something between us. We haven't really talked about it."

Another sigh-like wheeze in the respirator. "Ted, you met Lo-ren in the world out there as it exists right at this moment. You met because of the explosion. When the overload is fixed, and time is healed—" She cuts off her words, waiting for me to complete the thought.

"That world won't exist anymore." I straighten in my chair as the reality of what she is saying hits me. The devastation of the Cataclysm is what brought Loren and me together. Without my world of living on the streets and her hiding as a nurse while running from her father, we may never have met.

Tash'jya grabs my hand in hers. Her skin's warmth surprises me as she squeezes my fingers. "I am sorry, Ted. My sister shared with me that they have discovered that the human brain cannot retain the information of both timeliness. Skya'ja are different. We will remember. You will not. Nor will Lo-ren. If they fix the explosion, you will have no memory of each other."

The truth hits me like a sledgehammer to the chest. All at

once, I feel my head grow hot and the air leaves my lungs. The world spins. This last hour has brought me such relief and joy, and now I cannot sense the presence of either.

"But you'll remember, right? You can tell us about ourselves. How we met. How we worked together. How we fell in love." Is that what we have? Love? "Can't you?"

"Ted, from what I understand about human coupling, the relationship between you both cannot exist on the basis of information alone. You might learn that you were together, but it will feel like a story about someone else. Without the shared experience that brought you together—" She pauses, allowing her words to trail off.

"The feelings won't be there." I finish her thought.

"Exactly. Sharing the information might only cause you harm. You both would be conflicted and perhaps attempt to force something that is no longer there."

I never expected saving the world to cost me so much. Yeah, I'm sure my new life might allow me to meet someone special, but Loren and I had bonded through adversity. Our few days had been packed with years of pain, wonder, and lessons learned. How could I trade that for another?

Not that I would remember. But that doesn't mean I cannot feel the crack forming in my heart.

"Do you believe that people are meant to be together, Tash'jya? Do the Skya'ja believe that there is one person meant for them when they—couple?"

"My people are promised from birth. We do not couple the same as your speciess."

"Promised? Like an arranged marriage or something?"

"Marriage is human, but you are correct. The Skya'ja equivalent is arranged."

"Are you—promised?"

Tash'jya glances down at the table. "Y-yes."

"Why the hesitation?"

"My mate wass indeed arranged at my birth but he is no

longer alive." She pauses. "He iss—wass—out there." She nods with her head toward the window where the blue-green shimmer of the Bubble can be seen. "He did not survive in the fight with humanity that is taking place."

"But if we restore the timeline, and the world resets? Won't he be back, and you'd be reunited?"

Tash'jya's face darkens. "Yes. That iss true. But he will not have the memory of the time that has passed. He died early in the battle. I, on the other hand, will have two yearss of memories. Two yearss of accepting that my mate has died, and I will be alone. That my progeny will never exist."

Again, Tash'jya's femininity hits me. I never thought of her as having children one day.

"I'm sorry, Tash'jya. I'm not sure what to say."

"We do not practice love as humanss do, but the loyalty to our mate is built over a lifetime. Accepting life without my mate was difficult, and once restored will be impossible to forget." She folds her hands on the table. "So you see, Ted, there is a cost for both of uss. Yet I envy you that you will forget whereas I will not."

I drop my chin and stare at the table. My desire to finish my sandwich is gone. "Wh-what am I supposed to do with this? Why did you tell me? You could have simply allowed me to forget."

"Because you deserve to know. Because when you see Loren soon, she deservess to know—from you."

I raise my head to look Tash'jya in the eye. My lips tremble. My anger is not at Tash'jya. She did not create this problem, and as she's explained, she's not immune from it. My anger is at the cruel world that would exact such a price from us for helping save it.

"You are saying this is the last time I may ever speak to Loren?"

"I am sorry, Ted. Truly I am."

With a final squeeze of my hand, Tash'jya rises from the table, leaving me to myself. I want to vomit. I want to turn the table over. I want to slink out of my chair, onto the ground, and sob.

I want to see Loren.

Neural Implant Log: Entry 146
Officer: Tash'jya, daughter of Sun'tssh
Rank: Tactician

On the advice of my sister, I have informed Ted, whose name I know, of the reality of the cessation of time expansion. I cannot help but grieve the loss he will experience. Yet I am struck by the human notion of a destined partner. Ted is not the first human I have heard express such sentiment. Previously, I dismissed it as a result of humanity's immaturity as a species. I accepted that the Skya'ja were more evolved.

And yet, is this not what we Skya'ja practice? While our expression may be different than the human experience of love, we arrange our mates from birth and never veer from that plan. Skya'ja whose mates die before the proper age leave their designated partner alone for a lifetime. There is no hope of finding another mate.

Even now, as I wrestle with the complication of my own coupling, should the capacitor right the timeline as we hope, I do not accept another plan. I will spend the rest of my life managing my memories of life without him, even as I build my life with him.

If this is what I—and all Skya'ja—believe, how then can I dismiss the idea that Ted and Loren are meant to be together simply because they will have never met. On this, I will need to give some consideration.

End of log.

Chapter Twenty-Eight

My chest feels heavy as I push open the door of the medical facility. Here and there, human and Skya'ja physicians tend to various needs. Machines beep in corners, a blending of human and Skya'ja medical technology. Next to one bed, two Skya'ja doctors study an x-ray of a leg. There was a time when I'd have found seeing the physiology of a Skya'ja skeleton fascinating, but nothing like that is of interest to me now.

I pass by rooms, some occupied, others empty. Approaching the desk, I can barely lift my eyes enough to meet the gaze of a Skya'ja woman sitting at a computer. "Loren Westfield?" My mouth feels chalky as I say her name.

A couple clacks on the keys of the computer tick away the seconds before she answers. "Lo-ren Westfield is in room 311. She's located that way and to the right."

I mutter a quick thank you and begin the march in the direction she'd indicated. Laughter echoes down the hallway—the kind that lights up a room and all who are inside. I recognize that voice. Pain jabs at my heart like I'm being speared from behind. She's awake and happy, probably full of hope that the world is about to right itself. I'm about to smother that hope with the knowledge that our relationship—though fast and furious—will be over. It shouldn't be this hard to end things with someone I've known for days, but I have never connected to someone like I have with Loren. Approaching the room, I can see her through the curtains smiling as she speaks with doctors next to her bed. She is reclining in a hospital bed and wearing a robe. I can barely tell she's been through surgery except for the monitor beeping next to her, displaying her vitals.

My throat goes dry at the thought that such connection may never come again.

I never believed in soulmates. Relationships are work. Even at my age, I see that. Loren is different. We fit each other in that crazy way that old people describe meeting their spouse of seventy years—a look across the room, a glance at the local diner, an accidental bumping into each other in line—where sparks fly, and love is born out of nothing.

I love Loren. I finally admit it to myself.

But I won't after today. Not if my father is successful. For a moment, I entertain the idea maybe we shouldn't fix the world. That maybe all that has happened for two years should be allowed to exist. That Loren and I should continue.

I shake my head to clear my thoughts. That would mean not undoing the death of millions around the world. All for the sake of two-day-old love. How selfish am I? No, fixing the world is the right thing to do, but it doesn't mean I have to like it.

With a hand, I part the curtains and step through. Loren's gaze finds me, and a smile spreads across her lips. I offer one in return, but I fear mine is weak with the emotional storm inside me.

"Ted! Come here." She extends her hand and wiggles her fingers for me to take it. I slide my hand into hers and feel the warmth of her palm against mine. I brush the back of her fingers with my thumb. I want to run away from the room and stay forever in this moment all at the same time. Without warning, her hand grips mine tightly, and she pulls me toward the bed where she is reclined. With her other hand, she grabs the back of my head and pulls me into a kiss.

We drink in the kiss for a long moment, long enough we both have to take deep breaths in the middle. We part leaving our foreheads touching. Her hand runs through the hair on the back of my head.

"We made it," she says, smiling again.

"Yeah." My voice is breathy, and I wonder if she can hear the doubt in it. I kiss her forehead and stand upright. "Doc says you're going to be okay?"

She nods. "Skya'ja medicine is incredible. I can barely feel what they did to me in surgery. I feel good enough to walk, but they're insisting I stay in this bed for now. Something about the fragility of human anatomy or something like that."

"That's good." Circling the bed, I find a chair in the corner and carry it to her bedside. I sit and retake her hand in mine. Silence fills a long moment between us. How can I love her and not talk to her?

"So, what's the update on the capacitor? Everyone seems upbeat around here, but the hospital staff knows little of what's going on. Did it work?" Her eyes are wide with anticipation of the good news that the overload will be fixed.

I sigh, grateful for something to talk about other than the doom of our relationship. "My dad said the capacitor should probably take about an hour to install, and that was more than forty-five minutes ago. I'd imagine they're close."

"Really? We're that close?" She begins to sit up before pausing to place a hand on her abdomen as if reminding herself of the doctor's orders to stay down. "You mean to say that the world might be saved any minute?"

"I guess so. There's still time before the explosion is beyond containment, so my dad wants to thoroughly test everything to be sure the capacitor is enough. They've got one shot to get it right, and he doesn't want to mess it up." I can't meet her eyes. She's staring at me, searching for some kind of reaction, but I can barely stare at her hand in mine.

"Ted, what is it? What's wrong?" Her eyes droop in concern.

There it is. From the day we met at the clinic, she has been able to see right through my façade. I can't hide this from her despite the part of me that wants to enjoy my last untainted moments with her before the magic of time extension erases our connection forever.

I force my eyes to travel the length of her arm to her shoulder and neck and finally to her face. Our eyes lock on each other, and

I can sense the welling of grief in my gut threatening to overwhelm me. Her eyes search my face for answers. Her smile has melted, leaving her biting her lower lip on one side.

Here it goes. I'm not certain of the words to say, so I take a deep breath and hope they will come. "If all goes as we hope, the capacitor will hold the overload, and the explosion will be contained. The Skya'ja time extension machine will turn off, and the world as we know it will change into the world as it would have been." I pause, searching for how to go on. Loren, for her part, waits patiently. "I guess we will all wake up where we would have been had the last two years passed uninterrupted. Our lives will be rewritten, and we will have no memory of what has happened to the world. Tash'jya says her people inside the Bubble will remember. It's something about how their brains handle the time expansion, but what they tell us will only seem like a story to us."

"Ted, what are you saying?" She asks the question, but she is smart enough to have already guessed the answer. I can read it all over her face.

"Nothing that has happened over the last two years will have happened. People who died from the war will be back. Food shortages will be gone. The pain and suffering of the wasted world will be gone." I swallow hard. "But so will the memory of anyone we've met during that time."

She presses her lips together, and I can see the glassiness of her eyes. Her fingers grip mine. I breathe in to speak, but she shakes her head as if to say, "don't say it." I must say it. It's the truth, and truth must be spoken—even the painful truth.

"We won't remember each other." The words escape my mouth like breath forced from my lungs from a punch to the chest. My heart splits as the silence grows thick in the hospital room. I glance at Loren in time to see a single tear plummet down her cheek. I want to reach up and wipe it away with my hand, but I am frozen.

With a sudden sniff, she rubs her eyes and fixes her hair to compose herself. "Well, then, we will have to make the most of these final minutes then, huh?" Letting go of my hand, she sits up in the bed and twists to allow her feet to hang over the side.

I straighten and extend my hands, to stop her or catch her, I'm not sure which. "Are you sure you should—"

Her look cuts me off. "Yes, I'm sure. I can stand, and I'm not spending our last moments together laying in a hospital bed." I wince at the words 'last moments.' She slides off the bed, her bare feet hitting the floor with a quiet slap. For a moment, she teeters, and I'm convinced she is going to sit back down on the bed. To my surprise, she pauses and stills the sway of her body. Reaching her hand out for me to take, she turns to me. "Take me for a walk, Ted. Let's get some fresh air."

I stand, blotting away any dampness on my face with my sleeve. I interlace my fingers in hers and gaze into her eyes.

"If this is our ending, let's make it a happy one." A smile spreads across her face that warms me inside.

I find myself smiling. "Okay. A walk then."

Kaboom!

The building shakes beneath our feet and the windows rattle under the vibration from the explosion. Rushing to the window, we take in the scene a few floors down in the plaza where we'd entered. A plume of smoke rises from the building next to us, the source of the explosion.

For a moment, I fear we are too late. The overload has gone too far. The explosion that ultimately destroyed the world has taken place.

"Was that—?" Loren asks, sharing my fear.

"It's too early. My father said there was more time before the explosion happens."

Was that it? Did the Cataclysm happen? For a moment, I'm happy. I will be able to stay with Loren. I chide myself for my selfishness. "It-it can't be. Seems too small to be a world-ending catastrophe. And look." I point to the blue-green haze. "The Bubble is still working. If that had been the explosion, would the time expansion have ended?"

"Then what is it?"

"I'm not sure." But the truth is that I do know. I see it, right there by the edge of the Bubble.

A truck, the kind that used to be used for moving furniture, idles in the center of the plaza. Men brandishing weapons pour out of the back of the truck, creating a perimeter around it. To one side, a man with a rocket launcher is busy reloading. *Where did they get a rocket launcher?* In the middle of the circle, a man stands with his hands on his hips surveying his surroundings.

I recognize that stance.

I know that green scar.

Revon.

Chapter Twenty-Nine

"What is he doing here?" I ask the question already knowing the answer. Some part of me thought that the fear of entering the Bubble would be enough to keep Revon from following us. Around his circle of men, several humans and Skya'ja scientists, who'd rushed to welcome the visitors now cower on the ground at gunpoint. Revon turns to the buildings, and we can hear the muffled sound of him shouting. Stepping back from the window, so we can't be seen, I slide open the ventilation window slightly. The muffled sounds clear.

"—you're out there, Rookie. Nice place you have here. You took my daughter from me into the hands of these monsters. I've come to reclaim her and put a bullet in your head as repayment." He pauses before laughing to himself. "Doesn't sound enticing? Didn't think it would, so I'll make you a deal. Give yourself up, and I won't shoot every Fishface here. Easy decision if you ask me. The life of a human versus the meaningless waste of breath of a few invaders."

I retreat further into the room. What am I to do? I look at Loren.

"Ted, you can't." She shakes her head. "He won't keep his word."

"He's going to shoot every Skya'ja down there. And he might not stop there."

Loren swallows as she nods her head. Her voice shakes with emotion. "Yeah. And he'll probably do it anyway when you give yourself up to him."

My mind races faster than I can keep up with the thoughts hammering at the side of my skull. Loren's right. Revon will kill everyone here if he gets the whim to do so. Every Skya'ja. And any human who works with the Skya'ja. I'm not sure who he hates worse.

"Dad." The name crosses my lips in a whisper like I'm afraid to say it.

"What?" Loren turns away from the window to gaze at me.

"He'll kill my dad. He's been working with the Skya'ja from the beginning. If I give myself up, he'll kill everyone working with the Skya'ja before they can finish testing the capacitor."

"And the explosion will never be contained." Loren finishes my thought.

"The world will stay a wasteland. We can't let that happen." An idea forms in my brain, and I'm certain I appear like a crazy person as I have a silent conversation with myself. Loren's confused gaze confirms the impression I must be giving off. "We have to buy time. Give them something to do, so they don't start executing everyone they find. Keep them on the run until my dad can finish, and—"

"—and the world resets. No explosion. No Bubble. Problem solved. But how do we keep him that busy?" Loren cocks an eyebrow. She's probably guessed my plan.

I bite my lip before daring myself to say what I'm thinking. "We don't give him what he wants, but we tell him where it is. Focus his attention."

Loren sighs. "Not how I planned to have us spend our last moments."

I take her hand. "Save the world one more time?"

"Why not."

I turn to the window and step forward, putting myself in full view of the plaza. Revon stands below, checking the safety of his pistol. He stands over a Skya'ja woman in a lab coat. "Rookie, I'm a patient man, but not that patient. Your time is running out." He points the pistol at the woman, who throws her hands up in vain defense. "Five…four…three…"

"Revon." My voice croaks, so I repeat myself louder. "Revon!"

The nose of Revon's pistol wavers as he looks upward in the direction of my voice. I pound on the glass and shout again through the cracked window. "Commander, I'm right here. Your daughter is here. She is healed thanks to Skya'ja surgeons. Just leave us alone!"

I have no expectation that he'll leave, but my purpose is accomplished when he holsters his pistol. Turning to his men, he barks orders, pointing to the building we're in. Facing us again, he shouts. "Rookie, no such luck. You're not a father, so you wouldn't understand." He nods to his men. "Third floor, guys."

Revon's men rush the building, abandoning their hostages who begin to scatter to the edges of the plaza. Revon glares up at me, and a smirk finds his lips. Slowly, he strides toward the door of our building. He's in no hurry. He realizes his prey is caged, and he can take his time.

"Well, you got his attention. That what you were hoping for?" Loren asks breathlessly, already glancing at the doorway and ready to leave.

"Kind of thought he'd come after us by himself, but that was probably too much to hope for."

"What now?"

"Time to run." Taking her hand, we sprint from the hospital room.

Stair after stair, we climb the high-rise building. Loren's feet slap the floor with each step, and I'm amazed at how she's able to keep up barefoot. We can hear the footfalls of Revon's men as they swarm the staircase. As I hoped, their advance is slowed as they stop climbing to enter the third floor to find us.

We need distance…and a good hiding place. Wasting time, that's the goal. With luck, word will reach my father of what is happening, and they'll forgo the final testing of the capacitor. There's nothing Revon can do if the explosion is prevented and the time expansion ceases. We'll all relocate to wherever time would have brought us after two years. Loren and I will lose our memories, but so will Revon.

We don't need to escape. We have to drag this out.

"Ted, can you slow down?" Loren's words come between breathless gasps. Sweat trickles from her hairline down her face. She holds her back with one hand, and I turn her around to examine her. Blood is starting to soak through her robe.

"Your wound is reopening. We can't keep going at this pace." I look at the door in front of us, which reads *Floor 11*. It'll have to be enough. Throwing the latch, I fling open the door. Inside, we're greeted by an unfinished office space. I wrap my arm around Loren, and we stumble onto the eleventh floor. Scanning the room, I search for hiding spots.

"What about the supply closet over there?" I ask.

Loren shakes her head. "We'd be cornered in there if they found us. We need a place to run if necessary."

I point with my free hand to what would have been a conference room. Half walls circle the room beneath what would have been windows. The ends of the room each have an opening where a door was meant to be installed. "Let's duck in there. If they come out of this staircase, we can make a break for the other one by the elevators. And vice versa."

"Such a glamorous, well-thought-out plan." Loren smiles between pained breaths. Somehow, her sarcasm gives me courage. If she's strong enough to joke around, then we may make it.

We scurry over to the conference room and duck inside. Finding a corner out of view of both stairwells, we slide down the wall and huddle out of sight. Loren relaxes into me, and I'm grateful not to push her to run for a moment. I take several deep breaths to calm my racing heart.

Minutes tick by, and I find myself praying for the time expansion to cease. What will it be like? Will I feel it? Will the world flash before me or fade slowly? Will I see the transformation of the world as the Bubble falls and the wasteland morphs into the thriving city it was two years ago?

Or will it be the blink of an eye? One moment in this reality and the next in a new one.

The pain of what will happen to Loren and me hits again, and I choke back the emotion. I need to stay clear-headed should we be found. All we want is a quiet moment to be together before we are torn apart, but fate seems bent on preventing that. It's then that I realize how much of our relationship has been in the midst of trauma and flight. My heart aches for one normal moment with Loren before we're parted.

My attention is snapped back to the present by the sounds of footsteps and muffled voices on the stairs.

"They've reached our floor," I whisper.

Loren nods, and I can feel her body tense in preparation for fleeing again.

The latch of the door makes a metallic clink as the emergency exit swings open. Peering over the half-wall, I can see three men with rifles pour into the room. I recognize two of them…Chambers and Matthews.

"Sweep left, and check that corner office." Matthews orders the third man. "Chambers, go right to the restrooms at the back. I'll head up the middle toward that conference area." I duck down as Matthew's finger swings in our direction and pray I haven't been seen. "Eleventh floor, Commander."

"Sweep that floor and keep moving." Revon's voice squawks on the radio. "They can't have gotten far, and I don't want to do this all day. And Matthews, not a scratch on my daughter, you hear?"

"Understood, Commander."

Footsteps fall in different directions as the men divide. A moment later, the man checking the corner office calls out, "Clear!" Seconds later, I can hear Chambers kicking open the doors to the bathroom stalls. I can't hear him, but I guess Matthews is nearly upon us.

I stand.

I don't know what I'm thinking. The tug on my pant leg from Loren confirms she doesn't understand either.

"Found them. Conference room." Matthews shouts. A

moment later, his compatriots are by his side. Three rifles all train on my chest. I hold my hands out to either side. Matthews reaches for his radio. "Commander, they're here. We have them."

"Look, Matthews, give me a second. You don't understand." My voice shakes as I try to explain what is happening. "My father has almost fixed everything. The whole world was destroyed, but it doesn't have to stay that way. This Bubble is time slowed down. In minutes, the overload that destroyed everything might be fixed. The Bubble will fall, and the world will return back to the way it should have been." My explanation is partial, but I hope it's enough to get through to them.

Matthews' face twists as he processes what I have said. He glances at Chambers who gives a confused shrug. Turning back to me, he lowers his rifle an inch. "I'm not sure what you're talking about kid. Commander wants you, and you can try to explain it to him."

I raise my hands in surrender to keep him calm. "Matthews, I'm guessing this isn't you. Before the Cataclysm? Who were you?"

Matthews gives another nervous glance to Chambers. "I-I was a landscaper. Owned my own company. Wife. Kids. What's it to you?"

"And what happened to them?"

"Fire. House burned down after explosion sent pieces of downtown flying through the air. I worked the night shift and wasn't home yet. All three of them died in the fire because of those Fishfaces." He juts the end of the rifle at me. "Now quiet. I have orders to take the Commander's daughter in alive, but I don't think he'd mind you dead."

"Would you like to see your family again?"

Matthew's hardened expression fades, the corners of his eyes drooping. I can see the years of pain and loss surface, and I'd swear his eyes are watering. Yes, he would very much like to see his family again.

"Please, we simply need time. If this works, all that has happened in the last two years will have never existed. No explosion. No house fire. Let us go. Pretend you didn't see us. Tell Revon you were mistaken, and you merely thought you saw us." Sweat rolls down my back. I'm painfully aware that we've ticked too little time off the clock. Unless someone has told my dad what is happening, he's still cooped up in his lab running tests, oblivious to the need to throw caution to the wind and throw the switch. "Please, Matthews."

A tug on my hand brings Loren to stand beside me. She steps forward and slightly in front of me. All three men lower their rifles halfway. None of them are eager to point a gun at Revon's daughter.

"You're going to let us leave, guys." Loren's voice is shaky, but she speaks with authority. "You shoot him, you're likely to hit me. You realize what my father will do to anyone that harms me."

The three exchange glances. Chambers and the third man completely lower their weapons. Matthews keeps his half-raised. "Loren, come with us." His brow furrows in concern. "Your father—er, the commander—wants you home. You guys can explain that time thing to him. M-maybe he'll listen. Everything you said—if it's true—I-I just can't let you go."

"Last I heard, he wants to put a bullet in my head." I glare at Matthews. "Doesn't sound like a lot of opportunity to explain. And then your family really would be lost."

Loren extends her hand backward and places it against my chest. She slowly pushes me toward the other exit of the conference room. Seeing our slight retreat, Matthews raises his barrel again. Loren raises her other hand in his direction.

"Don't do it, Matthews. You're not going to shoot us." Loren continues to step backward, urging me to do the same with her hand. Step by step, we approach the other doorway. Matthews' face contorts as he struggles with what to do.

Chambers slaps Matthews' shoulder. "Dude, you can't, bro. Revon would kill you if he even found out you were pointing that thing at her. Don't worry. They can't leave the building."

With an exasperated grunt, Matthews lowers his rifle. That fills me with courage, and we retreat faster. Exiting the conference room and keeping the three men in our vision, we back toward the staircase near the elevators. I envision the metal door of the staircase meeting my back, throwing the latch, and retreating to the safety of the stairwell. I imagine our flight up the stairs. Time. That's all we need. A few more floors up might buy us that.

The floor changes beneath my feet from carpet to tile, and I recognize I'm in an elevator lobby. Steps away is the stairwell. Matthews, Chambers, and the third goon haven't moved. We're going to make it.

Ding.

The elevator doors next to us open. I turn to see a green-scarred face appear. A second later, the barrel of a pistol strikes my head. Bright light flashes in my vision. My knees buckle involuntarily, and I collapse to the floor. My head screams with pain, and I clutch it with both hands. One hand comes away wet with blood.

I crack an eyelid to see Matthews and Chambers run to either side of Loren, grabbing her arms in their giant meat hooks. Revon places a hand on Loren's cheek in a sickly paternal gesture, and she shakes her head to retreat from it.

"St-stop." I can barely speak. My head hurts like it's splitting open.

Revon turns to me and crouches. He taps the barrel of his pistol on the end of my nose. "You're a lot of trouble, Rookie. I'll give you that."

"He said something about his father and fixing the world." Matthews blurts the words out almost like he didn't intend to. I can see desperation in his eyes. He may not understand what I was telling him, but *fixing the world* is something he comprehends.

"Is that so?" Revon's smirk returns. "Your old man is here? Well, we wouldn't want him to miss the moment when I end you, now would we? Where is he, Rookie?" He leans in closer.

I spit in his face.

I'm rewarded with another pistol whip.

Chapter Thirty

The floors ding one after another as the elevator plummets to the ground floor. I was already woozy from the pistol across my head, and this stomach-dropping sensation is not helping keep the vomit down. Revon's iron grip wraps my neck with five calloused fingers. I can breathe, but I'm conscious that Revon is strong enough to squeeze the life out of me if he chooses. That thought is the only thing keeping me on my feet. My head is spinning, and I would love nothing more than to collapse to the floor and perhaps lose consciousness.

Behind him, Matthews and Chambers continue to keep a hand under Loren's arms. She glances at me. Without a word, I can understand her thoughts. *Sorry.* And then a wide-eyed glance brings me back to the present situation—there hasn't been enough time. We didn't keep them on the run long enough.

The doors slide open, revealing the main lobby of the building. Revon's men bracket the front doors. Several humans and Skya'ja are gathered on their knees at a round receptionist desk at the center. Two more guards stand over them, rifles trained on the group.

Revon grabs my shirt sleeve and pushes me in the direction of the table. My feet wobble beneath me, trying to keep up, lest I fall and end up dragged by the Commander. Reaching the table, he shoves me, doubling me over the desk. I push up slightly and meet the eyes of the frightened group under guard. Their expectant looks ask me for explanation. I don't have one that would offer any comfort.

"Take a good look people." Revon grabs my chin and forces my head upward. "This here troublemaker is the reason for all the stress you are under at this moment. From what I hear, his father is here somewhere, and I'd like to know where. Anyone who wants to offer me that information could be considered under my good graces for the remainder of our time together." He turns my head from side to side so the entire huddled group can get a glance at my face.

"Dad, stop!" Loren shakes her head. "This isn't helping anything. I can't even go with you if I wanted to. We're trapped inside the Bubble. If we could simply let them finish the work they are—"

"That's enough out of you." Revon shoves my head away before releasing me. Approaching Loren, he points a finger at her face. "In the end, all this suffering is on you. If you had stayed like a good daughter, then I wouldn't have had to come for you. Now would I? You keep quiet, or—"

"Or what?" Loren interrupts. "You'll shoot me…again?"

The question takes Revon aback. Pain washes over his face at the reminder. "That was an accident."

"The gun didn't pull its own trigger. You did." Loren's chin quivers as she speaks. "What would Mom think, huh?"

"You leave her out of this. She has nothing to do with this."

Loren straightens and meets Revon's eyes for a moment. "No, Dad, she has *everything* to do with this. You were always a hateful person, but your rampage began after she died. Your crusade to rid the world of the Skya'ja has been in her name." With a shake, Loren frees herself from the shocked Matthews and Chambers. She takes a step toward her father. "And what has your pursuit of 'right' gotten you? Violence. Racial cleansing. Taking from others. Forced recruitment into your posse." She pauses and lowers her voice. "A bullet in your daughter's back."

Revon's shoulders drop, and his posture stoops ever so slightly. His resolve withers under Loren's indictment. Amazingly, he takes a half-step backward. It is the first retreat I've ever seen from the man.

"I-I didn't mean—I would never—" Revon stammers unable to put a sentence together.

"Exactly, Dad. Too much is happening that you didn't mean

to happen. You're drowning in your own fight—a fight that doesn't even need to be fought." Loren's voice softens, and she reaches for Revon's shoulder. "The Skya'ja are not bad people. They mean well. All this"—she nods her head toward the shimmering Bubble outside—"is their attempt to fix what has been done. They aren't the monsters in this scenario. I wish you could see that. Mom saw it. She saw them with eyes of wonder. If she were here, she still would."

Whether it is to stall for time or to actually confront her father, my heart soars at Loren's confidence. Wounded and barely out of surgery, she is taking on the hardened militia leader before her. And he is wilting.

Revon's face contorts, as if choosing what emotion to land on. The result is a dark shadow that passes across his face. "Your mother isn't here. She didn't get that choice. She's dead because they came here." Revon jabs a finger at the closest Skya'ja crouched behind the desk. "*They* came to our planet. *They* intruded upon our lives. *They* messed up our world and sent it into ruin. *They* are why your mother isn't here."

In a flash, he unholsters his pistol and points it to the Skya'ja he'd gestured to. "The rookie's father. Where is he? I'll give you a count of three, and then we all get a firsthand demonstration of how well a Fishface can bleed."

"Dad!"

"One."

The group behind the desk retreats from the threatened Skya'ja, who holds her two hands up in pleading surrender. "Nuni sen manna passten." Her words repeat over and over, begging for mercy.

"Two."

"Dad, don't do this." Her lips tremble in desperation. There is no more appeal to be made to her father.

"Three."

With a shriek, the group retreats from the impending report of the pistol. "Wait!" A man half-stands from his crouched position, both hands raised. Revon's finger hovers a hair's distance from the trigger. "I'll tell you what you want to know. Just please don't shoot her." Visibly trembling, he glances from Revon to the Skya'ja woman.

Revon's pistol lowers. "Finally, a reasonable person." He turns the pistol on the man, who ducks in fright. "Start talking before this gun makes you do more than wet yourself."

The man's face flushes at the realization that he, indeed, has lost control of his bladder. "D-Dr. James' research lab is—is in building three. That way." He points a shaky finger out the door and to the right.

Loren's face drops. My heart sinks. The one advantage we had is gone.

"See? Was that so hard?" Revon holds both hands out to his side and scans the crowd. I'm painfully aware that the safety is still off on his pistol as he points it at me. "No one need get hurt here, except those who deserve it. Start walking, Rookie. It's time to pay your father a visit."

Chapter Thirty-One

The march across the plaza takes far less time than I would like. I keep hoping to see the Bubble fall and time correct. If only the capacitor had been installed and activated right away. None of this would be happening. My father is too careful for that. He will want to get this right the first time, and Revon's presence has simply been limited to the plaza and the medical building. The likelihood that my father is engrossed in testing every possible parameter multiple times increases with every moment as time here continues at a crawl. Matthews and Chambers have retaken their place at Loren's side, and I can see her out of the corner of my eye. Her eyes search the ground for answers. As we approach building three, I can't help but rehearse what is about to happen.

Revon is going to murder me in front of my father.

My father will probably be next.

The explosion will still happen. The Bubble will fall with nothing changed. Those outside the Bubble will go on fighting over the few resources left until they're gone, and everyone starves to death together. And Loren, she'll die here in the Bubble.

"Revon, you're going to die here." Each word makes my headache pound harder. "You're trapped in this Bubble. If we don't reset the timeline, anyone here will die in the explosion. You. Loren. Your men. All of you."

Revon turns, one hand on the door to building three. "They tell you that, Rookie? Those Fishfaces? And you believed them?"

"I'm serious. You can pass into this place, but not out of it."

"Gag him. I don't want to hear another Fishface lie out of his mouth." A second later, a dirty cloth is shoved in my mouth and tied around the back of my neck. Pain explodes as my headache reacts to the tight knot clamping down on the base of my skull.

We enter the building. Revon fires two shots into the ceiling, sending everyone present ducking and screaming. He points the pistol at the closest person, a woman in a lab coat clutching a pair of glasses that hang around her neck.

"Dr. James' laboratory, if you please." Revon stares the woman down.

"F-f-fifth fl-floor." She points to the elevators.

Revon's pistol returns to my back. Boarding the elevator, the five of us say nothing as the doors close, and the floors pass by. On the fifth ding, the doors slide open.

Several humans and Skya'ja in lab coats are huddled together around my father as he sits at a computer. Text and data scroll by on the screen, presumably the results of the latest test on the capacitor. On the wall, a compartment is opened, the newly installed capacitor gleaming silver under the laboratory lights. To the left, a large flat switch with a thin red handle protrudes upward behind glass. Warning labels litter the circumference of the glass window.

The switch. I guess I never thought the switch would be so literal, but there it is. One movement of the handle would pass power through the capacitor and either prevent the overload or not. I shudder at the gravity throwing that switch holds. The actual fate of the world depends upon it, and I can understand my father's caution.

The lab coats are so engrossed in their work that they don't see our approach until we have closed half the distance. As I feared, they have been singularly focused and have no idea what has been taking place. One of them looks up, and my heart sinks even further at her look of recognition.

"Ted. Lo-ren." Tash'jya sucks in a sudden breath through her respirator.

The group glances up in unison, finally breaking out of the spell of the screen before them. Several take steps backward, eyeing Revon's gun. My father rises from his chair slowly. Tash'jya stands defensively right in front of him.

"Ladies and Gentlemen," Revon begins, "a moment of your time. I'm here to take care of some unfinished business, and I would like to have a word with Dr. James, who I'm guessing is the center of attention there." He raises a brow and points to my father.

"Please, sir, we cannot be disturbed." Dr. Smythe steps from the crowd with both hands raised. "You don't understand what we are on the precipice of here. Time is short, and we stand to right the world to its—"

Bang!

I duck involuntarily as the blast of the pistol rings in my ear and echoes off the walls. The sound is sharp and causes actual pain in that ear. For a few seconds the world is muffled, and I shake my head to clear my thoughts. When I can finally take in my surroundings, I wish I hadn't.

Dr. Smythe lays on the floor, blood soaking across his chest into his white lab coat. His hands shake as he clutches the arms of another scientist to kneels next to him. "Why? Why?" His voice is barely a whisper. "We are trying to save everything. We were going to make it right—" His eyes roll back into his head as the words trail off. His arms fall to the ground limp, and I see his chest fall as his last breath seeps out of his lungs. Whimpers come from a couple of scientists. The rest are deathly silent.

Revon sighs. "We have very different opinions on what it means to make the world right, and my version does not include humans working with Fishfaces in any capacity. Now that you see that I mean business, back to the matter at hand."

"You are a savage animal! Have you no pity for your own kind?" Tash'jya spits the words at Revon.

"Ah, I recognize you." A smirk spreads across his face. "You're the Fishfaced friend of the little rookie here. Well, if that doesn't make the reunion a full family affair, I don't know what will. This is going to make this far more fun."

"What do you want from us?" My father steps out from behind the protective cover of Tash'jya. "Please, we don't want anyone else getting hurt." He glances down at the body of Dr. Smythe. I'm amazed at his calm in the face of Revon's gun.

Revon rubs his brow. "I wish that were possible, but I'm afraid your son here has been more than a thorn in my side for the last few days. I cannot let his actions go unpunished." With a nod of his head, Matthews and Chambers approach the group on either side. "Dr. James, your son has essentially stolen my daughter from me. She may be here"—he motions to Loren—"but she'll never fully come back home. As a father, I imagine you can resonate with how painful that would be. It's an injustice to me, and it must be atoned for. Eye for eye. Tooth for tooth. Child for child."

"No!" My father lunges forward, halted by the grip of Chambers hand. "You can't!"

"Believe me, I take no pleasure in it, but I made a promise to your son that there would be suffering from the trouble he's caused. I'm nothing if not a man of my word." He turns to me. "Any final words for your daddy, Rookie?"

Revon's attention turns to me, and Tash'jya seizes her chance. "Shya-sii!" Her battle cry echoes as she leaps in Matthews' direction. Her fist finds his throat, and he doubles over gasping for air. His hands clutch at his collapsed windpipe. Spinning, her foot connects with Chambers' arm. Letting go of my father, he retreats, his rifle clattering to the floor as he reaches for his broken forearm. She doesn't give him the chance. Another kick finds his chin, and he crumples to the floor unconscious. Matthews drops to all fours sucking violently to get air into his lungs, equally incapacitated. She turns to lunge in our direction.

Bang!

Bits of ceiling crumble around us from the bullet. I involuntarily clutch my right ear. Again, my ear rings from the blast right next to my head, and I'm certain my eardrum on that side is blown. Revon chuckles as the smoke from the pistol clears. "Not bad, Fishface. You have a knack for getting the drop on my guys there. Count me impressed." He lowers the barrel of the gun in her direction.

Tash'jya turns to Revon. Her eyes darken, if that's possible, as she rises to her full height. Whether she believed she could get to Revon before he could act or whether she intended to get the pistol trained on her, I can't tell. Her glance in my direction communicates it's enough for her for now.

"Human," she hisses, "you have no honor. You would sacrifice the world for your own prejudice. You force your own daughter into captivity rather than allowing her to have her own voice. And not because you are incapable." She takes a long breath through her respirator. "I have seen that your people are capable of kindnesss and friendship."

She glances at Loren.

"I have seen humans capable of mercy even before they fully understand uss."

A glance at me.

"I know humanss can see the greater good and fight for it."

A slight turn toward my father.

"But you—you see only your own endss. We are trying to save the world for everyone, but you simply want your version of it. You are short-sighted and weak and incapable of—humanity."

Revon's body tenses at the charge. Somehow, Tash'jya has gotten under his skin. What can offend a racist human more than to convince them they are less than human for being so? Did she actually get through to him? Revon readjusts his grip on his pistol, and I silently plead that he will relent and let the scientists finish.

Revon's jaw flexes twice as he looks down.

Please see what they are trying to do here, Revon. We can all live.

He looks up, pursing his lips to one side. He sighs deeply. "Fine. You want to paint me as the monster here?" A long pause. "Then, I'll be the monster."

The barrel of the pistol flashes.

Chapter Thirty-Two

All of us gasp as our bodies twitch in surprise at the report of the gun. I whirl back in Tash'jya's direction, expecting to find her dead on the floor. Instead, I find my father, wide-eyed as the shock of the moment washes over him. He stands between Tash'jya and Revon, one arm outstretched, having pushed her back and to the side.

A red stain begins to spread on the left side of his lab coat.

"Dad! No!" I shout through the gag. Not caring about what happens to me, I run toward him, ripping the cloth out of my mouth.

"Not so fast, Rookie." Revon grabs at the collar of my shirt, holding me in place. "You can watch this from right here. This isn't the order I wanted things, but perhaps this works just as well."

"Let me go." I squirm, but Revon's grip is iron.

My father falls to his knees, and Tash'jya catches him. She lowers him to the floor, cradling his head. Other scientists whimper as they cower nearby.

"Dad." My voice comes out as a weak moan.

"Sorry, Teddy." Tears fall from my father's eyes as he looks at me. "I don't think I'm g-going to get to finish what I started here." His breaths come in shudders, and his body begins to tremble.

"Watch and understand the cost of idealism, boy." Revon shakes me violently. "Because you and your Fishface friend are next."

Looking down at my father, Tash'jya touches her forehead and chest, honoring his sacrifice for her. "I am pleased to know your name, Kenneth James." My father's body stills. One final exhale slowly escapes his lungs. Tash'jya gazes up at me, a single tear leaking out of her midnight eye. "I am sorry, Ted. Your father iss gone."

My gut turns, and my chest feels as though it may split open. I stare at my father's lifeless body, willing it to start moving again. I cannot contain the despair, and the tears begin to plummet down my face. It is the second time I've lost my father. Only this time, there is a body and the certainty of his death.

The ball of anguish in my gut ignites and rages into fury. I turn to Revon, wrenching my shirt from his relaxed grip. My teeth grit hard enough to feel like I might break a tooth. Breaths seethe from between my lips. I want to rip this man limb from limb. Instead, I allow a single word to slip through my clenched jaw. "Murderer."

Revon's eyes turn to me, their expressionless deadpan enraging me all the more. *Does this man not feel?*

"Rookie, every battle has its casualties on both sides. Collateral damage is part of the process. Your father got in the way like all the sympathizers do. When we met, I thought you had a promising future with us." He nods with his chin in Tash'jya's direction. "You had this ugly Fishface on a leash, and I was impressed by your initiative. Instead, you fell in love with their kind. And so, like your father, you are in my way."

Out of the corner of my eye, I see Tash'jya gently rest my father's head on the floor and slowly rise to her feet. Revon notices and snaps the pistol in her direction, a warning to stay put. My hands ball into fists.

This man has killed my father.

He will kill Tash'jya.

He will sacrifice Loren as they remain trapped in this Bubble.

He will kill me.

I have nothing left. The realization fills me with a hollowness that makes me worry I might implode. My breath escapes me in a shudder. I shut my eyes, accepting my fate. I no longer want to live in this world if it means this kind of loss. It is doomed anyway. Revon has seen to that.

A hush falls over the room as if the entire group is holding their breath, willing the next moment to stay away as long as possible. The electrical whirr of the computers and machines in the room drones in the background.

Blip.

The tiny electronic note disrupts the steady noise of the room. I open my eyes and turn to the computer my father had been working on. The scrolling data, which had been running the entire time in the room, has ceased. At the bottom of the screen, a single phrase blinks.

Device Compatible.

I glance back at Revon, whose attention alternates between me and Tash'jya, as if unsure who to kill first. With my eyes alone, I gaze at Tash'jya, darting my eyes once at the computer screen. Her eyes follow mine to the screen. Her gaze returns to mine, and we silently communicate.

There is a chance.

We can right all of this. We can change this outcome. We can alter the history of the world with the flip of a switch.

As long as we can do it without Revon killing us both.

It is the silent agreement between Tash'jya and me. Killing one of us will not be enough. He has to take us both down. And I am closer to the switch on the wall.

I take a deep breath, trying my best to disguise my muscles which twitch for action. Anticipation causes all the nerves in my body to fire.

"Shya-sii!"

I don't wait to see what happens. I turn to run to the wall, knowing that behind me Tash'jya is lunging at Revon. The gun fires. Something hits the floor with a heavy thud. Another shot.

"Father, no!" Loren's voice screeches.

I'm steps away now.

Another blast. Something hot rips through my left arm, and I let out a cry. Still, I move forward. Balling my fist, I slam my knuckles into the glass cover of the switch. All my body momentum goes into the strike, and shockwaves of pain shoot up my arm as something in my hand breaks. The glass shatters, and I feel the shards tear into my skin. I scream to release the pain lest I give into the urge to yank my hand backward.

What feels like a sledgehammer hits me in the back, throwing me forward. Fire rips through my gut as the bullet passes through me and into the wall. My back arches involuntarily as my mouth forms a silent scream.

I've been shot.

I'm going to die.

My knees give way, and I begin to plummet to the floor. I have no strength to stand. My body will not obey me to stay upright.

Cold metal meets my fingers, and they curl around the switch. With my broken and bloodied hand, I grip the switch as my body crumples toward the floor. For a moment, I hang from one arm, suspended mid-fall. With the tiniest of lurches, the switch gives under my weight and flips flat in its closed position with a satisfying snap.

My head hits the floor, and I slump onto my side with my back against the wall. My vision alternates between cloudy and hyper-clear like my eyes can't focus. With my sideways view, I stare at Revon. He stands like a statue, smoking pistol still outstretched. His eyes widen as what I've done sinks in. At his feet, Tash'jya lays in a heap, purple blood pooling beneath her. Loren kneels by her side, her face twisted in distress.

Our eyes meet.

We gaze at each other. Her brow turns upward in the middle, and her lip trembles. I gather my strength to offer her the slightest smile.

I mouth the words 'see you later.'

I close my eyes as a bright flash fills my vision.

Chapter Thirty-Three

Sunshine filters in through two of the mini blinds in my bedroom that haven't quite closed. The ray of brightness, of course, finds its way right onto my pillow. I scrunch my face at the blinding light and rub my eyes. Glancing at the clock, my vision clears, and I can make out the time. Seven thirty-two. Way too early for a Saturday.

I roll onto my back and let out a deep sigh. The bed is the perfect temperature, and I want to enjoy it a few moments longer. I rub my stomach as if expecting to find something there, and I wonder why. I shake my head and run my right hand over my face. My right hand. I turn it back and forth, studying it with my eyes. Why do I feel like it should hurt? I wiggle my fingers a few times to make sure they're working.

I stretch out until my limbs are satisfied, and the blood is moving again. I contemplate rolling over and trying to fall back asleep when the smell hits me. Bacon. Somewhere in the house, someone is cooking bacon, and it smells amazing. My stomach gurgles its agreement with my assessment. That's it. No going back to sleep now.

Sitting up, I throw my legs over the edge of the bed. The floor is cool under my bare feet, but I don't mind. I curl my toes a few times to make sure they're ready for me to get up and walk. Grabbing a pair of old jeans and a t-shirt, I dress without getting cleaned up. It's Saturday. Dad will probably ask me to mow the lawn, so there's no point in getting ready for the day yet.

Glancing at my mother's concert poster on my wall, I remember how much she loved Saturday mornings. Sitting outside with a cup of coffee as the morning dew evaporated was her favorite. I miss her. She'd love what is happening in the world and all that dad has accomplished with the Skya'ja people.

When I open my bedroom door, the smell of breakfast wafts heavier into my room. Bacon. Coffee. And what I think is pancakes. All worth getting up for.

My bare feet slap heavily on the wooden floor as they continue to be the last part of me that is waking. Approaching the kitchen door, I can hear a radio playing with a voice humming along. Humming? My dad doesn't hum.

Turning the corner, my face spreads into an amused grin at the sight. If he didn't hum before, he is today. And dancing. My dad is actually dancing while he makes breakfast and hums along to the radio playing on the counter. The song is more my generation than his, so his humming is all wrong as he anticipates the wrong notes. The dancing is worse. What could have gotten him in such a good mood?

I lean against the door frame with my arms crossed trying not to laugh out loud. How long will he go like this before he knows I'm here? I watch him bop over to the sink to wash off a spoon. He twirls before cracking an egg over a hot pan. He reaches for another egg.

I can't help it any longer. "Don't hurt yourself, Dad. At your age, you're going to pull something." I can barely get the words out amid my laughter.

He startles at my words, dropping the egg on the floor. "Teddy. Oh my, you surprised me." He holds a hand over his chest while reaching for a paper towel to clean up the mess.

I push off the door frame and walk fully into the kitchen. "Trust me, Dad. You're not half as surprised as I am." I guffaw again. He joins me in the laughter.

He shrugs, a slight blush on his face. "Well, you caught me having a little celebration. Can't a man enjoy his successes?"

I smile. "Sure can. But that dance was anything but successful if you ask me." I grab a bar stool and pull it away from the counter.

My father clutches his chest mockingly. "Ouch. That one hurt, Son. You know, in my day I could cut a rug with the best of them."

"In your day, dinosaurs roamed the earth, but they've gone

long extinct along with the phrase 'cut a rug.' Seriously, Dad, how old are you?"

My dad makes a bowing motion to me. "Old enough to realize when he's beaten in a war of wits. Seriously, someone woke up today sharp as a tack. What's got you all cognizant on a Saturday morning?"

There he is. It was only a matter of time before the scientist and inventor in my dad showed himself and threw out a big word. "I'm not sure, honestly. I'm normally a pile of mush on a Saturday morning, but I woke up feeling like I had nitro in my veins. Some kind of adrenaline rush. Maybe I'm coming down from a wild dream. What's got you so"—I search for an equally big word—"exhilarated this morning?"

"Glad you asked." He slides a fried egg onto a plate and hands it to me. I mutter a thanks and grab two pancakes. "Things at the lab are going very well. In fact, we started energy production early this morning in a new plant in Beijing, and everything is holding up perfectly."

"No worries about an overload this time?" I pour way too much syrup over my pancakes to the point that it's spilling into my eggs.

"I'm impressed. Didn't think you were always listening." He flips a couple pieces of crispy bacon onto my plate, one of which I promptly grab and begin munching on. "Man, that takes me back. Two years ago, this was all theoretical. Everyone, human and alien alike were ready to throw the switch."

"But my dad, ever the hero, made everyone stop to think about what they were about to do." I point my fork at him and smirk. "You've told this story about a thousand times, Dad."

"I know. I know. I still don't understand how it all came together. I was certain this was going to quite literally blow up in our faces. That was until my colleague, Dr. Smythe, complemented me on installing my prototype capacitor. It made the difference, so—no overload." He stops and stares at the griddle in front of him as if lost in thought. "I—I don't even remember coming back to my shop to grab it, much less installing it. I mean,

I had the idea to do so, but don't recall following through." He shakes his head. "Whatever. I'd been working so many hours at the time, I was basically a walking zombie. Probably grabbed it and installed it half-asleep. No matter, two years in and all the data is saying the grid is holding up with no issues. That's why they are ready to bring Beijing online. Berlin and Tokyo will follow in a matter of months."

"And hence the breakfast and dance party."

He points a plastic spatula at me. "Exactly. So allow your old man a minute to celebrate." He slides his own egg on to a plate and sits down next to me at the counter. Taking a bite, he savors it for a moment before turning back to me. "Teddy, I'm sorry I've been so absent these last few years. This project—it's consumed me. It's going to change the world. So much of the bickering and fighting in the world is over energy resources. This could end all that. The Skya'ja are committed to ensuring this tech is made available to every nation now that we've figured out how to make it compatible with our unique planet."

"Skya—ja." I slowly pronounce the awkward name. I've heard my father use it before. It doesn't exactly roll off the tongue. "I realize this has been important to you, Dad. I've been okay."

"But you shouldn't have to be okay. That's my point. Since your mom passed, it's been you and me, and there hasn't been a lot of me lately. You've been forced to be on your own a lot since our friends from above came to visit, and I'm sorry for that. I was barely there for your graduation, and I regret that."

I shake my head. "Stop beating yourself up. I see how important this all is and how badly it could have gone if it didn't work." Why did I say that? Something in me knows how bad the world would have turned out if the power grid had overloaded, but I'm not sure why I know that. Dread fills me as I am convinced the world would have been devastated. I sigh heavily. "You needed to be there. This is global-level stuff, and you were on the front lines. I'm glad you got to be a part of it."

He smiles at me. He takes a bite and doesn't wait to swallow before responding. "Still, it's going to be different. I've been asked to oversee the installation of the facilities all over the world and begin construction of my capacitor designs for each unit."

I raise my eyebrows. "Big responsibility. And travel, that will be fun."

"I was hoping you'd think so because I have an idea." He swallows. "What would you think about taking a gap year. Postpone college for one year and come with me. We could travel the world. London. Paris. Moscow. I could hire you as an assistant. You'd make crazy money for school as the world is going to throw every dollar at this thing. And—we could make up for lost time. See the sights. What do you think?"

I hesitate. I'd been looking forward to college, but seeing the world on someone else's dime sounds incredible. "Well, Mom always did want to show me the places she'd visited when she was younger and traveled. In a way, we'd be doing what she always dreamed. Plus, it would be fun to hang out."

My dad sighs contentedly. "Your mom did always dream of this kind of trip. That settles it. We need to do this. Are you in?" He holds out a hand to me.

I take his hand and shake it. "Promise me the dance moves stay stateside, and we have a deal." I smirk, trying to hold in a laugh.

"Promise." I can tell he's holding back his own laughter. "Besides, I can always show off my singing voice if I need to celebrate again."

I roll my eyes. "Dad, you can't sing. You can't hold a note to save your life."

He wags his finger at me. "Nope. A deal's a deal. No altering the terms once the agreement has been made. Not singing was not part of the terms. We'll have to work on your negotiating skills while on this trip." After a moment, he can't hold it any longer and bursts out laughing, the kind that comes all the way from the bottom of the gut.

I join him. We laugh until we're sweating, and our outburst ends in a sigh. I wipe the tears of laughter away from my eyes.

"See," my dad says, "we're going to have a great time." He

gets up from the counter. Grabbing our empty plates. "Hey, I've got all this. Mind mowing the lawn for me?"

I nod. "No problem. Figured you'd ask."

"Thanks, Teddy." He hesitates. "I promise. Things are going to be different from now on. I feel—I feel like we have a second chance at life. I don't know why, but that's the only way that feels right to express it."

I pause for a moment. "I'm not sure why, but I sense the same thing."

He smiles. "Tell you what. Why don't you come with me after you mow and clean up? I need to pop into the lab for a few minutes to make sure things are still humming. You can come look around. Then, we can go play a round of golf or something."

"Golf? Really? You don't golf. Neither do I."

"Well, maybe we should start. Father and son need some kind of shared activity. Unless there is something else you young-uns are into?"

"For starters, don't say 'young-un.' If I have to work on my negotiation skills, you have to work on not sounding so old. Golf sounds like fun."

"Agreed. Ready in about ninety minutes?"

"I better get started on the lawn then. Thanks for breakfast." I approach the door from the kitchen to the garage ready to exit. Remembering my bare feet, I spin back around. I snap my fingers and tap the side of my head. "Might make more sense if I grabbed some socks first."

I cross the kitchen and step into the living room.

My heart skips a beat at the shadow of a figure standing in the room. The lights are off, and my eyes take a second to adjust. The man has a grizzled face and is unshaven. He's dressed like a truck driver with the insignia of a distribution company stitched on this shirt. A long, greenish scar stretches the height of one side of his face. In his hand, he holds a pistol.

"Good morning, Rookie."

Chapter Thirty-Four

"Dad?" I barely get the words out. My feet are frozen to the spot, and my heart is racing.

"What is it, Teddy? Did you already forget to—" His words stop short as he enters the living room and sees the man standing in the corner. The dish towel he was drying his hands with drops to the floor. "Who are you? What are you doing here?"

A smirk spreads across the man's face. "Well, if it isn't my favorite father-son duo."

"Do we know you?" my father asks, eyeing the pistol.

"We have met before, but I'm guessing you have no memory of our encounter or how it ended." The man sighs and rubs his chin. "Reset has wiped your minds of everything—of the truth of how things really were."

"I-I don't understand. Please. You have the wrong house. Please leave my son and me alone. We don't want trouble."

"No trouble?" The man screams the words as the pistol levels itself at my father. Instinctively, my father and I both put our hands up. "You don't want trouble? Then why did you ever play nice with those—those—freaks?"

"Dad?" My words are breathy plea. Who is this man? Why is he threatening us with a gun? The green scar on his face seems so familiar. Why is that?

"Please." My father's tone is frightfully calm. "You are scaring my son. I don't know who you are, but I'm sure we can get you the help that you need. Please just put the weapon away."

The man grits his teeth. "You shut up. You don't remember me, but I sure as heck remember both of you—a little gift from their blood transfusion." He runs the finger of his free hand down the length of his scar. "I remember what they did to our world. I remember the wars. I've held dying soldiers in my hands. I watched as people starved and scrapped for food. I've seen the death of earth. And your smarmy do-gooder mentality that wants to play nice with invaders. Slavery. That's what they are offering. Turning us into them. I've seen the world in their hands, and it's hell on earth."

"Are you talking about the energy project? It's working. Clean, renewable energy for the entire earth. The end of wars for resources. How can that be slavery?"

"Because it means trusting them."

"The Skya'ja?"

The man winces at the name. "The freaking Fishfaces don't deserve a name." He shakes his head as if having a conversation with himself. He relevels the gun at us. "I tried to stop you once before and was seconds away from doing so. I've been here long enough to listen in on your little plans to travel the world and put the world in bondage to this alien tech. You may have gotten this one up and running, but from how it sounds to me, they can't do this without you. That'll buy me enough time to gather the folks that feel like me. I won't miss this chance."

My father takes a step away from me, drawing the sight of the pistol. "Please, I don't understand what you're talking about, but if you have some beef, it sounds like it's with me. Do what you will to me, but my son has done nothing wrong to you."

"Dad, no!" I start to approach him, but he holds a hand up to stop me.

"Please, leave my son alone. He's innocent."

The man's eyes ignite with rage. "Innocent? You think your boy is innocent? He's the reason you all are blinded to the truth of how things should be. He threw the blasted switch and erased everyone's memory of how bad it was. He's the one who stole my daughter from me. Had it not been for him, our eyes would be opened." Slowly, he turns the gun in my direction.

"No." My father, hands still raised, steps between me and the pistol. "Leave my son alone."

The man's face grows remarkably calm. "No. I don't think

so. You're going to step aside and watch as your son dies. That will be your punishment for cooperating with the freaks. Then, you die so this madness can end before it goes any further."

"Please." My father's voice is shaky. "Please, don't."

"Step aside."

"I won't."

The man sighs. "Fine. You die first. Funny how this went down the same way as before. No matter. It's all the same to me in the end." His arm extends, and his finger reaches for the trigger.

"Shya-sii!"

A blur of motion comes from the hallway. A figure, too fast for a human, leaps at the man with the gun. The muzzle flashes, and my father and I both jerk in surprise. Drywall dust falls from the ceiling where the bullet struck above our heads. My father retreats to our corner, keeping me mostly behind him.

Across the room, the figure is on the back of the man, two hands gripping the pistol arm to keep it from pointing in our direction. The man shouts in frustration, firing two more shots in the ceiling. They spin, crashing into walls and furniture. Pictures fall off the wall, shattering on the floor. A lamp bursts with a flash of light before going out.

He finally gets a grip with his free hand and pulls the alien over his shoulder. It crashes to the floor before immediately twisting over into a crouch position. The man fires his pistol, but the creature is too fast. Leaping to the side, it meets the wall only to spring into a second lunge. The man fires wildly, missing each time.

The alien's second leap throws all its weight onto the man, who tumbles backward. The two writhe in a mass of violence. The gun goes off, and the Skya'ja cries out in pain before recommitting to the fight. With a strike of its arm, the Skya'ja knocks the pistol clear of the man's grip, and it skitters across the floor on the far side away from us.

Both hands available, the man fully commits to the melee fight. With one hand, he grabs the throat of the wounded alien. The other balls into a fist and strikes the Skya'ja's face. Pulling his knees up, he forces his feet into the alien's gut and thrusts outward. The creature flies backward, hitting the wall and slumping to the floor.

In an instant, the man is on his feet. Grabbing the piano bench, he lifts the seat above his head. The Skya'ja, dazed from smashing into the wall, can do little more than gaze up at him. One hand covers its abdomen from which purple blood oozes.

The man snarls as he glares down at the alien. "Freaking Fishface. I recognize you, too. I'm going to enjoy this." He brings the bench down on the head of the alien. The crack of wood against bone sickens me. Amazingly, the Skya'ja is still conscious after the first blow, holding one arm up in feeble defense. The man begins to raise the bench a second time.

Electricity shoots through my nerves as my body acts almost independent of my will. Swatting away my father's hand as he tries to restrain me, I leap forward. In two strides, I've crossed the room as the bench comes down a second time. I skid to a stop, my bare feet getting the traction they need on the wood floor. Bending over, I grab the pistol.

With a flick of my thumb, I check the safety is off. How did I learn to do that? I raise the pistol in the air and fire once. Dust and debris fall from the hole in the ceiling.

The man freezes and turns slowly to me. I level the gun at his chest.

"Stop." My voice shakes, so I swallow hard to calm it. "Just stop."

The man eyes me, a darkness in his gaze. He is unmoving. In one hand, he still holds the remains of the piano bench. "Rookie, you don't have the fortitude to wield that weapon."

"Why do you keep calling me 'Rookie?'" I don't know what he means, but each use of the word rings with familiarity—and not a comfortable one. Danger. That's the word that comes to mind.

He shakes his head, "Pity. You could have been one of my best. You have guts, I'll give you that. Could've used more of that on my crew." He holds out his hand. "Now hand me that thing before you accidentally shoot yourself in the foot." He steps toward me.

I straighten my arm to get him to stop. Will I really shoot a man?

"Son, be careful." My dad is frozen to the spot, his eyes wide as he takes in the reality of his son pointing a pistol at another human being.

"Listen to your dad, Rookie. I can see that maybe we should have talked this out first. I *promise* I'll not harm you or your dad."

Danger. The word comes again. Don't trust this man.

"Give me the pistol."

My hands shake. I'm not sure I can shoot a person down, no matter what they were about to do. I try to take a breath, but it shudders through my windpipe. I'm showing my cards. He knows I won't hurt him.

He takes another step toward me.

"Stop right there." My voice trembles. He won't believe me. "I mean it. Stop."

His lips spread into a smirk. "I don't think so." Another step.

Behind the man, a shadow rises silently. Pale green skin oozes purple blood as the battered Skya'ja stands. Reaching behind, the alien grabs a vase off the piano. A second later, the vase shatters over the man's head.

The man crumples to the ground with a grunt. In a flash, the alien is on his back, binding his hands behind him with bracelets that slap around his wrists. The same is done with his feet. Woozy and barely conscious, the man mutters something garbled into the floorboards.

"Hello, police?" My father has produced his cell phone. "We have a home intruder." His voice fades to the background as he begins giving the 911 operator our address.

The Skya'ja stands and gazes at me. For a long silent moment, we stare at each other. I realize I'm still pointing the pistol, and I lower it and click the safety in place.

"Th- thank you," I say. I'm unsure what else to say. Whoever this is, they saved our lives.

Still clutching her stomach, the alien touches her hand to its bleeding head and then to its chest. My father has mentioned this gesture before, and I realize it carries some kind of important meaning. "My name is Tash'jya. I am pleased to know your name, Ted."

Am I right? Was the voice female? And the name sounds so familiar.

"Psst, Teddy." I glance over at my father, who still holds a phone to his ear. With one hand, he mimics the head and chest gesture and then holds his hand out as if to say, "Well?"

Turning back to Tash'jya, I touch my forehead and chest. "My name is Ted. I am pleased to know your name, Tash'jya." Somehow, the name rolls off my tongue as if I've said it before. I want to say more, to thank her for what she did for us. I don't get the chance.

With a grunt of pain, her legs buckle. She crumples to a knee unable to break her fall. I race over and help her lay backward.

Tash'jya smiles in the way Skya'ja do. Her voice is garbled as blood seeps out the corner of her mouth. "You don't remember what happened or what you did or how it saved us all. But I do. My people do. I guessed that this human"—she glances with her gray pupils at the man—"might also have his memoriess, as our genetic code hass mixed with his." She doubles over in pain, tightening her grip on her bullet wound. "Our blood and his have become one. I knew he would come after you and your father, and there was no time to do anything other than to come here myself."

She turns to my father. Her long fingers tremble as she touches her head and chest. "I am pleased to know your name, Kenneth."

My father places the phone on speaker phone and rests it on the end table. He repeats her gesture. "I am pleased to know your name, Tash'jya." Kneeling next to her, he takes her hand in his. Her respirator wheezes loudly as she gasps for air.

Sirens begin to wail in the distance.

Several moments pass and her complexion pales. Tears leak from her eyes, and I find myself crying over this alien I've never met. Her gray pupils gaze at me before rolling backward.

Her respirator goes silent.

Chapter Thirty-Five

Police mill about our house, taking pictures and interviewing my father. The man, called Revon, is taken into custody. He is handcuffed to a gurney and is being loaded on an ambulance to receive medical attention under guard. I sit in the corner of the living room, sipping on a glass of water.

In front of me, a group of Skya'ja have gathered around Tash'jya's body. Each kneels by her side and touches her head. Whispers of her name come from the circle. Holding each other's shoulders, they sing. First out of tune, and then into one beautiful chord.

Her body is covered and carried by the Skya'ja to their own vehicle. One of the group remains behind. Standing across the living room, she stares at me. If I hadn't seen Tash'jya die, I would swear this was the same Skya'ja.

"I'm sorry about your friend." I'm not sure what else to say, and the staring is unnerving me.

"Tash'jya was not my friend. She was my sister."

"Oh. Wow. I didn't realize. Really. I am sorry for your loss."

The Skya'ja woman crosses the room in two great strides and stoops before me. She touches her head and chest. "My name is Tash'jyi."

I repeat the gesture. "I am pleased to know your name, Tash'jyi. My name is Ted."

She smiles. "I am pleassed to know your name, Ted. You are well known among my people."

"Me?"

"Yess. You saved our people. And yourss."

"Your sister said the same thing, but I'm afraid you must have me confused with someone else."

"My sister would not give her life for a mistake. She died with honor saving the one who saved all of uss, and thuss does not pass nameless." She takes my hand in hers as my father comes to sit next to us. "May I tell you a story?"

For the next half hour, we listen as she tells us about the world ending and time expansion and the delivery of the capacitor in time to prevent the overload. She describes the war between our peoples and my own capture of Tash'jya. She doesn't withhold that Tash'jya hated me as much as I hated her. Her description of our escape from Revon and flight to the Bubble makes my head ache as I try to understand it all.

"Do you believe all that I am telling you?" Tash'jyi gazes at me with obsidian eyes. I stare out the window in the direction of where Tash'jya's body was loaded.

Me? Capturing a Skya'ja? Standing up for a people group when men threatened them at the arena? Finding and delivering the capacitor? Running for my life? "Honestly? It's hard to believe all that." I shrug. "I don't remember any of it, but I have to admit that certain things *feel* familiar. It's like some sort of déjà vu."

She smiles. "In a way, it iss exactly like your human *déjà vu*, only you've *actually* done this before. You simply don't remember."

"I'm not sure I can believe all this."

"Wait," my father interjects. "You said it was Teddy that brought the capacitor to the lab?"

"Yes, he helped my sister find it for you and delivered it inside the Bubble."

"Wow." My father smiles from ear to ear and shakes his head. He places a hand on my shoulder and squeezes it. "My son, the hero."

"Yeah. Let's not go assigning that title." I roll my eyes. "Doesn't sound like everything I did was perfect." I turn to Tash'jyi. "I'm sorry for what I did to your sister. I must have been pretty angry to treat her so poorly."

Tash'jyi is silent except for a head and chest gesture. I return it. After a long moment, she speaks. "Ted, you are a hero. To your people and ourss."

The word 'hero' sits uncomfortably in my gut. I'm not sure I like the sentiment, but I don't say anything. Instead, I touch on a topic that is bothering me. "Tash'jyi, you say I did all these things with your sister, but sometimes, your wording makes it sound as if there were more of us. Was there someone else involved?"

Tash'jyi's smile disappears for a moment. She lowers her head. "There wass someone else."

"Who?"

Another long pause. "It is not for me to tell you this story. That honor belongs to my sister."

I straighten in my seat. "I don't understand."

"You will, Ted. Let me finish the death ritess for my sister, and I will explain."

My father sighs. "Of course. After the police are done here, I think it's time to head to the lab and see if we can put the pieces of this together. Maybe we'll have more déjà vu moments that will make sense. You can find us there."

"Very well." Tash'jyi stands, her hands folded in front of her. She strides with grace from the room and joins the other Skya'ja waiting for her on the front lawn. In moments, they board the vehicle with Tash'jya's body and drive away.

I turn to my father, who doesn't say a word. He puts his arm around my shoulder and squeezes. It's been a long time since my father hugged me. I've missed it.

An hour later, after countless interviews from the police, we finally roll up to downtown Charlotte. Our vehicle pulls over in front of a plaza that sits outside a high-rise building. The door opens, and we pile out onto the concrete. Everywhere I look, people are going about their business. Traffic streams by. A man on a motorized scooter zips down the sidewalk. Commuters make their way to work in any of the tall buildings all around. Various people mill about with their morning drink of choice in their hand.

To me, it doesn't fit. I stand in the plaza feeling like none of this should be here. Dread fills my gut, and part of me wants to run. All this normality feels off to me. Good, but out of place.

"Hello, Dr. James. This must be Teddy. It's so good to finally meet you in person!" A man with a British accent grabs my hand and shakes it vigorously.

"Dr. Smythe, this is indeed my son." My father claps Dr. Smythe on the shoulder. "I brought him to see how things are going. We're talking about having him come as an intern or assistant on the global installation."

Dr. Smythe smiles broadly. "What a completely bonkers, yet wonderful idea! I love it."

"I trust everything is still working as I left it?"

"Of course. You've been gone hardly a few hours, chap. You were supposed to return home to rest. We did not expect you until much later." He shakes a finger with an amused smile on his face. "But some part of me knew you couldn't stay away."

"We've had a morning of—adventure. I'm not sure I could sleep if I wanted to at this point."

"Very well. Very well. Let's go inside." He waves a hand toward the door as he turns.

We follow Dr. Smythe, who enters through a revolving door. As we make our way through the door, my vision of the lobby clears. People line both sides of the entryway. Upon entering, thunderous applause erupts. Cheers and yells fill the room. I glance at my father who looks as bewildered as I do.

Dr. Smythe turns to me, a mischievous smile on his face. "What can I say? The Skya'ja informed us what happened during the time expansion and what you did, young lad. And as one who can say they owe their very life to you, this was the least I could arrange." He offers a slight bow, which only encourages the crowd even more.

We slowly walk through the gauntlet of cheering people. Humans are clapping and cheering. The Skya'ja present are far more solemn. Each turns to me and touches their head and chest with both hands. At the end of the line is Tash'jyi.

I don't deserve this. "I don't remember the time expansion. It's just a story to me. It doesn't feel real."

Tash'jyi gently grabs my arm and turns me in her direction. "Ted, storiess have great power to offer hope, even workss of fiction. This is true in my culture as much as it is in yourss. Your story may not feel real to you, but that doesn't make it less true."

"I didn't actually do anything."

"Many of us were there, Ted. You were willing to sacrifice yourself for family and friendss and those you formerly hated. Among our people, that brings great honor."

We step into the elevator, and I hesitate to meet the eyes of all the celebrating faces in the lobby. I breathe a sigh of relief when the doors close. "I don't feel like a hero."

"I don't imagine most heroes do." My father places a firm hand on my shoulder.

Chapter Thirty-Six

The lab is bustling with activity. My father is greeted with more than a few congratulatory handshakes and claps on the back. Everywhere, excitement exudes in the conversations and postures of the scientists. The concept of taking clean and completely renewable energy worldwide has them understandably motivated.

In one corner, a table of people in business attire study a projected spreadsheet displaying names and flight numbers of world leaders traveling to come see the new power grid. One thing is for sure, the world will never be the same.

Here and there, I am greeted with a thank you or pat on the shoulder, but I am relieved that my father seems to be the greater celebrity on this floor. I need a break from the attention. Finding a corner table, I slump down in a chair and do my best to become invisible behind a table full of prototype contraptions. On the wall, a removed panel reveals the gleaming metal of the capacitor. I can almost sense the cool metal on my fingertips.

A presence hovers to my left, and I turn to see Tash'jyi take a seat next to me. She gazes at me silently, seemingly knowing I'm overwhelmed and don't want to hear more from any more admirers. After an awkwardly long pause, I let out a breathy laugh.

"What is it? Looking to escape the craziness of all this, too?" I feel my face flush when she does not smile at my humor.

"Ted, I made a promise to you to reveal the rest of what happened during the time expansion when the moment was right."

My stomach drops. I'm not sure I can handle more revelations, and the fact that she has waited to tell me makes me dread what's coming. Did something bad happen? Did I hurt someone else?

"Ted, there was another person who helped us. Neither of you remembers the other, but I believe it is important for you to meet each other."

"Who? And why?" I'm intrigued but still nervous.

"I should not say anything more than that."

I scrunch my brow and offer a confused smile. "Really? That's it? How mysterious of you. A random person I don't remember exists. That's all you're going to give me? Why tell me at all?"

"The story is not mine to tell." She hands me a tablet. On the screen, a single line displays in the middle. *Neural Log of Tash'jya, daughter of Sun'tssh.* "This is the log of my sister, and I have tagged the entries that pertain to her time with you. It contains her thoughts on her mission as well as her confession of what she intended to do to you. As it was stored in her brain, the entries survived the time reset. It is the final entry that will explain to you what I have held back."

I swipe at the screen, painfully aware that Tash'jyi intends to sit and watch me read the log. My eyes take in Tash'jya's account of her mission, her failure, and her intent to bring me to the Bubble. But there is a name that makes my heart flutter—Loren. I have not met this woman, and yet I see Tash'jya's wonder at how human relationships work. Then, I arrive at her final entry.

Neural Implant Log: Entry 147
Officer: Tash'jya, daughter of Sun'tssh
Rank: Tactician

The mission was a success. Ted, whose name I know, has started the energy unit with the capacitor installed. The Bubble has fallen, and the two years of devastation are nothing more than a distant memory. It has occurred to me that the one who attempted to thwart our efforts to save the world may have retained his memories as we Skya'ja do. Our blood has mingled with his, and he has become part Skya'ja, the very people he hates. Even now, I make my way to Ted's home. I fear for his life.

Ted, I make this log as my final gift to you, my friend. I do not fully understand the nature of human relationships, yet I am struck by your sense of destiny in it all. I am convinced you are not wrong, and there may be a greater power at work behind the scenes.

Loren, whose name I know, is a woman you have no memory of at this point. Yet, she was there and assisted in our efforts to bring the capacitor to your father. She did this at great risk to herself, rejecting her father's hatred for the hope of a better world.

Human love is foreign to me, but if it is what you and Loren shared, then I think our people could learn from humans in this regard. Despite the trauma you lived through, you and Loren found each other and shared a bond stronger than any Skya'ja coupling.

I cannot in good conscience allow you have your memory reset and deprive you of the gift of what you found in each other. She is out there, Ted. You may not remember her, but I am convinced you share a bond that transcends the rewriting of your history. Find her, my friend.

No doubt, my fellow Skya'ja have informed others of your heroism in those final moments. I expect that you are wholly uncomfortable with the attention and filled with regret for your actions against me. You once asked me for forgiveness, and Ted, I give it to you completely. You are my friend. There is a book that some of your people read that says there is no greater love than being willing to lay your life down for a friend. Truer words have never been spoken. You gave everything for me and my people. When I arrive at your home, if it costs me everything, I will be content to understand that I have reciprocated your friendship.

Thank you, Ted. Each of us was captive to our anger, and through your actions we have been able to find relief from it. May you always remember that I will forever know your name.

End of log.

Tash'jyi doesn't answer my questioning look. She folds her hands on the table and simply glances to her left. I follow her gaze to a man in a lab coat. He is speaking to someone I can't see when suddenly he turns and directs the person to our table.

I see her.

A young woman approaches, maybe a year or two older than me. Her blonde hair is pulled neatly into a sensible ponytail. She wears blue medical scrubs under her jacket. She is beautiful despite having minimal makeup on. When she reaches our table, she smiles. Something in my stomach flutters at the sight of her smile.

Nodding at me politely, she turns to Tash'jyi. "Excuse me. I'm sorry to interrupt, but I'm told you are the one I need to speak to. I have to admit, I'm a bit confused. My professor told me I'd been requested to consult a patient with memory issues, but—I'm only a nursing student. I'm not sure I can help you."

Tash'jyi turns to her. "I am Tash'jyi. I am pleased to know your name, Lo-ren."

Again, something inside of me jumps at the pronunciation Tash'jyi uses for Loren's name.

Loren startles at the words. "Oh, yes, wow. Thank you. I mean—." She pauses to collect herself. "I am Loren. I am pleased to know your name, Tash'jyi." I'm impressed with how well she pronounces Tash'jyi's name.

Tash'jyi gestures with a hand toward me. "I have asked for you, Lo-ren, not because you need to diagnose or treat the patient, but because I was able to convince your teacher that meeting him would make an excellent case study for your education."

Loren studies me with her eyes. "Really? That's great. Thanks for thinking of me." She pauses and glances around the room, which is still a flurry of commotion. "This place is crazy. Isn't the new clean energy being developed here? I remember following the news that there was some kind of last-minute miracle to make it work. Never thought I'd get to see it close up. Is this related to that?"

Tash'jyi nods once. "In a manner of speaking. Now, I think I will leave you both to it." She pushes back from the table and rises to her feet. She offers a slight bow with her head and walks away.

I turn to the woman across the table, who appears as confused as I am. Still, my gut leaps as I study her features. I can't put my finger on it, but it's more than an attraction.

She holds out her hand. "Well, I guess this is 'hello.' My name is Loren—as you of course just heard." Her face reddens with embarrassment, and her smile returns to her face.

I grab her hand and shake it gently. Electricity courses through me at the touch of her skin, and my heart melts. "Hi, Loren. My name is Ted. And I'm pleased to know your name."

Acknowledgements

Praise to God the Father and his son Jesus Christ for the grace to continue to put words on the page. Writing was God's gift to me in the darkest of seasons, giving me a beacon of hope when I had none. Each work that I complete is for Him and His glory, and the joy I receive in return is grace upon grace. The fact that anyone reads and enjoys what He has given me brings me more joy than I can truly express.

To my wife, Tirzah, who never allows me to cease pursuing my publishing dreams. You are my best friend and greatest support when I am tempted to give up. You never fail to help me celebrate the smallest of victories throughout the process of each book. Thank you for being by my side with every word on the page. Love always, T.

To my children, Samantha and Hunter, who make me proud every day at the authentic Jesus-loving adults they are becoming. I am humbled that you would express your pride in me as my books make it to the shelf. Your affirmation leaves me at a loss for words. I love you both.

To Miralee Ferrell and the team at Mountain Brook Fire that continues to believe in me and the stories I write. The fact that you came to me asking for this work will forever make me grateful. I hope it lives up to your expectations and does MBF proud.

To my community of writers at Realm Makers, you are my family. The shared laughter, tears, and experience of taking our off-the-wall ideas and putting them on the page has been life-giving for me. I would not be where I am without you.

And no acknowledgement would be complete without mentioning my readers. I love writing and publishing, but you multiply my joy every time one of you shares that you loved my books. *Captive* is a very different project for me, and I hope you enjoy spending some time in Ted's shoes. Thank you for your support, encouragement, and love of reading.

Author's Note

The birthing of *Captive* into the literary world has been a rollercoaster of emotion for me. It was during the writing of this manuscript that my agent, who has done so much for my journey, needed to change careers (I wish her and her family all the best), and what seemed like a free-flowing journey toward my dreams became an endless series of closed doors. There were times when I wondered if *Captive* would ever see the light of day. Yet hope shines its brightest when we become convinced we are out of options. Only in the complete darkness does the light of God's plan display its fullest brilliance. To receive word that I would not only get to publish this work but also get to be reunited with the team that gave me my first publishing opportunity reignited my passion for this craft in a way for which I will forever be grateful.

Friend, whatever journey you are on, I suspect that it has not gone according to plan. It's easy to become discouraged when our best laid plans do not go as we so thoughtfully mapped them out. We can become captive (forgive the play on words) to the despair and/or anger it produces. I want to encourage you to keep pressing forward while becoming unbearably patient. Your plan may not come to fruition, but that only means a better one lays in wait right around the corner, only to surprise you with joy when you least expect it.

Such is Ted's journey in this book. He believes he knows the truth and only wants answers, a feeling familiar to those of us with unfulfilled dreams. Yet, it is when he finally opens his eyes that he experiences something far better.

Friend, your journey is not over, but it may take a turn you do not expect. Rather than fight the unexpected, learn to embrace the change. It is a lesson I learned far too slowly, and I pray you will trust that God's best is waiting for you.

I hope you enjoyed this work. I am cheering for you.

I would love to connect with you and hear what you thought of Ted and the world he lives in. Would you have made the same choices? How would you react to a world in which you needed to survive on your own in a wasteland? In all honesty, would you make it?

If you'd like to know more, the best thing you can do is visit my website and sign up for my newsletter. I send out occasional updates on what is happening with my books as well as the first glimpses of what is to come! In return, I give you a free novelette, *Kane: A Chase Runner Story*, which is a prequel to my debut trilogy.

Here's how to connect with me:
Website/Newsletter/Free Book: *BradleyCaffee.com*
Facebook: *@bradleycaffeeauthor*
Instagram: *@bradleycaffeeauthor*
Tag me in a picture of you with the cover of *Captive!!*
MOST OF ALL, the best compliment you can give any author is to leave a positive review and pass on the word about *Captive.* Reviews are the lifeblood of authors like me, so if you loved *Captive,* please consider saying so on Amazon and Goodreads.
Until the next book…thanks for reading, friends.